FIRE FEUD

FIRE FEUD

Thomas Roehlk
A RED DEUCE NOVEL

For information about this title contact the publisher:

Red Deuce Publishing, LLC
Winter Park, Florida
www.reddeuce.com
reddeucepublishing@gmail.com

ISBNs:
979-8-9924015-2-3 (hardcover)
979-8-9924015-1-6 (softcover)
979-8-9924015-0-9 (eBook)

First edition

Printed in the United States of America

FOR MY CHILDREN, MIRANDA AND LANE

Also by Thomas Roehlk

Red Deuce

CONTENTS

Great Chicago Fire of 1871

area burned

LAKE MICHIGAN

Chicago River

map by Chicago CartoGraphics

1

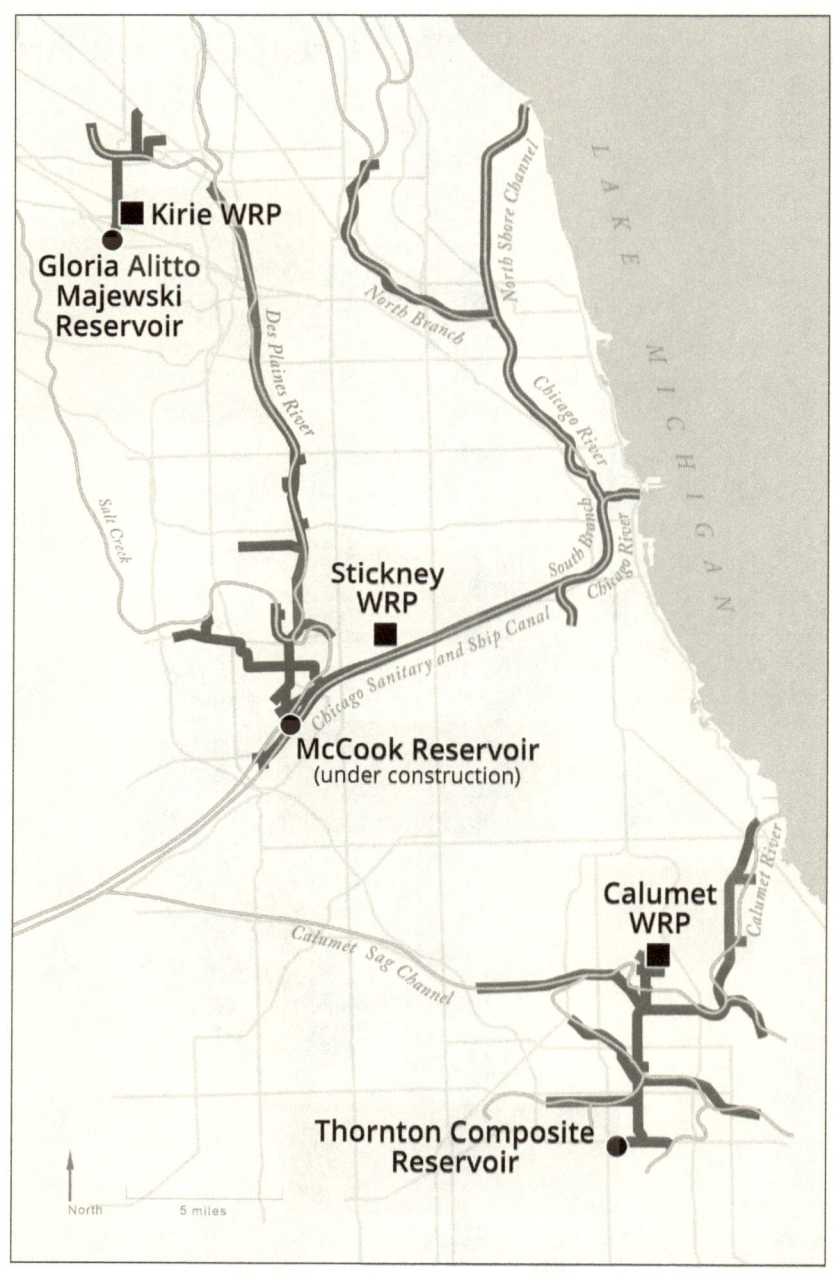

Water System Map
(Source: Metropolitan Water Reclamation District of Greater Chicago)

Old Bones
June 2010

A FRANTIC EMERGENCY at one of the company's construction sites started off Mandy Doucette's workweek. She was a corporate lawyer for LaSalle Enterprises, a large Chicago multi-national company with a history going back to the 1830s. As Vice President and Chief Compliance Officer, she regularly got such calls. This call came from one of the company's site superintendents managing a large project on the southwest side of the city. It was the southwest terminus of the Deep Tunnel project, a multi-decade water management system for the Chicagoland area. Though its proper name was the Tunnel and Reservoir Plan, the Deep Tunnel nickname had stuck.

One small part of the site was an ongoing excavation of an old scar from the nineteenth century. Directly in the way of the massive expansion of the McCook Reservoir, a part of the Deep Tunnel project, was an obsolete bridge structure buried under a grassed-over mound. An equipment operator of a large claw-arm tractor had knocked open a portion of the buried structure, revealing a human skeleton. The site superintendent had assembled several of the LaSalle Enterprises employees at the scene to protect the discovery after a terse radio message from the cab of the tractor.

"We have a 10–24 at the bridge site. Assistance requested." That "trouble" code would get immediate attention. Soon flashing lights and vehicles approached and zoomed through the entrance of the thirty-acre site. Off to one end of the site the earth rose above the north bank of an adjacent canal. A security tent blocked the rain, and the area would soon be swathed in yellow crime scene tape. It stood over an open excavation showing the partial skeleton. The weather had produced a string of storms, and LaSalle was protecting the remains until they could be handled by the authorities.

The site superintendent's call to Mandy was concise and to the point. "We've found a skeleton in a structure we broke open, and it looks like it's quite old and very suspicious."

Mandy said, "Have you reported it to the police?"

"We called the Water District police, and once we identified the issue they opted to involve the FBI."

"Leave that to me. I've got very good contacts there. Just keep the site protected and don't touch anything. We'll be there shortly."

She pulled up her contact list and punched in Steve Baker's number. He was the agent-in-charge of the Chicago FBI office, and a good friend. Steve had worked with Mandy on two previous crimes involving her company. The first was an interstate, inside-theft ring of diesel engines from one of the company's factories. Mandy had enlisted the FBI to break up the ring.

But it was the second crime that ensured their friendship. Despite a happy ending, the consequences had been significant for many. Not the least of them was LaSalle Enterprises itself. It had almost lost its government contracting credentials in that case. Mandy and her twin sister Reggie, an FBI pathologist, had found themselves in the middle of an international spy scandal. Reggie had nearly lost her life. Mandy called Steve and repeated what she'd learned and asked him to meet her at the site.

"I can think of better ways to start my week," Steve said. "Let's get down there and check this out. I'll bring Reggie too. It sounds like we need a pathologist. We'll swing by and pick you up."

Reggie had been an FBI pathologist at the Bureau's Quantico, Virginia lab for five years, but now worked in the Chicago office. Their involvement the year before had bonded them together even more than being twin sisters, if that was possible. Mandy and Reggie were red-headed, blue-eyed and freckled sisters who were striking in appearance. Tall at five feet seven inches, the thirty-year-olds lived together in the near north area of Chicago known as River North. They were both curious problem solvers. Mandy was the more intense and aggressive of the two, though introverted and uncomfortable in groups. Reggie had a more amiable personality and a willingness to throw herself into the mix with others. Mandy loved words and had been a literature major and went on to law school after undergraduate school. Reggie was a science nerd and headed to medical school. They had the maddening habit of dressing alike whenever they could, making it nearly impossible to tell one from the other. No one had ever been able to dissuade the sisters from dressing alike, though many had tried. They took great pleasure in befuddling everyone, though they realized it was time they grew out of the habit.

The problem of telling one from the other pales in comparison to contending with the twins' fiercely protective nature toward each other. Their two boyfriends had found out the hard way not to take sides, even if their support was expected. In a sister conflict, the men quickly found out they should stay out of it. Any disagreement between the two would blow over with blinding speed, but the rebuke for boyfriend interference could linger.

This morning's trip to the site was in a black FBI SUV, but it wasn't flashing blue emergency lights since a skeleton obviously meant an old set of remains.

Reggie poked Steve from the back seat and said, "Tell me why the Bureau is getting involved in this skeleton business?"

"The Deep Tunnel is connected to the Chicago Sanitary and Shipping Canal. The canal is part of the U.S. navigable waters, so the Army Corps of Engineers has jurisdiction. That's why the Water District police handed it off to us. The FBI is the law enforcement arm of the Corps."

Reggie said, "I have no problem with handling the bones. If it's truly old remains, they'd probably have called on our forensic anthropologists. But please tell me I won't have to go into a tunnel." Reggie's abhorrence of going underground focused her attention.

"No tunnel activity today," Steve replied.

They pulled into the site, located the protected area where the skeleton had been uncovered, and made their way to the tented spot. LaSalle workers were milling around awaiting their arrival, anxious to get back to their own pressing duties. Once the sisters came to the tent the attending workers gave them a long stare. They were used to the stares. At least on this occasion they were dressed differently, making their appearance together less striking.

LaSalle's site superintendent met them and led them down to the tented area. They climbed down into the hole and looked over the scene. A concrete structure was partially shattered, revealing a cavity and the remnants of a large oaken barrel. Its staves were broken and askew, barrel rings bent and in a pile. They got closer for a better look at the skeleton, and a shattered skull and knees protruded out of badly decomposed cloth. It might have been a rug. No flesh or tissue remained.

Mandy asked the superintendent, "What is this place?"

"What we're standing on is an old, buried bridge abutment from a long-ago dismantled bridge. It spanned the old Illinois and Michigan Canal but was removed over a hundred years ago when the old canal was replaced by the Chicago Sanitary and Shipping Canal. Whenever the bridges were removed, it looks like they left the buried abutments, probably concluding it was not worth the cost to remove them."

Steve asked, "Then why would they disturb them now?"

Pointing to the west from the tent, the superintendent said, "The Deep Tunnel project is now being completed; they needed this area to complete the expansion of the McCook Reservoir, so it had to be removed."

Off in the distance on the other side of the site was the opening of an underground shaft nearly twenty feet in diameter. Reggie looked over at it and was relieved not to have to go down that shaft. Her fear of heights and depths was pronounced.

Mandy asked, "What does the Deep Tunnel do?"

The superintendent said, "It collects billions of gallons of rainwater when there are big storms. Without it, stormwater and sewage sewers would overflow riverbanks and flood streets and basements. Then they would have to open the locks and release contaminated water into the lake. Beaches would close and drinking water would be threatened. Someone came up with the idea of the Deep Tunnel so the flooding and contamination could be avoided once and for all.

Reggie said, "How does it work?"

"If the flooding risk is imminent, special drains are opened to a one-hundred-mile-long system of tunnels buried three hundred feet underground. The excess water fills the tunnels, and they carry the water to one of several huge collector reservoirs. After the storm, the water gets pumped out, treated and released into the river slowly." Just the thought of that underground tunnel system made Reggie shiver.

The superintendent was ready to keep explaining, but Reggie was impatient and wanted to concentrate on the skeleton. She said, "We can get into all that later. Let's focus on the remains. When I first heard about this, I guessed that a cemetery had probably been disturbed by the construction crew and a casket had broken open. But this is no cemetery, and that is no casket. A skeleton couldn't have gotten here by accident either."

They had climbed down into the cavity and were within feet of the remains. Pointing to the skeleton, she added, "I'll bet this guy was murdered. It looks to me like he was intentionally dumped here and buried. Okay, there's a lot to do before we can get to the cause of death."

Mandy asked, "How do you know it's a guy?"

Reggie just shrugged her shoulders. "It's the knees that give it away."

Steve Baker said to Reggie, "Isn't that an anthropologist's area?"

She answered by taking a close-up photo of the protruding knees and sent it to her boyfriend Dan, now a forensic anthropologist professor after working with Reggie for years as an FBI pathologist.

Steve said, "This is now officially a crime scene."

Reggie stepped off to the side and called Dan, briefing him on the photo. "Did you get the photo I just texted over?"

Dan told her, "Yes, you wanted gender? This guy was a male. Too big for a female. You shouldn't do anything until a Smithsonian team gets there and handles the bones. I assume you want anthropology protocols used?"

Reggie said she did, and she'd make the call to get a team sent out from DC immediately. They left the evidence techs to deal with the remains and the crime scene.

Later on, the sisters rehashed the trip they'd taken that morning. Reggie was enthralled with remains that old and had goaded Dan into speculating about the death. Dan had traveled to the site and spent time with the techs at the bridge site. Dan was excited as an anthropologist. Mandy wished she could share this with her boyfriend Patrick immediately, but she knew this would have to remain a closely held secret for a while. Patrick loved the prospect of finding a great idea to start one of his novels, but Mandy was determined to keep things confidential until much later.

2

Invitation

AFTER WORK THAT NIGHT, Mandy made the short walk to the apartment from her office, a premiere location in downtown Chicago. It was at the intersection of the Chicago River and Michigan Avenue, neighboring the Wrigley and Tribune buildings with Pioneer Court in front of her building. It formed the southern gateway to Chicago's Magnificent Mile. In that exact spot three hundred years before stood the cabin of Chicago's first resident, the non-indigenous pioneer, Jean Baptisté Point du Sable, a Haitian immigrant. Mandy's office was in the thirty-five-story steel and glass building towering over pedestrians scurrying about below like ants.

In her role policing LaSalle's far-flung worldwide operations, she contended with lies and deception every day. Compliance work left no one, especially Mandy, positive about human nature. The tone of her life had been set as a sixteen-year-old. She'd had an unfortunate experience with some coworkers in a job at the Wilmette Harbor Yacht Club in that near-north suburb. The scheme involved one of the high school-aged workers. Mandy had taken the initiative to alert the harbormaster, and when he had ignored her alert, she summoned the police. Her reward for revealing the embezzlement scheme was harassment for her final two years at nearby New Trier High School. The harbormaster she'd informed had turned out to be one of the embezzlers and he'd been convicted and received a short prison sentence. It was later revealed that he'd had a record of similar criminal behavior in Oklahoma and had served time there.

The student involved had been ejected from New Trier. His friends terrorized her over her vigilante actions. The kid had been popular, as well as being an accomplished football player. The New Trier team had suffered from his absence. Her sister Reggie had gotten her share of abuse too, given that she was identical to Mandy. But Reggie was less affected by the experience than Mandy and actually had coached Mandy through the ordeal.

The experience had been one important factor that led Mandy to law school and then on to law enforcement. So far, she'd been the only one of the ten Doucette children to follow their father's career path in law. But she wouldn't be the last, as her youngest sister was set to take the law school plunge soon. Before taking the compliance officer job at LaSalle, Mandy had spent her first three years after law school working for the Department of Justice in Washington, DC. She was one of the lawyers in a prosecution trial unit concentrating on anti-corruption. It was there that she made herself an attractive prospect when LaSalle began searching for a compliance officer.

Now, almost fifteen years after that Wilmette Harbor nightmare, unlawful conduct had become Mandy's entire career. Righting the wrongs she found at LaSalle was lucrative, but she was growing weary of it and ached for a more uplifting job. She was thankful she had Reggie, who could always be counted on to force some balance into her life and serve as a sounding board. Mandy was conditioned to be suspicious and cynical because of her position, but Reggie always looked on the positive side of life and tried to pull Mandy into her camp. Reggie's influence would keep her away from the edge.

The sisters worked off their anxiety and kept fit with long-distance running. They had been on the track team at New Trier and had eventually been challenged by their coach to push past typical track distances and take on the longer challenge of the 26.2-mile marathon race. They were now members of the 50-State Marathon Club and were slowly checking off the states from their list. They were also working on the *Marathon Majors*, consisting of Boston, Chicago, New York, Berlin, London, and Tokyo.

Mandy also credited her boyfriend Patrick's influence for keeping her steady. He was a successful historical novelist, and his family was a significant shareholder in LaSalle. Totally by coincidence, they'd met the year before in a Chicago River kayaking group. Patrick had aggressively pursued Mandy, and they had become a couple. It was only afterward that she learned of his family's history as the founding family of her own employer. He was expected for dinner with the sisters that night.

Mandy entered her apartment and found Reggie sitting on the balcony, taking in the stunning view of the Chicago Loop to the south. The sun in the west constantly created changing window reflections on the high-rises across the river in the Loop. Chicago's architecture provided an impressive steel and glass jewel to give sunrises and sunsets something to paint. Sitting on the table next to Reggie was an unopened envelope addressed to Mandy. It bore the return address of Northwest Engineering Company, at 150 North Riverside Plaza.

She picked it up and when she saw the return address pointed south across the river and said to Reggie, "This letter is from that building right there, across the river from Wolf Point. It's the one they built on a forty-foot base, then cantilevered out on each side, using air rights over the commuter rail lines. I hear it has a massive water tank in the middle of the top stories, to counteract wind force."

Reggie said, "I like the dark blue glass. It reflects the sky and clouds."

"I can't imagine what this letter could be about." Mandy opened the envelope and took out a single sheet of paper on the letterhead of the Chief Executive Officer, Franklin Wagner. She read it out loud.

Dear Ms. Doucette:

We have never met, but I am very familiar with your admirable achievements at LaSalle Enterprises. I have an urgent matter I wish to discuss with you that I think will be of great interest. If convenient, I would appreciate your presence at our offices on Wednesday morning at 9 a.m., so I can explain. I promise to make it worth your while. My apologies for the last-minute approach, but time is critical to us. You of all people will understand once you hear me out. Please let me know by email or text my cell number if you can accommodate me.

Sincerely,
Frank Wagner

"Huh," said Reggie. "What a brownnose. '*Your admirable achievements.*' Maybe he's hitting on you."

"He isn't hitting on me. I recognize this company. It's as big as LaSalle, but private. If I take him up on this, I'll need to do some quick research first. Patrick may be able to help with this too. This has to be about a job."

Reggie stood up and put her hands on her hips and leaned into her on the balcony, saying, "You wouldn't think of going, would you? You'd turn your back on LaSalle after it's been so good to you?"

Mandy waved her off, went inside and logged in to her computer to study the Northwest Engineering website. She started with the *About* tab on the company's website and read that Northwest Engineering had begun life in Chicago as Northwest Drayage and Tunnel Company in the 1830s. That roughly matched LaSalle's own timeline. LaSalle had gone public over six decades ago, though, while Northwest was still a family-owned company. The two companies had been head-to-head competitors in the beginning, but LaSalle had morphed over the years into mostly a transportation and technology company. Also, a public company was much different than a private company.

Northwest was a heavy-duty engineering and construction company, engaged in major capital projects around the world, including bridges, tunnels, and canals. LaSalle still had its little toe in the capital projects business, but had diversified and gone in different directions from Northwest. Mandy had no appreciation for Northwest's size or market presence. It wasn't unusual for private companies to be somewhat mysterious. Many private companies flew under the radar and enjoyed a degree of anonymity from the general commercial world, except within their own circles. She wondered who did the compliance work for Northwest Engineering. Often it was left to the in-house lawyers to prevent and cope with ugly scenes from compliance problems.

Mandy next turned to the *Executive Team* tab. Most prominent among the executives was Franklin Wagner, a great-great-great grandson of the founder, Maximillian Wagner. From the company website page, a photo revealed him to be a tall, early-forties man with streaks of gray in his hair and a confident pose. He reminded her of Tim Robbins, the actor. Mandy pulled up another tab on her browser and searched his name. Up popped a series of pictures of him with beautiful women on his arm as the couples were caught in society shots. It was a different woman in each shot, all attractive. Apparently, he had quite an eye for the women, and they for him as well. No mention was made anywhere online of a wife or family. He looked like a guy in the prime of his life who liked to live it up

Reggie looked on as she paged through the pictures and said, "This guy looks hot, and probably rich as hell too."

Other Wagner family members held top posts at Northwest, with one sitting on the board. A key officer was Carl Wagner, the general counsel. Carl's mother Gretchen Wagner was listed as a board member. Mandy recalled her dad's old friend John Booth telling her how he'd served as Northwest Engineering's general counsel. It was for a brief time after his retirement from another Chicago company. She'd been puzzled by why he would retire then take another job. When she asked about it, he'd explained it was a favor to a friend. He was a temporary stand-in for another Wagner family member who wasn't yet ready to take the position. Could that have been Carl? John Booth had either left or been let go when he'd seen some troubling signs and had started asking questions. She would love to be able to call him to discuss this further, but that was impossible. Mandy had pulled him into her due diligence project on an acquisition of Allzient Corporation.

Too late, she accepted that she'd unwittingly painted a bullseye on his back. He'd been murdered at his Sarasota home, in a staged drowning. She still felt guilty for exposing him. Drawing him into the case had been her idea. She couldn't avoid taking the blame.

Mandy stopped there for the night. She shut down her computer and sent Frank Wagner a text message accepting his invitation. Her apartment doorbell rang, and she buzzed in her boyfriend Patrick. After he came in and kissed both sisters, Mandy showed him the letter. "I just got this invitation to meet Wednesday with Frank Wagner of Northwest Engineering. Do you know him?"

When Patrick heard that name, a wry expression came over his face and he said, "Only by reputation. The family nemesis. My dad is no fan of the Wagner clan and warned me about them. His family has been an archenemy of the Carneys going back generations. What does he want?"

"I'm not sure. His note is very mysterious, and he apologized for the last-minute invitation."

Reggie said, "Watch out, Patrick. He's making a move on your woman."

Mandy said, "Don't listen to her. She's just taunting you. That would be too weird, anyway. It must be about a job. I'm going just to see what it's all about."

Patrick said, "My mother was friends with Gretchen Wagner years ago, but I think their friendship blew up. Maybe she can be helpful."

"What about the family nemesis thing? Does that affect you and your parents?"

Patrick said, "It's nothing to do with me. I've never even met the Wagners. My parents, on the other hand, did have a history. Why do you want to bother with this, anyway? If he's looking at you for a job, you wouldn't abandon LaSalle, would you?"

Reggie threw up her hands in the air and said, "Thank you. My point exactly." She had an annoying know-it-all smirk on her face.

Mandy said, "Abandon is a pretty strong word, don't you think? Dad always told us to give everything a fair hearing in case it was a good opportunity. He thinks opportunities are put before you for a reason. Besides, I'm bored, and compliance is more of a rut than it used to be for me. I can't do this cop stuff the rest of my life, anyway. And I don't need you two ganging up on me."

Reggie said, "What's wrong with cop stuff?"

Ignoring her comment, Patrick said, "What if Reggie's right and it's you he wants, but not for a job?"

She smiled at him and wagged her finger. "Do I sense a little jealousy here?"

Patrick said, "I've heard he's a confirmed bachelor always on the prowl for ladies. Don't you want me to be concerned about other men?"

She said, "Of course I do. I can appreciate a little jealousy. You need to explain about your parents' history please." She wanted to change the subject.

"Why don't you have your meeting with him and if there's some interest, we can talk it over with my parents." He was clearly troubled by the notion of the Wagner family entering Mandy's orbit, but tried not to let it show. He knew for a fact that his father had serious fears about the Wagner operations, past and present. But neither he nor Mandy could possibly anticipate what would happen.

3

Meeting Frank

WEDNESDAY MORNING Mandy crossed the Franklin and Lake Street bridges spanning the river to get to the Northwest Engineering office. She rode up to the fifty-fourth floor in the elevator bank dedicated to Northwest Engineering's headquarters, and in the mirrored elevator cab she looked herself over. Her red hair cascaded over the shoulders, framing her blue eyes and freckles. The hair worn down hid her good luck red-chili-pepper earrings. There was no need to reveal her superstitions to this man, so leaving the hair down kept the earrings hidden.

She was also packing her St. Dymphna holy card. The patron saint of the anxious, she routinely carried it to help with stressful situations. She came from a family of two superstitious grandmothers who instilled their own distinctive ancestral quirks. The earrings were a traditional protection against evil that came from her Italian side, and St. Dymphna came from her French-Canadian side. She was not about to forego her protections.

A receptionist greeted her and led her back to Wagner's office. He stood up and came from behind his desk and shook hands. He had one of those firm but not crushing handshakes that conveyed a desire for control. He also worked in a slight pull toward her, as if to throw Mandy off balance. She immediately felt uneasy.

This was the man she'd seen in glamour photos with a parade of women, during her research the night before. It was easy to see why he commanded female interest. He was dressed casually and stood six foot four inches tall, with the gray-flecked brown hair and brown eyes she'd seen in the internet photos. He was giving her an intense examination that he tried to disguise. He couldn't be expected to appreciate her perceptiveness, though, and she had read him like a book. His office looked out the northeast corner of the building, giving him a clear view of the main stem of the river east to the locks and beyond into Lake Michigan. Below them, the main stem of the river met the north and south branches, forming the "Y" which had become a symbol throughout the city's official emblems. From here it would be possible to count most of the bridges over the river if you were a bridge counter. Mandy noted that she could see her own apartment building off to the left, and the LaSalle headquarters to the east at the Michigan Avenue bridge, producing a twinge of guilt in her. She had to compartmentalize.

After the uncomfortable handshake, Frank said, "Ms. Doucette, thank you so much for coming on such short notice."

She said, "Please call me Mandy. Your message was very mysterious, so naturally I was curious. I've always wanted to come inside this building anyway. I hear there's a big water tank inside to counteract wind forces on the building."

He had a broad, charming smile and flashed it for her. It was almost another kind of invitation. "Yes, we engineers call it a *'tuned liquid damper'* and it's one of the techniques common for tall buildings in windy places. There are a number of them, but the water tank is indeed what we have."

He motioned to the wall of photos behind her, saying, "Have a look around at all the big projects. Northwest was responsible for many of them. LaSalle's had many of its own, in fact, but I'm sure I don't need to tell you that. You made your own interesting news last year. I suppose you're quite busy at LaSalle these days?"

She didn't want to waste time dwelling over her past corporate adventures, but she had to answer. "It was quite a year for me and my sister, and you're right about me being very busy." Both sisters had their lives threatened the year before, with Reggie almost losing hers in a very public way.

"LaSalle is an active player, so I suppose you do some very interesting acquisitions and mergers work. But I think I have an interesting opportunity for you. We've been in business for over 170 years, owned throughout the whole time by successive generations of the Wagner family. It's quite a feat for a family to continuously run a large business through so many generations. It's difficult to cultivate family members to work in the business. But we've done it and been quite successful. Yet now we have quite a few family members who wish to move on, for a variety of reasons. They've driven us to look for ways to unlock value from the company. We studied our options for some time and selected a path forward—we're going public."

Mandy blew out a breath, hoping to disguise her excitement, and said, "That's a big undertaking."

"I'm learning that. To be honest, if it were solely up to me, I wouldn't have made that choice. I think we've done well for generations, with no other constituencies except the family to satisfy. I don't know how we'll operate or who we'll have to listen to, but I guess it's all beside the point now. It was NOT solely up to me. The decision was made, and now it's up to me to execute."

"Did you consider a sale rather than going public? That would have unlocked value as well."

"One of my ancestors tried that and it didn't go anywhere. He was rudely rejected and didn't take it well. The bankers did an analysis for us and persuaded us to take the company public. I wasn't a fan of either route. Maybe someday I'll be able to say '*I told you so*,' but for now I need to buckle in and get it done."

Mandy smiled and said, "I'm sure it will be very exciting though."

Frank got down to business. He wasn't much for chitchat. "Maybe. We have a lot to learn, and you may be one of the people who can help us. Since you understand how a large, international company in our line of work might function as a public company, you've drawn our attention." He paused for Mandy to react.

"What kind of attention?" she asked.

"My cousin Carl, our general counsel, recommended you for a new role we're creating. He felt that you would have the public company expertise we need, but that being from the same industry would make you the ideal candidate. I agreed, and I asked you here to offer you that position. It would be a very senior role. First, to help get us launched and establish a corporate staff and prepare us to operate as a public company. After we're launched, I would want you here succeeding Carl as our new general counsel and corporate secretary. Carl would then become a group president overseeing a division of the company," he said.

Mandy had some tingling at what had just been said, even though she expected it. She put her hand on her forehead and said, "I didn't see this coming. Obviously, you're taking me by surprise, and I've got to think about it. I'm humbled that you're asking me, though." She was just relieved that Reggie's idea had crashed and burned.

Frank said, "Don't you want to ask some questions about the company, first?"

"I spent some time last night researching your company after getting your invitation. I think I have a pretty good grasp of it, but of course I'll have questions."

Mandy had gone through as much as she could about the company's history and lines of business. As a private company, though, its financials were unavailable. The kind of inside information she needed wouldn't be easy to get, even if she asked the right questions.

She had a niggling sense that this guy wasn't trustworthy. During her years as a prosecutor and a chief compliance officer she had developed a sixth sense about liars. After she crossed through the portal from government to corporate work, she'd expected her cynicism to diminish. But she'd had a rude awakening when she got to the other side. She didn't really want to believe a CEO would be lying about anything, especially in a job interview. But once the niggle of lying began, it monopolized her thinking.

She said, "There might be a hurdle for me since I'm under LaSalle's non-compete agreement. I might not be able to get over that until I can see your financials. I'll need to measure competitive overlap to see if the agreement is even invoked. Can you help with that?"

He said, "Of course. I wasn't expecting you to accept the offer on the spot, but can I ask you to consider it and give me an answer soon? Next Monday morning we're issuing a press release announcing that we're going public, and this place will be chaos. Only a handful of people are aware of this, but my investment bankers and outside lawyers urged us to get a running start on preparing to be public. They laid out some key positions we would need filled, and yours would be one of them. That's why I am reaching out to you with some urgency."

Mandy said, "I'd have expected to be contacted first by a headhunter and then interviewed by your general counsel. I'm surprised to be contacted by the CEO directly."

"If you join us, you'll see I'm a very hands-on type, especially when it comes to senior hires. Carl is the current general counsel, of course. He's been with the company since law school, but he doesn't have the kind of background for this. We can't afford to do on-the-job training. If you want to take the position, you'll meet him, and he'll have to be on board to hire you. He can give you the financials. But like I said before, Carl recommended you for the job, and I wanted to have the first conversation with you. I'd encourage you to look at it as an adventure, since you seem to be an adventurer."

This guy liked to control things, she thought. It still bothered her that his general counsel cousin wasn't here with him. She also detected a little more interest from him than she welcomed. She was used to being looked at, especially if she and Reggie were together. But she didn't expect it in a job interview. Maybe that was why Carl wasn't here.

She said, "I suppose that's one way of looking at it—an *adventure*. I'm still not happy about all the attention the last one brought, though."

Frank said, "I imagine you've both had constant attention, given your good looks and your prominence. It's going to be awhile before the limelight dims, I'm afraid. Better embrace it."

He couldn't resist commenting on her appearance.

Just then Wagner's assistant opened the door and said, "Excuse the interruption, Mr. Wagner, but your Aunt Gretchen is on the phone and insists on speaking to you immediately. She said it's important."

Frank instinctively glanced up at the ceiling, sighed and said, "I'll talk to her. I'm sorry, Mandy, this is my high-maintenance aunt and board member, and I better talk to her."

Mandy got up and headed toward the door. "I'll step out."

"No, no. Please have a look at the photos if you don't mind. Should only be a minute."

She shouldn't be here, she thought, and he'd told her volumes about himself by having this conversation in front of her. He shouldn't have done an eye roll about his aunt and let her see it. Clearly Frank Wagner lacked self-control, or just didn't care. Either one was a problem.

From Patrick's mention last night, Mandy knew his aunt was a director and an old friend of Patrick's mother too. She heard Frank say, "Aunt Gretchen, is everything OK?"

Frank listened to his aunt, facing out at the panorama outside the windows. Mandy swung in the opposite direction facing the wall of memorabilia so Frank could not watch her reflection in the windows. But she listened carefully. She surveyed the inside walls of the room while the conversation was taking place. Framed photos of gigantic construction projects occupied most of the wall space, many sepia-colored and obviously vintage. The subjects were bridges, tunnels, canals, and buildings, and a familiar stone high-rise building caught her eye. Conspicuous by their absence were any photos of a wife or kids, though there was an abundance of ancestors from prior generations. Apparently Frank Wagner was all business, unless he was busy womanizing. He wasn't the marrying type, it appeared.

Frank said into the phone, with an edge to his voice, "I'm sorry about this, Aunt Gretchen, but it's necessary for the public offering. As a director you'll have to sign a registration statement too, like all the board members. There's no getting around that. Need I remind you that this was all your idea? We wouldn't be going through all this if it weren't for you. I was the last person on earth who wanted to do it, but since I was outvoted, I'll make it happen. I would like your cooperation, please." That last sentence was delivered with his voice rising.

Frank's momentary display of anger swiftly receded as he shifted back to listen mode, and he was clearly getting an earful. She glanced back at him and saw that he had a white-knuckle grip on his chair arm as he took the tongue-lashing his aunt was administering.

Suddenly he angrily said, "Who's she?"

After getting another earful from his aunt, the next thing he said was, "Stay away from the press, especially that history journal rag. I promise you that Carl and I will make your involvement as brief as possible. Let's not argue about this. Let our team get the info they need, and we can leave you alone to count your . . ." He hesitated, awkwardly, and then said, "Alright then, we'll talk soon."

Mandy guessed that the aunt had hung up on him. She understood that Frank Wagner had been outvoted by most of the shares owned by the family, led apparently by his Aunt Gretchen. She also knew a little about the *Chicago History Journal,* being that it was published by her boyfriend's mother, Beth Wagner. Instantly it struck her that he could have done a background check on Mandy and known of her connection to Beth.

Putting down his phone and turning to Mandy, he said, "Sorry. My Aunt Gretchen is one of our directors and she's a little stressed out with all the activity going on. She doesn't like all the prying, as she puts it."

Ignoring Frank's comment, she pointed to one of the photos and said, "These are impressive. These are your projects, I assume, including this one?"

"Correct," he said, "that's the Monadnock Building, one of the first skyscrapers in the world. We didn't build it, but we own it and were headquartered in it for many years. As a matter of fact, its centennial celebration is coming up soon and a hundred-year time capsule will be opened."

Other items were framed and interspersed on the wall among the sepia-tinted photos—swords, knives, pistols, rifles, a Civil War uniform, and other memorabilia. Looking at the combined framed photo and pistol, Mandy said, "Who's this?"

"Gus Wagner Senior himself in his Union Army uniform. The very same uniform hanging next to the photo," he said, pointing to another spot on the wall with the actual blue uniform enclosed in glass.

Looking next to the photograph of two men, Mandy asked, "And these two?"

"On the left is John Roebling, the famous German canal and bridge builder best-known for starting the Brooklyn Bridge. He'd left the repressive Prussian empire just like Max. He's standing next to Max Wagner, Gus's father and the founder of this company. Roebling mentored Max when they were constructing the Delaware and Hudson Canal after the Erie Canal. Roebling taught him to be aggressive and not kowtow to authority. If he was his own boss, Roebling said he'd never have to ask permission for what he wanted to do. That governing principle lasted many generations after Roebling planted the seed."

Mandy said, "That's a compliance officer's nightmare—people who don't ask permission when they should."

"You've dealt with that kind of thing a lot?"

Mandy wanted to change the drift of the discussion, so she said, "Enough to know about it. But it does seem that Northwest has a long, impressive history. Not unlike LaSalle," she said, hoping to sound impressed.

"True." He seemed distracted and started moving them toward the lobby area, and quickly changed subjects, saying,

"I'm going to be optimistic here and say *when* you join us, we'll have plenty of time to talk about all the rest of these photos and mementos. Meanwhile, I should let you think this over. I assure you that we'll make it worth your effort and promise you very interesting work."

She said, "I have a number of things to consider, but I'll get back to you as soon as I can."

He said, "Thank you. I wish I could give you more time to consider, but I need to hear back by next Monday. If you can't do that, I'll have to move on to plan B. We're in a big hurry to staff up for the launch."

By Mandy's thinking, Frank had been surprisingly abrupt for this level of job. If the roles were reversed, Mandy was certain she would have talked about a lot more things. Cousin Carl would be assigned that role, she thought. Frank was making the first pass, establishing himself as the master of the enterprise.

As she got in the elevator, she wanted to test if she could feel some water splash in the big tank. She began jumping and thrashing her arms around. Red hair danced around her shoulders and the red chili-pepper earrings swung wildly about. It was one of the most spontaneous things she had ever done and was thankful no one could see her gyrating. Nothing happened in the splash tank though, at least that she could detect. By the time the elevator reached the ground she was composed and calmly walked off into the lobby.

She had to admit to herself that she was excited about the offer, but also tormented at the thought of leaving LaSalle. It had been so good to her over the years, but she was serious about being bored and was looking for a new challenge.

The contentious telephone call she had just witnessed intrigued her. That was some obvious family drama. Frank clearly had been distracted after his aunt's call. She felt as if she'd been pushed out the door. She was expected to make a big decision almost immediately without adequate time to consider.

She rushed off to her office at LaSalle and immediately called Reggie at work. Reggie answered the call with a question. "What did Mr. Arm Candy have to say?"

"It was a job offer, alright. And a good one, at that. But my first impression of Frank Wagner is not a good one."

"Why? What did he do?"

"He openly disparaged a relative—a board member even—in front of a complete stranger. Not sure what that says about how he'd treat an employee. He was inappropriate in undressing me with his eyes, too. Let's kick it around tonight."

C H A P T E R

4

Disagreement

AFTER MANDY LEFT HIS OFFICE, Frank sat at his desk and pondered his problems quietly to himself. He routinely voiced his dilemmas aloud and tried to resolve them as if he had an audience he was addressing. Now he controlled himself, and no sooner had Mandy left the building than Frank pulled up a closed-circuit feed from the elevator. There on the monitor, a red-headed elevator passenger started to do a wild, almost maniacal dance in the car, heavy on arm movements. Just before the elevator reached ground level, she stopped and walked out like a normal person. He wondered out loud, "What the hell are those red dagger earrings she's wearing? Is she some kind of wild woman? Damned good looking, though." He froze the screen and replayed it a couple times, then saved it, deciding it might be a good thing to have.

When Northwest Engineering became the premier tenant in the building, Frank asked to have the building equipped with the latest monitoring capabilities. Carl had instructed his technical guru, an old school friend, to install inconspicuous cameras throughout the common areas of the facility, including the Northwest Engineering elevators. Frank could monitor his departing visitors or employees, or just get a good look at the women who frequented the building. If nothing else, Frank was intent on creating any advantage he could for himself. His father had taught him that the founder, Max Wagner, had used spies to monitor the company's competitors in the early days, and the tradition continued. Lessons from the past were not to be ignored.

Those lessons weren't lost on Carl either. The company and the family might not survive the kind of scandal Frank could produce, since he was known to think with different parts of his body. With that risk in mind, Carl designed his video system to include Frank's private chambers, but only he and his IT friend knew it existed or how to access what it had captured. It was quite eye-opening to later view the clip of Frank in his office slobbering over the idea of Mandy Doucette. Carl was playing with fire by filming his cousin's private office area, but he justified it by the knowledge that Frank was just plain dangerous. Carl had to know whether Frank was creating a high-risk situation for the company.

Frank couldn't dare say some things in the presence of others, particularly cousin Carl, but he could say it privately as much as he wanted. His cousin had harangued him about making unwanted advances. Once an attractive woman was in Frank's mind, though, some comment usually came out of his mouth.

Carl monitored Frank's soliloquy. He didn't want a high-profile sexual harassment complaint on his hands. He'd already had to broker potentially noisy departures of other women with generous severance payments and non-disclosure agreements. On several occasions they came from events captured by his very secret surveillance of Frank's office. The problems Frank had caused so far had flown under the local media's radar, but Carl couldn't be sure that would be the case once they went public. He didn't need anyone targeting the CEO of a new public company or landing the company in court. That kind of problem would just fall into his lap to handle. The investment bankers had drilled into him that once public, Northwest would be living in a fishbowl. It was another reason to keep clear of negative media.

Frank's father, Gus Jr., had taught him to keep his own counsel, whatever the subject might be. Those were more like a lawyer's words, and he wouldn't allow himself to be kept bound and gagged. If his father was the CEO and chose to keep his mouth shut, that was his business. But he was the CEO now, and if he wanted to say something, then it got said. Let Carl clean up after him if he wanted. And his father had drilled into him the ancient advice from John Roebling to be aggressive and do whatever it took to win.

He didn't think his casual comment about Mandy's looks was troublesome. In fact, he intended to push the boundaries a bit for Carl's benefit. He was well aware of how much it troubled Carl, so he was happy to throw out a decoy for Carl to worry about. Frank didn't want Carl to pay too close attention to other issues that were much more significant to the company than a little flirting. What Carl didn't know wouldn't hurt him. Frank had studiously watched his father hamstringing his own brother Klaus for years and keeping Klaus off balance so that Gus could get his way. The Deep Tunnel debacle, though, had threatened the golden goose when Klaus had refused to follow the usual manner of dealing with bids.

Frank was aware of the devious bugging of his office and left it in place and used it to mislead Carl. It was still treason, though, and not one Frank would easily let pass. But he could bide his time on avenging Carl's treachery. Carl could play the role of useful idiot for a while.

Frank pulled up the contact number for his private investigator. He'd used Jack Greer over the years for sensitive assignments, and Greer had been very good at surveilling people Frank needed to influence. In fact, Greer had been the one to sniff out the bugging of Frank's own office. Frank's father, Gus Jr., had also taught him to use any means available to study his adversaries so he could get the best of them. After the bomb Aunt Gretchen had dropped on him this morning, Frank had the need for eyes-on work. Greer could investigate, track, watch, and provide security. Frank needed some of those skills now after Gretchen's threat.

Frank was a poker player, and he studied the habits of his fellow card players in the games he played at his site. He kept index cards on each player with notes about their idiosyncrasies, like "tells," if they had any. That was a good investment. He'd contacted a very discreet organization online bearing the Middle Eastern evil eye logo. Frank had enabled a dial-in video connection to the poker room he used. He would identify the table seats of the players he wished to be profiled. He would get back profiles with any tells the players might exhibit. Carl had been one of the players, and Frank had gotten insights into his own cousin from the poker experiment. He would use those insights into the cousin to guide his tactics, like he tried to do with others.

Frank was preparing to shed his corporate feathers so he could fly away when the need arose. He'd never really enjoyed it, anyway, like his father had. But with his resources, carefully accumulated over the years and strategically located in several spots, he was in excellent financial shape. Without the distraction of a wife and children, he had many options. Right now, he was focused on launching the company, staying awhile to assure a smooth transition, and cashing out. If he could settle a few scores on the way, then all the better. After the public offering launch, he'd have such a pile of cash that if he didn't like the new environment, nothing could keep him there. He just needed to make sure that none of the attention being drawn to the offering went into dangerous areas.

Frank went down to the plaza outside the office and got Jack Greer on the phone and explained what he wanted done. Carl didn't need to get any of that. On the call, Jack told Frank he'd be happy to help and just needed the specifics.

Frank told him, "For the moment, it's a straightforward job of shadowing someone. It's a woman in her late seventies living here in Marina City. I'd like to see where she goes and who she meets. That kind of thing. Depending on what it produces, there may be more to do.

"I'm particularly interested in whether she meets with anyone from the *Chicago History Journal*. I'll send over the name of a woman to watch out for." Minutes later Jack's phone chirped with an incoming text message from Wagner with contact information for Aunt Gretchen and Beth Carney.

———

Mandy's return to the apartment at the end of the day found Reggie sitting on the balcony waiting for a debrief.

She wasted no time. "Tell me everything."

"Reggie, he's a predator. I'm sure of it. He thinks he's subtle about it, but he's not. And I'm pretty sure he's in this public company play only for the short run. Once Northwest is public, I think he'll cash in and skedaddle. He probably had to promise the investment bankers he'd commit to stay and run the company."

"So, you told him you weren't interested in a job, right?"

"No. I told him I'd think about it and get back to him by next Monday."

Reggie had been drying her hair in the open air. But now she stood up and threw her towel at Mandy, shouting, "Oh come on. You can't do that to LaSalle. After all the support they've given you, you'd consider dumping them for a snake?"

Mandy pushed her hands down to get her sister's volume under control and then said in a normal tone of voice, "No. I wouldn't dump them for a snake. But I would like a chance to become a general counsel of a public company. Remember what Dad always preached about opportunities? This would be a big one for me. It's every inside counsel's ambition to become a general counsel. How can I pass it by without giving it a chance? YOLO?"

Reggie said, "So, if I got an offer to leave the Bureau, after they'd accommodated me with a Chicago office, I should just turn my back on them?"

"Why are you so upset?"

"Because this has a bad smell to it. I'm shocked you're not getting a whiff. I certainly have it, and your own boyfriend said it." They were rarely angry with each other, but this had set Reggie off.

Mandy sat quietly and explained her willingness to look into it. She had gotten control over things at LaSalle. After last year's espionage case had broken, she'd spent the last year digesting the chaotic acquisition of Allzient. But now she was looking at an unending plateau of corporate compliance grind and not feeling any enthusiasm for it. Suddenly popping up out of nowhere was a gift opportunity to go in an exciting new direction. She had to go through the process.

In a worst-case scenario, she could see suffering through the birthing process, and after Frank's departure, conditions would even out and eventually she could leave with a nice financial reward and with a good resumé enhancement. She explained all that to Reggie with no response. When the silence became awkward, Reggie stood up and said, "I have to go out. You're making a big mistake. I suggest we do a long run tomorrow morning and then check in with the Oracle. He's good at looking around corners." That was their father, Bob Doucette, to whom each of them turned for advice when things got too difficult to work through.

5

July 4th

BOB DOUCETTE WAS A SILVER-haired, intellectual type, sporting tortoise-shell glasses and always attentive to his twins. He'd served for many years as a corporate in-house counsel and eventually became a general counsel. Now he was the chief executive officer of a telecommunications company that had once been part of AT&T. He took the call from his front porch looking across Linden Street in Wilmette at the magnificent Bahá'í Temple and the swaying masts in the harbor across Sheridan Road. He said, "So what's this all about?"

Mandy laid out what had happened with the Northwest offer. He immediately reiterated his longtime mantra about accepting opportunities when they came up, if there was a good chance of a big gain. Sitting next to Mandy, Reggie said, "Dad, this is so disloyal of her to LaSalle. I don't like it."

He was surprised. "What would you have her do? Reject it out of hand? What if it was the key to a fabulous next step? Becoming a general counsel of a public company is a huge career leap, especially for a thirty-year-old woman."

"Don't you respect loyalty?"

Bob said, "Sure I do, but I value self-respect over loyalty to a company. Both of you were put at risk last year because Mandy went out on a limb to serve LaSalle's interests. Look what both of you got for that. If there's any loyalty owed, I think it should run the other way. These days there's nothing wrong with changing jobs frequently, anyway. You should know that better than me. I'm just an old baby boomer. Loyalty to companies by your generation is uncommon. HR is constantly telling me how your generation hops like rabbits from job to job."

Mandy reached over and took Reggie's hand and said, "What do you think I should do?" She didn't want to reignite the emotion from the day before.

Reggie said, "You're asking the wrong person. I think you should stay where you are. I don't have an open mind on this. But you heard what Dad just said, so it's up to you. And talking to the two of you is like being in an echo chamber. The apple didn't fall far from the tree."

When it came to answering Mandy's question of what she should do, Reggie was just not going to support the idea. She was too stuck.

Reggie said, "I just know how I'd feel about leaving the FBI after they've been so good to me. What's important is how you feel about it after all this haggling. You're the one who has to live with that decision."

Mandy wanted to stab back at her with a criticism of Reggie's government-minted loyalty mindset, but she didn't. Having once been a government employee herself, she could understand Reggie's thinking, but Mandy had already passed into the private sector and had shamelessly adopted the attitude of self-interest. Mandy let go of her sister and took a couple steps back and said, "I'm leaning toward it. From what I've seen in initial public offerings, the owners selling into the market become fabulously wealthy overnight. The management team is rewarded through stock options and restricted stock awards they offer the top people, and I'm expecting to be included. I've seen corporate deals rain money on people. But besides the money, it's interesting work and a big sense of accomplishment to take a company public."

"Are you just in this for the money? Don't you love LaSalle?"

"I do love LaSalle. There's a lot to do there, and I have a lot of future opportunities, if I'm patient enough. But right now, it seems like a never-ending mill of liars and cheaters. This has adventure written all over it, and I'm a sucker for that. And it gets me to a general counsel spot right now. I can't be a compliance cop my whole life. And I could labor in the trenches for decades before getting a GC opportunity like this. And what's so bad about wanting money?"

Bob said, "Amen."

Ignoring him again, Reggie said, "I guess you need to weigh everything, but I'd be careful about throwing away a proven fit like LaSalle, to try and grab some brass ring. Good jobs like LaSalle are hard to come by. Of course, you're a national celebrity, so maybe jobs would be yours for the picking." Now Reggie was just needling her. Mandy threw a paperback book at her and Reggie ducked as it flew by.

Bob, still on an open phone line, said, "Just be careful. A company with such a long history as a private, family-owned operation could have plenty to hide. You may have to navigate a minefield. John Booth left there with nothing good to say about it on his way out."

Mandy said, "John never had a chance to tell me about that before he died. I agree it could be a challenge, especially given that I'd be struggling with disclosures. I have no idea whether the insiders are on board with going public either. I've already gotten a distinct whiff of intra-family discord, though."

Bob said, "On the good news side of the equation, you'd have more public company experience than anyone, and you would be controlling the process. You'd just need to strap in for a turbulent ride and keep your eyes wide open. Unless they've got some people who've been in your shoes before, you'd be all alone. No allies other than outside advisors or other new hires who get the drill. Everything could be an uphill battle. But if you could navigate through all that, there could be a nice reward at the end, if nothing more than being a young general counsel of a major public company. Worthwhile on its own, in my opinion. The rest of the good news is the jackpot, if things go right."

Mandy said, "That's what I hoped. Weren't you in the same position when you helped separate the Baby Bells from AT&T? You were basically making new public companies out of the original parent company, so there must have been lots of blank stares when you were trying to get things done."

Bob said, "Right. But the regulations were much less onerous back then. It was easier terrain, but yes, it was the same idea. I took the same risk you're thinking about, and it paid off nicely."

Bob Doucette had been a risk-taker back in the 1970s and 1980s, and it had turned out well for him. He'd been opportunistic and climbed through the management ladder when he could.

He'd taught his children to be observant in life, and to accept opportunities put in front of them. And if they didn't find opportunities when they expected them, they might have to create some. Mandy had taken his advice to heart, and it put her in some uncomfortable situations over the years. Luckily, she had Reggie to help extricate her when she needed it.

At Northwest, she would be facing one of those opportunities by jumping midstream into a securities registration process for a company she knew little about. She'd have to rely on insiders who could have a lot to gain by deception or simply clamming up. Taking this job could mean engaging with dishonesty on a grand scale.

Bob added, "I don't like it that they expect you to decide in such a short time, either. You don't have time to do any investigating. Having a short time frame makes it harder, but once a company decides to go public, it has to move fast."

"I've got a little FOMO going on, and I need to either resist it or embrace it and hope for the best."

Bob said, "What's FOMO?"

"Fear of missing out. C'mon, get with it, Dad."

Bob said, "I'm with it enough, thank you. I just don't talk in acronyms."

Mandy said, "Spare me. Your generation gave us *SNAFU* and *FUBAR*, didn't it?"

"Hell no, that was in World War II, before my time. I'm a boomer, remember? Anyway, you need to think this through carefully, but I'm sure you'll make a good decision. Look, I've taken my gambles in the past, and I did it when I had ten kids to feed. You'd be taking a risk, but nothing you couldn't bounce back from if it went south. If it were me, I'd go for it, but it's your decision. Just get them to give you a sign-on bonus and bake a two-year salary payout into your employment contract if they terminate you. It's very common for new public companies to have a high turnover in the top ranks, because the personalities may clash and you could get pushed out just for rubbing someone the wrong way,"

"Great idea."

"Remember, ladies: There are two ways to go through life. You can wait for things to happen and react to them, or you can make a plan and let others react to you."

Mandy said, "Reggie's not wrong, though. I do have a lot to thank LaSalle for, but I feel this is worth a serious look."

Reggie put up her palms outward and said, "OK, OK. I'm on board with it." She recognized a clear outcome ahead and chose to slam on the brakes. A graceful surrender was necessary. "But if there's any buyer's remorse from you, I'm not shedding any crocodile tears for you. And I think you should appreciate a little JOMO."

Their dad said, "What's that?"

"Joy of Missing Out."

Mandy said, "I think I could use some help from your researcher, if you don't mind."

Bob said, "Of course. I'll let Sammy know to look for a call from you. By the way, you know she's involved with your old friend Ray Hanson, right?" Ray Hanson was a former FBI investigator who had gone private and done some work for Mandy.

Reggie perked up at this news and said, "How did that happen? Involved how?"

Bob said, "Not in the platonic way. Apparently, they set off some sparks with each other last year when they helped you out."

———

On the Fourth of July, the two couples headed up to Wilmette to meet with the Doucette clan. Patrick had met Mandy's parents earlier on the trip out to Washington, DC, when the sisters were at the White House, but none of the other siblings were present. Dan had been around longer and had met some. They sat on the porch, and they talked for a while, but soon Mandy and Reggie took Patrick up to show him their room. He loved the immersion in their youth. Dan had seen it all before, so he stayed downstairs and entertained Bob on the porch.

The siblings in the Doucette family fell into two categories—the *Uppers*, or the four older siblings, and the *Lowers*, the four younger sibs. Mandy and Reggie were in the exact middle of the brood. Among the Lowers, Sarah was a twenty-six-year-old postgraduate student at the Medill School of Journalism at Northwestern. Will was a twenty-four-year-old commodities trader at the Chicago Mercantile Exchange. Jake was a twenty-two-year-old engineering major at Purdue, and maybe soon a physicist. Prudence was the youngest at twenty-one, and an English major and pre-law student at DePaul in the city. They were all introduced to Patrick for the first time, and again to Dan.

The room was unchanged from their teenage years. It was a Mandy and Reggie museum and Patrick marveled at the wall decorations: preserved insect collection, medals and finish line photos from races, photos of the sisters doing American Sign Language at New Trier High School events, and even a mural made of sea glass they'd collected from Gillson Beach. The sign language skill was one the sisters had picked up when New Trier was looking for signers to assist hearing-impaired students at student gatherings. The school had them trained, but they used it to help them have private conversations amidst the crowd of ten siblings. Life in a family as big as the Doucette's meant that privacy was a precious commodity.

Patrick noticed that in all the photos the sisters were dressed identically. Though he'd seen them doing that plenty of times since they'd met, they were growing out of that habit. Now that they had their own boyfriends, Mandy and Reggie had loosened up the sisterly bonds, at least where looks were concerned.

Mandy and Reggie spent some time catching up with some of the Lowers one-on-one, with some questioning and encouragement involved. They had a very lively discussion with Jake, now an enthusiastic intern with LaSalle Enterprises at the Fermilab National Accelerator in southwest suburban Batavia. He was going through Purdue's engineering program. He was practically vibrating just being at Fermilab and having the unique experience of working at a particle accelerator facility. He could rub elbows with all kinds of engineers.

Mandy only had one piece of advice for him. "Just so you know, Arthur Ross heads up that unit for LaSalle, and he was cranky about the internship. Keep your head down."

"Will do, and thanks again for getting me the internship."

Soon Prudi changed places with Jake and updated them on her progress through DePaul. She'd suffered through Scott Turow's early book about the law school experience—*One L*. She was having some hesitation on that career choice and wanted some reassurance from Mandy that it was the right thing to do. Mandy tried to be upbeat about it, but it was still a vivid memory for her just how hard that first year of law school had been. She didn't like to think back on that phase of her education either. It was too painful.

They soon made the short walk over to Gillson Park, the sixty-acre lakeshore area east of Sheridan Road. After finding a good viewing spot on the lawn, they all made a run to the food stands at the Taste of Wilmette. Some of their siblings strayed away and ran into old friends, neighbors, and former schoolmates. Other members of the family straggled over to join the group.

While the Doucette siblings were catching up, Bob and their mother Josie took the opportunity to get to know Dan and Patrick better. They covered their origins, their schools, and families. Both Dan and Patrick got the feeling that they were being interviewed, but that was fine. They were both only children, and were equally entertained and overwhelmed by the family dynamics of the Doucettes. Though it was relatively tame now with most of the children living elsewhere, they got the impression that the household back in the time all the children were living at home was anything but tame. Prudi told them that the twins had a pivotal role in the family, becoming persuaders and negotiators. Sometimes it was up to them to protect the *Lowers* from the *Uppers*, and they were also enforcers when times called for that. But when it came to relations between the twins, Bob was proud of their compatibility.

He said, "They were always there for each other and were a unified force. Fortunately, we never saw any lasting tension between the two. Considering the strength of their personalities, no one in the family wanted to see a fiery feud between them."

Changing the subject, Bob asked Patrick, "What was your major?"

Patrick said, "I double majored in history and English, and I write historical fiction now."

"You could have gone into law with that background."

"That's what my dad says."

He preferred to volunteer that up front, preventing the painful exploratory conversations he always had with people who wondered why he would pursue those majors. Bob Doucette was not one of those. They talked for a while about his books and what he was working on, and how historical fiction captivated him. He said he was drawn to stories about Chicago. They spoke of the dynamics of water in the Chicago area and how it affected the lives of the pioneers and the workers. His studies were leading to a story based on a theme of water, he told them, but it hadn't quite come together yet.

"I spend a lot of time on research to get a good grip on history, and eventually a story jumps out at me. It's a fun process, but because I have a book to deliver annually to my publisher, I'm usually working on at least two books at a time."

Bob said, "If you're interested, the harbor is past the trees there and leads to part of the overall Chicago water control system. Past Sheridan Road is the entrance from the harbor to the North Channel. It eventually connects to the Chicago River, and down to the canal leading to the Mississippi. I think the girls have even kayaked it down into the city."

Patrick said, "That's how Mandy and I met, kayaking on the Chicago River. She was in a kayaking group I joined awhile ago."

"Mandy joined a group? She always avoided groups."

"A friend of hers dragged her into it. She told me she had kayaking experience on the upper Mississippi where some ancestors lived."

Bob said, "Right. We have a long family history on rivers and lakes. I'm sure you can coax it out of her if you're interested."

"I may. I'm interested in everything about Mandy," he said, smiling at Bob. "Maybe it could even blossom into a story for me."

Jake jumped into the discussion and said, "You should let the Red Deuce tell you about the Mississippi and the Minnesota Doucettes. There was some wild paddling back in the territory days. They even got burned out in a Chippewa attack." Patrick hadn't heard the sisters referred to by their family nickname—the Red Deuce. It was charming to him.

Bob added, "And two of the daughters, twins in fact, were captured by the Chippewa. Their correct name is the Ojibwe, of course, and they survived the captivity. Those twin sisters were something to behold, according to family lore, much like the Red Deuce."

Just then the first fireworks went off, and oohs and aahs dominated the crowd for the next thirty minutes. After the finale they followed the crowd out of the park in darkness and across the bridge to the North Channel. On the way, Reggie pulled the other three over to the edge of the harbor and pointed down at all the boats.

Reggie said, "Patrick, here's where your girlfriend cut her teeth on crime-busting as a sixteen-year-old. This is the harbormaster's headquarters at the Harbor Club, right next to the Coast Guard station." She pointed to Wilmette Harbor below. "She worked there and busted the harbormaster himself for embezzlement. She's famous around here for it."

Having no interest in wading into that bog, Mandy rolled her eyes at Reggie and said, "It's a long story that we don't have time for right now." She dragged them away into the flow of the exiting crowd, across Sheridan Road and through the golf course. The two couples bade their goodbyes to the family and drove back downtown via Sheridan Road and Lake Shore Drive. Along the way, they could see neighborhood fireworks displaying along the entire drive from Wilmette to their River North neighborhood. Mandy, meanwhile, quietly reflected on whether her life was about to become a series of fireworks of another kind.

When they were alone after dropping off Reggie and Dan, they sat on the balcony of Patrick's condo overlooking the north end of Lincoln Park and the lake. Patrick asked Mandy about Reggie's earlier comments. He said, "Are you going to tell me what the harbormaster bust was all about?"

She sighed. "Look. It was when I was a teenager in high school, and I caused a big deal I should never have started. But it's ancient history anyway." Mandy didn't want to dwell on painful memories, regardless of her being in the right.

"I happen to care about you and want to know everything I can."

She pulled him in for a big hug and then told him how her dad had always pushed her to ask questions and do the right thing.

"He'd always wondered why things get done a certain way. How do things work? Where are we, and how do we get to places? He was a due diligence machine, and he said if you didn't ask the questions, you might never get the answers. It's what happened with me in the harbormaster situation."

Patrick said, "What did you do?"

"I worked there and saw some things happening with the cash. I didn't think it was making it to where it was supposed to go, so I spoke up and set off a bomb. I paid the price."

"How?"

Against her better instincts, she explained the events of her teenage experience and hoped that would put an end to the topic. Patrick said, "And yet you're still doing that kind of thing, but on a much bigger scale. I think that's great."

"I'm glad you do, but it's not so much fun to be charging after people constantly."

He didn't want to say that no one was forcing her to do that work, so he gave her a little smile and said, "You also need to tell me about the Minnesota Doucettes and the Chippewa Indians."

Mandy gave him a curious look back and said, "Where did that come from?"

"Brother Jake."

With her finger tapping her watch face, Mandy said, "All in due time. That's boring. Let's change the subject."

"OK. What do you want to talk about?" Patrick said,

With a big smile she said, "How about us? You just said you care about me." She had his attention, and he wasn't going to say anything until she kept going. "We've been together for a while, and I'm wondering what we're doing. I mean, are we headed somewhere as a couple?"

"I'm headed somewhere, and I hope you are too. I have a great time with you, and I want to keep going with this. What are you thinking?"

It wasn't the "L" word, but it was getting closer. She had to let it come out from him first.

She said, "Same here, as long as it's exclusive. Reggie likes you too. That's important."

"Exclusive it is. My parents really like you, and that's a huge compliment, especially from P5."

"What's *P5*?"

Patrick said, "P5 is my dad."

"You call your dad P5?"

"Yes. And I'm P6. It's a tradition in our family going all the way back to the original Patrick Carney in the 1800s. But you don't have to call us that."

Mandy said, "And I thought my family's nicknames were weird."

"What are they?"

"My dad calls my mom *Gabby*. Reggie and I call him the *Oracle,* because he can see around corners and tell you what will happen next. He calls Reggie and me the *Red Deuce*, for obvious reasons. My family is also very superstitious, so you should be prepared to see some serious quirkiness."

"How did your mom get the nickname *Gabby*?"

"It's probably not what you think. She was a spectator at one of Reggie's Ironman races, then watched later as Reggie got the Ironman logo tattooed on her ankle. She babbled nervously while Reggie was inked, and after a steady stream of that the tattoo artist told *Gabby* to keep it down."

Having had enough of that, she climbed onto his lap, and they kissed for a long time.

6

Meeting Carl

EARLY ONE MORNING Ray Hanson made a call from the pilot deck of his vessel, the *Bogie*. She was a forty-three-foot Nordhavn trawler yacht, now berthed at her summer home at Belmont Harbor on Lake Michigan. The boat could comfortably accommodate two adults with separate staterooms and was reputed to be the sturdiest vessel of its size. She was perfect for the Great Loop trip between Chicago and Florida every year. Ray was a regular *Great Looper*. He worked onboard, mostly, but he'd go ashore and even take trips for the right job. He was the sole proprietor of his own one-man surveillance firm, a service Mandy had used a year earlier.

Growing up in the Wrigleyville neighborhood, almost in the shadow of Wrigley Field, Ray had gone to Lane Tech High School and then DePaul University to get his dual degrees in criminology and information systems. From there it was on to the Cook County Sheriff's Office, and later the Chicago office of the FBI. He completed the intelligence training program at the FBI Academy and served as an analyst. Eventually Ray became more focused on his current specialties, hacking and tracking. Over time he had become an expert and jumped to the private side to pull in larger amounts of cash than he could have ever earned at the Bureau.

Having worked at Belmont Harbor as a kid he'd taken a liking to the nautical life, and he'd eventually gotten the bug to become a *Great Looper*. That meant he was a nomad, living on a boat and rotating between Chicago's Belmont Harbor and Key West. Each autumn he would pilot his boat down the Mississippi River via the Chicago, Des Plaines and Illinois rivers, and through the Gulf of Mexico to the Keys. Then in spring he'd go up the Atlantic coast through the intercoastal waterway, through the Hudson River, the Erie Canal and the Great Lakes, and return to Belmont Harbor. He was part of a community that made the same annual voyage. The *Bogie* was totally rigged for electronics work, bristling with antennae, video screens and surveillance equipment. Ray was excited to use his newest toys—his night vision drone and his new directional mike. He had already hatched a plan to add electronic countermeasures to his defensive arsenal during the winter months. If fighter jets and navy ships were armed with such defenses, why shouldn't the *Bogie*?

Ray called a number from his pilot bridge and when it was answered, he said, "Good morning, beautiful. Am I going to see you soon?"

Samantha Wong replied, "Aye aye, Skipper. Sooner than you think. Permission to board?"

As he came out of his bubble, he stepped onto the Portuguese bridge and looked down at the dock. Sammy stood there at his berth looking up and talking to him. She had a big smile on her face and waved to him. She was a beautiful Asian-American woman with sparkling green eyes, and Ray had been attracted to her instantly when they met.

"Ahoy. Permission granted. Get up here," he said. Sammy had many talents useful to Ray, beyond merely being a great researcher that Mandy's dad used and who did some work for Mandy last year. She now held several part-time gigs, ranging from doing high-level psychological counseling, to body language analysis, and lip-reading. She even read lips for law enforcement, viewing remote video feeds that lacked audio. Sammy had first met Ray in his prior life at the FBI when they had some contact. Sammy worked on closed-circuit video clips. It was very helpful to hear what people caught on closed-circuit film were saying to each other. Sometimes people did out-of-character things that got caught on video, and came to regret it. Sammy could pick those things up using her assessment skills. She had earned a psychology degree from the University of Chicago.

Her childhood had involved protecting and understanding her little sister, whose deafness had led to Sammy's communication skills. She was conversant in American Sign Language.

A later study of enneagrams gave her another assessment tool, but it required her to have some contact with her subjects and could not be done remotely. She had also studied kinesics, so she could look for the different kinds of body language that bespoke all manner of intentions and attitudes. Sammy's unique talents made her highly valued in the investigation community.

The lip-reading she did for the Cubs during home stands she couldn't really talk about. It was illegal under the rules of baseball but was done throughout the league. She once watched a pitcher, disgusted with some batter, say that a beanball was coming his way. It was a timely observation by Sammy, and she texted a warning to the dugout and the batter was forewarned by the third base coach. That was typical of her regular "consulting" work during home stands. Using a high-powered monocular she always carried with her, she scoured the dugout, the base coaches, and the pitcher for unguarded moments to see what they were saying.

After bumping into her one night at Toons Bar and Grille, a nearby Southport Avenue watering hole, she and Ray had gotten friendly. More than friendly, in fact. On this particular day, Sammy came aboard and joined Ray in the pilot deck and kissed him. She had walked the mile from her Wrigleyville apartment to Belmont Harbor. Ray said, "We should step into the pilot's cabin to release some stress."

Sammy backed up into the cabin and wiggled her finger at him. "*Smooth sailin',*" she said.

Later, a stress-free Ray was on the pilot deck again plotting his course across the lake, when he heard a pebble hit his window. Looking down, he saw Mandy and Reggie standing on his pier, in running clothes, waving at him. He motioned them aboard and joined them below at the surface deck with all the creature comforts.

Reggie said, "Is the name of your boat a comment on your golf game?"

Mandy quickly said, "Humphrey Bogart played Sam Spade in Dashiell Hammet's novel *The Maltese Falcon*. I'll bet that's where the name *Bogie* came from. Am I right?"

Ray replied, "Yes. Hop aboard."

Reggie said, "Why are you up so early?"

"Getting ready to head out across the lake to Saugatuck after the Cubs game. They head off to San Diego after this home stand. We're taking off for a couple of days of antique hunting and cherry picking."

Mandy cocked her head and said, "We?"

The harbor was calm but the boat rolled a little. Ray unconsciously glanced past the sisters, and Mandy and Reggie followed his gaze and saw a yawning Samantha Wong walking up the stairs. Not expecting to see them, she gasped. Sammy had some serious bedhead going on and wasn't moving too fast.

Reggie discreetly signed to Mandy that they must have just finished a morning delight. Both were stunned into silence when Sammy signed back at them that they were invading her privacy and should mind their own business. It was blunt, which was a Sammy trademark.

The sisters turned back to Ray, who was clearly embarrassed, and they all burst out laughing.

He said, "OK, OK, you caught us. I confess."

Mandy gave a tilted head look at Ray and asked, "You're not doing work for the Oracle too, are you?"

"Who?"

Reggie said, "Our dad? Bob Doucette? You know, the occasional client of Sammy?" as she hooked her thumb toward Sammy.

Sammy said, "I think I need to go freshen up. Excuse me. *Storm's abrewin'* up here. By the way," she said to Mandy, "your dad sent me a message saying you need me to look into something for you."

Mandy said to her, "Right. There's a company named Northwest Engineering. It's been in Chicago since the 1830s, when it was known as Northwest Drayage and Tunnel Company. I need a thorough search of its history to see if it ever did anything illegal or questionable."

Sammy asked, "When do you need it?"

"ASAP."

"Shouldn't be a problem. We'll be cruising for a few hours to Saugatuck and back, so I'll have some free research time. That should be enough to get a start on finding what you need. Text me some details. By the way, how do you two know sign language?" Saugatuck, Michigan, was sixty miles due east across Lake Michigan from Chicago and was a cherry orchard area and antique store haven.

They both said, "New Trier High School."

With that Sammy ducked down to the lower deck and the sisters turned to Ray.

Ray avoided discussing the scene that had just taken place and said, "About working for your dad, you know I can't disclose my clients. But I'm always available to you if you have some snoop work."

"We wouldn't want you violating any professional confidences, would we? I may have a job for you to help with soon. Looks like we interrupted something, so we'll be heading on. *Storm's abrewin',*" Mandy joked, mimicking Sammy. She gave an over-the-shoulder look back at Ray and a wink as they hopped off and ran down the pier.

Sammy had an interesting top-level situational assessment she went through. She called it the *vibe.* If she anticipated trouble the vibe would be *storm's abrewin',* and if it looked generally good it would be *smooth sailin'.* The only ones left were *don't care* and *not sure.* It was her trait to first assess overall whether what she was going into was good, bad, or worse yet, unknown situations. If she didn't care, the rest was irrelevant. Then at the next level she would assess individuals in control and see how they exercised it. From there she would study them and learn to read their body language. She could then be useful to people like Bob Doucette. He'd employed her to carry out very specialized services at annual meetings of shareholders. She would observe shareholders waiting to attend the meeting. A company's annual meeting frequently attracted an array of attendees, and some of them brought their own personal grievances against the company to air. If she detected someone with an issue, she could alert management and the shareholder could be approached discreetly and defused. It was always a good idea to avert disruptive meetings.

Mandy finally met Carl Wagner, Northwest's general counsel, for lunch at Gene and Georgetti's, Chicago's oldest steakhouse on North Franklin Street in the River North district. The restaurant was nothing to look at, but the food was great and it was convenient for them both. He was almost a look-alike for Frank but not as tall and had no gray hair yet. A little public company experience would change that, she thought.

Carl said, "It's such a pleasure to meet you. I know it struck you oddly that my cousin would start our contact, but he does that kind of thing. He told me you'd said that."

"Is it an alpha male kind of thing with him?" she said.

He just smirked in return. Carl couldn't very well admit to knowing what Frank was likely doing, though Mandy had already sniffed it out. She had a good nose for that kind of thing. Frank had made no effort to hide his attraction anyway. The constant torture Carl had endured from his cousin for years kept him in constant vigilance mode. Frank had been a frequent offender. Mandy was happy that Carl wasn't undressing her with his eyes, like Frank had done.

The server brought a *"No Horsin' Around Sangwich"* for her and the ricotta-spinach ravioli for him. Carl impressed her as straightforward without the type-A aura of his cousin.

She had to be certain that he'd be receptive to what would be involved in a public offering. That was on her agenda for this meeting.

To his credit, Carl was honest with her. "I don't have a background in public company law, so as soon as the bankers and deal lawyers told us we should staff up for the launch, I knew I couldn't wait for a headhunter search. You were my choice after I saw your escapade last year, so I served up your name and pushed Frank to go with you."

"Thank you. I suppose I should have guessed how you knew about me."

He said, "It's obvious, isn't it, with all your publicity last year? But it was serious bonus points that you had a history in our line of business."

"Why would you need to preempt a search?"

Carl said, "If a search was going on, it would take time that we don't have. It also meant Frank would be making the choice. There's no telling who we would have ended up with if he was driving the bus. If I'm going to get into line management and if Frank's pick wobbled for some reason, I can see myself being stuck with two jobs. At least for a while. I wanted to strike first and get who I wanted."

She said as tactfully as she could, "I appreciate your confidence in me. From my side, I need to make sure I'd be going into a deal where management appreciates what needs to be done."

"Please explain."

"I'd be joining a project that's well underway, if I'm not mistaken. Securities filings need to be thoroughly vetted for full and accurate disclosures. I would have to be dedicated to that from the outset." She was sure that he'd had a good primer on securities law from the outside lawyers and the investment bankers. But did he fully appreciate where it could lead if misleading statements ended up in a filing? Mandy was only trying to measure his appreciation of what he and his cousin were embarking on.

"My understanding is that you are already on file with the SEC waiting for comments on your registration statement. If I join you now, I will have liability for that document, and I'll need to do my own due diligence to be satisfied with it."

Carl asked, "It's not enough for you that our outside counsel has vetted everything?"

"I'm afraid not."

"You'd know best about that, I suppose. I can guarantee you'd have support for what you need." She wondered quietly to herself whether that guarantee spoke on behalf of Frank as well.

One of her goals for this lunch was to see if there were any omens she should identify and hear what Northwest Engineering was prepared to undertake. It's one thing to accept a family-driven exit from management, but quite another thing to get it done. She didn't want a reluctant management team to hamstring the process. From his own mouth Mandy had heard about Frank's reluctance.

She also needed to see if this job would be worth her while. Carl laid out the compensation package, and Mandy was very pleased. It nearly doubled her salary and added a hefty sign-on bonus and a significant cash and stock incentive program. If everything worked out, she would be very secure. Her title initially would be Assistant General Counsel, Corporate Law. She'd also be an Assistant Corporate Secretary and have a staff to help her manage the board of directors and regulatory filings. She would also continue to have the compliance role she had, but she could delegate the grunt work. No more speechmaking to large groups, especially unreceptive ones. As Frank had said, once the stock exchange launch took place, Carl would become a group president, and Mandy would become general counsel and corporate secretary. Mandy said her piece and Carl agreed not to hire other LaSalle employees if she joined, and added a two-year termination payoff for dismissal. When they left, Carl promised to get an offer letter to her later in the day, along with a copy of the draft registration statement now under review by the SEC.

She said that if it reflected what they had discussed and she was comfortable after reviewing the materials, she would likely clear her issues with LaSalle and sign it, then come aboard after a two-week notice period to LaSalle. Carl had no idea what he was getting into by going public, she decided. But then again, hardly anyone ever did. She hoped it made sense joining up with the Wagners. Her sister's strong reaction still reverberated in her head.

She said to him, "Are you happy about this or did you prefer the way things were?"

"I've got my reservations, but I'm happy to go public."

"You must know that your lives are going to change. You'll never be able to operate Northwest the same way."

"Meaning what?"

She leaned out over the table with her chin in her hands and said, "You'll be on duty twenty-four seven, for one thing. That's just for starters. Then there are the regulators, the shareholders, the stock exchange, the corporate governance people, and the gadflies. You've probably heard about them from your banker."

He was nodding and replied, "I'm going to do my best to deflect as much of it as I can to you."

They shook hands outside the entrance and went their separate ways. As Mandy walked away she studied the receding image of Carl in the store windows serving as mirrors, so she didn't have to turn around. She didn't want to be caught looking back at him in case he was watching her walk away. He wasn't, which confirmed for her that he didn't have Frank's lecherous character. Even if she had some concerns over Frank, Carl appeared safe to her.

CHAPTER

7

Acceptance

MANDY RETURNED TO HER OFFICE at the LaSalle headquarters after her lunch with Carl Wagner, aware that she had to switch from investigator to diplomat. An open, straightforward approach with LaSalle's general counsel would be best. Rick Crawford was a good friend, and she'd neither jeopardize that friendship nor put her friend and boss at a disadvantage.

She still stung from Reggie's criticism about disloyalty, but today she had to compartmentalize. She was preoccupied with the non-compete agreement she'd signed when joining LaSalle four years ago. Though she hadn't reread it since then, her guess was that the agreement should not pose a problem. Reggie had questioned her about it during their run.

"What's up with these non-compete agreements? I hear they're very common now."

Mandy had answered, "Corporations have gone overboard on non-compete agreements. It's anybody's guess how enforceable they are with courts. If they're overly broad in scope, courts won't enforce them. Courts have limited their use based on public policy."

"Public policy?"

Mandy said, "People shouldn't be unreasonably prevented from changing jobs."

"You're not worried about it?"

"No, but I'm not about to provoke a lawsuit and have a legal debate with LaSalle anyway. I've got too much regard for Rick and the company to start a war with them. Sounds pretty loyal of me, doesn't it," she'd said, giving Reggie side-eye as they ran. Reggie ignored the swipe at her.

Rick's assistant waved Mandy into his office. She'd worked closely with him over the years. He looked up when she entered his office and before she could say a word he said, "Guess what I'm realizing about Ed Rosen? He'd hardly finished drafting board meeting minutes and starting on his to-do list, and already he had to start working on the next board meeting."

Rick had inherited the job of corporate secretary along with the general counsel post when the prior general counsel, Ed Rosen, had left the company. That was in the wake of the spy scandal the previous year. Both Rick and Mandy had great respect for Ed Rosen.

Mandy said, "You have my sympathy. If you're not right there in the thick of it, you don't appreciate all the work a board creates. I'm sure you know the worst part is that the board is the CEO's boss. So, your mistakes as corporate secretary not only reflect badly on you, but on the CEO too. If it's not bad enough being under the spotlight by the CEO, then you've got the board members on your case too. At least you've got a good CEO to have your back."

He didn't seem comforted by that thought.

It was time to take control of the discussion. "Do you know anything about Northwest Engineering?" she said.

"Some. It's a big company, but private. It's a mystery unless you work in the industry. It's been around as long as we have. Why?" he asked.

"Are they much of a competitor with us?"

"Not really. After the Great Fire and Patrick Carney's disappearance, LaSalle just about folded. It started moving away from the type of projects it had been doing. Northwest kept on with the same kind of work. Is there a problem?"

"You know about Patrick Carney and his disappearance?" Mandy asked, looking incredulous.

"Sure, he was right there at the birth of this company along with his father Seamus," he said with a little smirk. "Any studious employee would understand that part of the company's history. He took over for the founder but then died in the fire. Afterwards the company started changing its lines of business and never looked back. Still hasn't. So, I repeat—is there a problem?"

Brushing aside his insult about her studiousness, she said, "Have you heard anything about Northwest currently?"

Rick said, "They just issued a press release announcing they're going public. What's this all about, by the way?"

Mandy was silent, struggling with how to get the words out. They would surely sting.

When she hesitated, he said, "Uh-oh. Wait a minute. Not another one. Don't tell me they're sniffing around you?" He held his forehead without looking at her. She'd been approached a few times in the past year and had been open about it. He should be getting used to it by now. Mandy was relieved Rick had sensed it and that she hadn't had to say it out loud herself.

She said, "They reached out to me out of the blue. I didn't have anything to do with it. I had no bait in the water, just like with the other offers I've had. Honest," she said, finally looking at him and crossing her heart. So much for the open, straightforward approach.

Leaning his head back and looking at the ceiling, he said, "Please don't let this be happening. Not now."

"I haven't given them a definitive answer yet. I told them I had some thinking to do, and that's what I'm doing. If you want me to shut it down, say so."

"They're staffing up, aren't they? What did they offer you?" Rick asked.

"They have no corporate staff with public company experience," Mandy said. "They've asked me to head up the internal team to take the company public. After they're public, I'd become their general counsel. I wanted you to be aware that it's out there and didn't want you surprised any more than you are already. I also wanted to make sure that leaving for Northwest wouldn't cause a violation of my non-compete agreement."

"Look, I'm in shock. I really rely on you, and I'd have some big shoes to fill if you left. Compliance officers are such a new thing, and we've been so lucky to have you. Let me think about it and get back to you. When do you need to give them an answer?"

"Today, actually. I'm sorry about this, especially the rush. Oh, and by the way, if I joined them, I'd make them promise not to raid LaSalle for anyone else."

"Just so you know, legend has it that stealing LaSalle employees was a tradition from the early days at Northwest." Mandy didn't know what he meant.

"Huh," she said, "that's news to me."

He said, "Let me think about the non-compete."

She made a beeline back to her office and called Reggie to report on the discussion. She and her sister spoke constantly throughout the day, and had for years, serving as each other's confidants and sounding boards. Even though Reggie was living with her, and they had plenty of together time, they still needed to talk during the day. It was a twin sister thing.

Mandy said, "The loyalty issue doesn't seem to be a problem. Rick will be fine. Are you still mad about my decision?"

Reggie said, "No, I can never be mad at you for long, but I still don't like it. Hopefully you'll see the light."

Three hours later, Rick came to her office, pointed to his mouth and said, "Let's go put on the feed bag." He was still a farm boy, at heart.

Once they sat down for lunch, Rick said, "You didn't tell me this morning about how Northwest got interested in you."

"Same as with the others. It was last year's media coverage."

"Makes sense. I'd probably go after you too." Then getting serious for a fraction of a second, he looked at her and said, "I'd miss you, but if you do this, I hope it works out for you. You deserve a big break like this."

She said, "I still need to be clear about this non-compete issue before I make a decision."

"Oh right. Sorry. We wouldn't stand in your way. After all, how would we look like if we went after a national spy-busting celebrity, relying on some flimsy non-compete agreement?"

She put her hands together as if in prayer and said, "Thank you."

"By the way, we're releasing some good news today, so don't buy any stock," he said.

"Tell me."

"We won the bid to supply equipment for the St. Lawrence Seaway upgrade project. Large-scale excavation equipment, lock systems, everything. It's a nice contract for us. The project is going to double the size of the canal's capacity."

"Congratulations. A nice piece of business. Did Northwest bid on it too? Is this why you brought it up?" she said.

"I don't know, but if they bid on the construction work, we'd end up being their equipment supplier if they got the award. About Northwest itself, though, I'm warning you that you'd have your hands full. It's been private forever. And there will have to be lots of due diligence done. If you go there, you and their auditors are going to have to turn over all the rocks and see what crawls out, unless it's already done. They've been audited by a public accounting firm, right?" Rick asked.

She said, "Of course. They need three years of audited financial statements for a public offering, so their investment bankers accomplished that so they could file a registration statement. They sent me their draft registration statement so I could see their sources of income. I wanted it to get comfortable on the competition issue with LaSalle. I did a limited litigation history search, as well. They had some cases in the past, but nothing significant pending. I've got somebody working further on that. On my own I found mainly minor commercial disputes but no big, risky bet-the-company cases. I have no idea about the individual family members, though. I'm only into this barely a couple days now, all of which has been spent thinking about my own personal issues," she said.

Rick said half kiddingly, "And you should also remember what happened to you the last time you did due diligence. Does attempted murder ring a bell?"

Deciding to kid him back, she said, "For a second there, I thought you meant it when you said you wouldn't stand in my way. Now you're trying to scare me off. That's heavy-handed to play the murder card. This is a public offering, not a gunfight."

Rick put his hands up in the air in surrender. "You never know. Just keep in mind that if it does turn out to be a gunfight, don't just bring a knife." She looked at him and blew him a kiss as he walked away, and wondered if that was his way of saying he'd take her back.

Mandy worried that she was making a mistake by rushing into this, and she should be much more deliberate. But Frank had made it clear that if she passed on the offer, he would move on quickly to someone else. She believed him, at least on that issue.

Her mental calculations over, she decided to take a chance. She composed a text message to Frank and Carl accepting the position, and just to show her sense of humor, she offered up one of her favorite Gary Larson *Far Side* cartoons—the one where two spiders had spun a web at the bottom of a slide with a little kid on top, ready to slide down into it. One spider told the other that they'd eat like kings if they pulled it off. Frank immediately sent back a message congratulating her and welcoming her aboard.

C H A P T E R

8

DNA

REGGIE WAS BUSY IDENTIFYING the skeleton. She used her technicians and a Smithsonian staff member for forensic anthropology needs. They had carefully coaxed away the concrete and gravel mix permeating part of the skull. Completing work quickly was important, but not at the risk of destroying evidence or sacrificing a ballistics test. The team re-articulated the skull, putting *Humpty Dumpty* back together again. Dan Aleri had worked with the team examining the skeleton. Though still teaching at Northwestern's medical school, he was now a forensic anthropologist. He and Reggie had met and worked together at the FBI's Quantico, Virginia laboratory as pathologists. He'd followed her back when she had transferred to the Chicago FBI office. Then Dan had left the Bureau to pursue

Reggie romantically and not be hamstrung by the FBI's anti-fraternization policy.

As a forensic anthropologist, he'd already made an important observation about the skeleton. The cranium had been re-assembled and showed no evidence of an exit wound, and certain of the interior surfaces showed graze marks. Dan theorized that the bullet had grazed the eye socket, then followed a careening path inside the skull before coming to rest in the brain. The severely cracked skull eventually fell apart—or *disarticulated* in Dan's terminology. The tissue was all that held it together. A relatively intact bullet rested below the base of the skull, having remained in the cerebral stew it had caused. No mushrooming or fragmentation had occurred, so it presented itself as a good candidate for a ballistics test. It rested there inundated with concrete when the bridge abutment work was finished.

The bullet was small, and to Reggie appeared to be a .22-caliber, so it would be entirely possible for the bullet to remain inside the victim's skull without exiting. Luckily for the victim, death would have occurred instantly once the brainstem was hit.

She said, "I thought someone might have rammed a sharp object through the eye socket. I didn't expect to see a bullet. Most likely a shooter would aim at the torso."

Dan said, "Maybe it was a second or third shot, like a kill shot after first hitting a bigger target. Or maybe it was just an incredibly lucky shot to the head. We should also X-ray all the additional material we've scooped up below in the bones."

"I wonder if we'll get some good ballistics if it's not too distorted. What does it mean to you that there's no exit wound?"

Dan said, "That a small caliber weapon was used. Probably a .22-caliber, just like you said."

Reggie's next concern was ballistics testing. The techs did a good job removing the cement encasing the bullet without marring the bullet itself. Under a microscope the striations were faint, but sufficient to test. The science of ballistics had been around since the 1830s. There was nothing questionable about the identification means, or its evidentiary value in a court of law. The problem was that, even though you might possess the ballistics from the projectile, you still needed a gun to fire a bullet that could be compared. She ordered the ballistics pattern of the bullet to be made by the techs. When the results came back, they could only be stored, awaiting a gun barrel with which to try matching them. That would be Steve Baker's problem.

From the FBI autopsy suite where they had been working, Reggie called her sister. "The techs finished laying out all the bones to reconstruct the skeleton. They were encased in concrete in the barrel, so it was a reconstruction project first. Some cloth bits were in there, so we've searched for biological material. With bone marrow, teeth and hopefully hair, we might find a clue to help us identify the victim. Maybe even the perpetrator."

"Even from over a hundred years ago? Does DNA last that long?"

"Look, they've been able to extract DNA from dinosaur teeth sixty million years old, so why not a mere hundred years?" Reggie said.

Mandy said, "Is that really true?"

"I'm the science geek, remember?"

Her lab had cleaned the concrete off the bones found in the barrel. The bones encased in concrete yielded a much better opportunity to find nuclear DNA, with some resistance to the normal decomposition processes. They extracted bone marrow and teeth to check for DNA. They might have nuclear or mitochondrial DNA, or both. Mitochondrial DNA is the most resistant to degradation, yet it only runs to the maternal side. Nuclear DNA would be used for paternal genealogy.

By Wednesday, the results were in hand. Reggie asked for them to be run through CODIS, the FBI's Combined DNA Index System. This was a national law enforcement database system which collected profiles through federal, state, and local law enforcement systems. It would be hit-or-miss whether the DNA from the skeleton could be matched to anything in CODIS. To be in CODIS a person's DNA would have been collected in a criminal matter. That system had only existed for a couple of decades. It was a long shot, but she ordered it to be checked. In effect, Reggie was looking for an ancestor, from whom a genealogy search up the family tree could be attempted to connect the victim to a family.

Also back were the radiocarbon dating test results, in which the carbon-14 element in the bones was analyzed for the half-life of the element in the test sample. The result showed the bones were approximately 170–180 years old, so the murder victim was in his early thirties at the time of death.

Mandy wished she would cut to the chase.

Reggie said, "We found a bullet below the skull, and then reconstructed the skeleton and found chipping on rib bones. After carefully examining the debris from below the body and X-raying it, another bullet appeared, almost intact."

Mandy said, "Another piece of the puzzle falls into place. What does that tell you?"

"We think this person was executed, with a chest shot followed by a kill shot to the brain."

The next day at the lab, Reggie got the results of the CODIS search. One match came up to a sixty-three-year-old male by the name of William H. Carney in the Chicago area. His rap sheet was for a rape committed twenty years earlier in Chicago. He'd been convicted and served ten years in the Joliet Correctional Center. He had been paroled and his whereabouts were unknown.

Reggie had to call Mandy to ask if Patrick had a relative named William in his early sixties.

Reggie said, "It may just be a coincidence, but we did a DNA search on the skeleton we found, and it matches a person who served time for a rape twenty years ago. His name is William Carney."

Mandy didn't know. She sent a text to Patrick to stop by, and when he arrived that night he found two somber-looking sisters in the living room.

He said, "What's up? Why do you both look like you've taken a gut punch?"

Reggie plunged right in. "I did a DNA test on some remains we found near the McCook Reservoir. I don't usually tell anyone about the stuff I work on. But in this case, I have to ask: Are you related to someone named William H. Carney?"

Patrick could not disguise his look of dread at that name. He said, "I'm afraid so. It's my ex-con uncle. My dad's little brother. He's estranged from the family because of his past. What's he done now?"

Reggie said, "Nothing. His DNA was collected in the process of his old criminal prosecution. All DNA from criminal cases is kept in a nationwide system these days. When new DNA is tested for a match, if it matches DNA found in the database, it's tagged and means there's a connection to the criminal."

"Meaning?"

Reggie said, "It means William H. Carney is a descendant of a murdered person we discovered from over 140 years ago. The victim apparently was a Carney, based on this DNA test."

Patrick asked, "How do you know it's over 140 years ago?"

"Carbon-14 dating of the bones."

Mandy said, "Reggie has a theory she's pursuing. Is it OK with you if she takes a DNA sample from you?"

Patrick's head was spinning. He said, "I guess so, but why?"

Reggie said, "If you and your uncle's DNA is the same, it will be an additional good indicator. I want to try matching it to the DNA from the bones. If it matches, my theory is that the skeleton might have been your ancestor Patrick who disappeared in the Chicago fire. Except I'm hypothesizing he didn't disappear in the fire at all. He was murdered, probably at the time of the fire, and his body has been hidden away since then. I'm sorry to have to tell you this."

Patrick said, "You're saying the skeleton you found is the original Patrick Carney?" He looked excited and energized by the idea. "Let's do it right now. You don't have to be sorry."

Mandy asked, "How would your parents react to it?"

He said, "First they would be shocked. But I think it would bring closure to a century-old family mystery. Sure, it's horrifying to think your ancestor was murdered, but if that's what happened, so be it."

Reggie said, "Alright, let's get some hair samples and some saliva swabs and bag them. And you should keep this quiet until we have confirmation. I also think I should huddle with Steve Baker and get his ideas on this."

Patrick said, "Meaning what?"

"If this was murder, and we identify the victim, shouldn't law enforcement take an interest in it?"

"Interest as in a murder investigation?"

"Right."

Patrick said, "We better visit my parents."

Patrick set up dinner Friday night with his parents at their condo and picked up some Portillo's beef sandwiches on the way over. They'd brought Reggie along, given that she would be the only one who could explain the DNA issue. He also noticed that they again were not dressed alike.

Patrick's parents had a choice spot overlooking the Magnificent Mile along Michigan Avenue. From their position on the west side of the street, they could see all the way from the Michigan Avenue bridge on the south to the Water Tower Place on the north. The stores were surrounded by hotels, universities, museums, and luxury high-rise residential buildings. Mandy had met Patrick's parents before briefly. She knew his father was a patent attorney with a big intellectual property firm, and his mother Beth was the publisher of the *Chicago History Journal*. Patrick and his father were the same height of about six feet with light brown hair. Beth was a good-looking blonde, a few inches shorter than the sisters and well put together. They spent some time discussing each other's families and their interests. Mandy and Reggie took a bit longer than the Carneys, since their family dwarfed Patrick's only-child family.

Beth complimented Mandy and Reggie on the red chili earrings they were wearing, and Mandy explained that "These are good luck charms from our grandmother."

"Superstitious, is she?"

"You could say that."

Mandy turned to Patrick's father and said, "Patrick has told me your family has an unbroken string of Patricks, and you're Patrick Carney the fifth? Should we call you P5?"

Patrick the elder said, "No, no, Patrick and Beth will be fine. By the way, we're very proud of LaSalle and its role last year, carried out by both of you, of course. We were sorry to hear you may be leaving LaSalle, especially for Northwest."

"Why '*especially*' Northwest?" she asked.

Beth spoke first, before her husband could answer. "He's never been at ease with the Wagners. There was always tension between him and the Wagner brothers before they died. I'm afraid he's not mellowed since then."

"What happened that caused that tension?"

Patrick the elder said, "It started in the 1830s. In my opinion, what happened then carried on throughout the years until the reign of Gus, Jr. and Klaus. I can't say about the current crop of Wagners, so I'll just leave it at that."

Reggie gave her sister a steady look, impersonating an exclamation point. Mandy avoided Reggie's laser stare and tried to steer the discussion away from a difficult conversation. She didn't want to ask what happened. "It's true. I've accepted the offer and will join them soon. They've also announced that Northwest Engineering is going public, so I'll be very busy, very soon. But enough about me. We'd love to hear about some of Chicago's history, Beth. We can never get enough of it."

Beth turned out to be a human encyclopedia of the City of Chicago. She pointed across Michigan Avenue and explained, "Well, to start at the beginning, this area to our east was the lakeshore that became a dumping ground in the late 1800s. As the city recovered from the fire, a kooky riverboat captain named George Streeter showed up. He beached his boat here and became a squatter. The city filled hundreds of acres around him with fire debris. Eventually surrounding his boat, the area became known as the Streeterville neighborhood."

Reggie said, "Then George Streeter must have been responsible for our alma mater's location of its law school and medical school."

Beth said, "In a manner of speaking."

She went on to describe the city as a marvel of human ingenuity which capitalized on the times and adapted to events, reengineering itself as needed. She explained that the spot was popular with the Sauk and other native American tribes because of the water route. River waters flowed into the lake. A traveler going west from the lake through the river system would end up eventually at the Gulf of Mexico down the Mississippi River. Just like the explorer and fur trader LaSalle did in the seventeenth century. In reverse, it led through the other Great Lakes and river systems to reach the Atlantic Ocean.

Reggie said, "We've been on the Mississippi ourselves. In northern Minnesota near its headwaters, we kayaked down to Minneapolis. We didn't go any farther because we didn't want to cope with all the locks along the river."

Mandy said, "Water was the whole game for transportation back then, right?"

"Right. Waterways were the dominant means of commerce, with livestock, timber, furs, ores and crops finding their way to or from, but always through, Chicago. This area was also a sponge, absorbing refugees from war and famine in the nineteenth century. Many of them were Irish and Germans. But railroads were coming on strong, which turned out to be good news for Chicago and the Carneys."

Reggie asked, "What do you know about the roots of the Carney family?"

Beth said, "Quite a bit. Seamus Carney immigrated from Ireland. A twenty-six-year-old from western Ireland, he found himself in the lead group of emigres to America. Ireland held no future for him. My dear son Patrick can cover that."

Patrick said, "Of course. Industrialization hadn't hit Irish shores yet, so Seamus had to look elsewhere for work. He scraped up enough money to buy a ticket across the ocean to America. Once off the ship in New York City, he ran into Erie Canal recruiters. He went to work right away on a crew digging the Erie Canal through New York."

Mandy asked Beth, "Do you know what happened since the time of Seamus?"

"Sure do. We're blessed with extensive family records and accounts that go back a long way. There are even some old letters in our office area, passed along through the generations. You may find them interesting. It's been ages since I read them. Maybe there's even some good material for a *Chicago History Journal* article or two, now that I think about it."

Patrick smiled and said, "Not to mention a novel."

Beth looked over at her husband and said, "There was tension between these families since their beginnings in Chicago, not just between my husband and the Wagner brothers—Gus, Jr., and Klaus. The one thing I can tell you is that we kept our son out of it and sheltered him from the feud mentality . . . I think." Now she paused to look over at him to see if she was getting a reaction from young Patrick.

The three women looked at the father and son. The father was silently nodding, and the son was shrugging his shoulders. Then Patrick the younger, like a frisky puppy, said, "I volunteer to go through all those records."

Mandy thought about her new employer's family having issues with her new boyfriend's family. What was she getting herself into? The boyfriend was uneasy with it, her sister was mad at her about it, Patrick's parents didn't seem too fond of the idea, and she'd disappointed Rick Crawford. Her dad was the only one supportive of her move.

Patrick's father asked Reggie to explain the DNA connection the FBI had established. She took them through the science and the connection to their relative William. When she said she was sorry to be the bearer of bad news about a possible family murder, Beth thanked her with a big smile and announced that it would be her next *Chicago History Journal* piece.

Mandy said, "Great idea!"

Patrick's parents were underwhelmed by the DNA news, and Mandy made a mental note to ask Patrick about this later. She didn't think it shocked them. When the sisters said goodbye to Patrick at their apartment, Reggie turned to Mandy and said, "You're provoking something again."

"How?"

"By encouraging that article."

C H A P T E R

9

New Start

MANDY'S EMPLOYMENT with Northwest Engineering began the third week of July. Her whirlwind wrap-up of activities at LaSalle had left her in need of some downtime, but she had to hit the ground running. Compared to LaSalle, the intensity she found at 150 North Riverside Plaza was at a whole different level. She was joining a staff whose members were a mixture of old hands at the company and new employees who held newly created functions in the organization. Going in, Mandy had to be sensitive to any reluctance from the old guard to cooperate with the new corporate staff. Resistance was a common reaction by organizations to a new authority, and it was most often seen in corporate acquisitions. Initial public offerings were the next most common. To a compliance professional, resistance would foreshadow difficulties ahead.

She had to construct an organization chart for her function, with duties, job descriptions and reporting arrangements, and most importantly, people. But that would have to wait. The new jobs were needed to operate the corporate functions of a publicly traded company. Right now, she had to roll up her sleeves and be single-focused on getting the offering done.

The pace of activity would not allow for anything that took time. Instead, she'd have to jump into the fire and handle it herself. Frank and Carl had managed the launch so far. They'd worked with investment bankers and outside lawyers who gave guidance on what was necessary. Even on the financial side, no one had public company experience, and the search for an appropriate chief financial officer was underway.

The principal financial person up until then had been an accountant without publicly traded stock experience, and he had been judged woefully inadequate for what was now needed. Financial accounting largely had been outsourced to an outside firm whose ultimate purpose was to prepare and file tax returns and support bank agreement needs. The search for a chief financial officer was being managed by Frank and the head of human resources. Until the new CFO was in place, Mandy didn't think things could be put into high gear. The need for an in-house accounting group schooled in financial accounting principles was dire.

Early on her first day, Frank called a meeting for the executives already in place. He introduced Mandy and several other new faces and spoke to the group. He welcomed everyone and told them that the process was moving quickly, and the company was leaning heavily on the new employees to work with its bankers, lawyers, and auditors.

"We have to hit the ground running as a new public company, so we are most importantly looking for guidance on how to operate once we're officially public," he said, directing the comment to Mandy.

He noted that most of this burden would fall on Mandy's shoulders and the new finance staff to handle as well, once all were in place. Frank expected everyone else to soldier on and hopefully not be too distracted from their regular duties. The company engine needed to keep running. He nodded to Mandy, saying, "You've hardly gotten through the door, but is there anything you'd like to advise the group about?"

"Thanks," Mandy said. "I'm thrilled to be here, and to get to know you all as time permits. The main effort is to review the registration statement already under review by the SEC, to make sure we're all happy with it. I expect to be completely absorbed in this process and want you to understand I will need to interview each of you to get schooled in the history of the company and its current activities. It's important for us to have an accurate and complete registration statement for the regulators to review and declare effective, so we can begin trading."

When the meeting broke up, Mandy told Frank and Carl she wanted to meet with the outside lawyers and the bankers, which Carl agreed to set up. She went to her office and tried to set up some space for herself, while looking out the window at the view down the river branches. She could see LaSalle off in the distance and had a pang of regret.

———

The night was perfect for pizza with Reggie at nearby Lou Malnati's in the Wrigley building. Reggie suggested that the FBI call in the Wagners for a discussion about the jobsite where Patrick Carney's skeleton had been found. Steve Baker had learned from

Cook County that the site had been a Northwest project in 1871. That opened the door to getting information from the company. Steve agreed it was a good idea and was moving forward on it.

Mandy said, "Don't get me involved, though. My hands are full. Just deal with Carl and Frank. I'm preoccupied with all this other stuff: board minutes, litigation, environmental history, and risk factors, plus looking at comparable companies' public disclosures."

"You need a team for all that, don't you?"

"Tell me about it. I don't have time to get caught up in some murder investigation where no perpetrators could be alive any longer."

Reggie said, "Wait a minute. Hasn't the company's outside team already done all that stuff you're talking about?"

"They did enough to get a filing made. I don't know how much confidence those outsiders have in the disclosures. After all, they're indemnified for fraudulent statements made by the company. We're not. I mean management and the board." She couldn't just rely blindly on outside lawyers who might have done the work to get to where things now stood. That just wasn't her way.

"Is this what Northwest expects from you?"

"Nope. They expect me to be concerned with the legal side of running a public company, not digging into the disclosures already loaded into the offering. Frank Wagner said so when he introduced me today."

"So how will they react when you start raising these issues?"

Mandy said, "Probably not too well. But I can't help that. Once I have the controls, I own what's in the document. If they didn't want me to do this, they should have held off on hiring me until they were public. I'm sure they think they're beyond that, and I wish they were. But they hired me now, and until I'm satisfied that the disclosures are adequate, I have to do the work to make myself comfortable."

"Nice. You're starting out your big opportunity by ruffling feathers? Are you sure you're not pulling another Wilmette Harbor trick, except this time on a much grander scale?"

"Don't taunt me. I'm starting out doing what I should be doing. I made it very clear to Carl before he hired me that this was going to have to be done. If he was going to choke on that, he and his cousin could have pulled back and brought me in later, or just gone with someone else."

"Whatever."

Lastly there was the board of directors. She'd gotten a lifetime worth of board wisdom while at LaSalle because of its former general counsel and corporate secretary Ed Rosen. He'd included her in the board process and she was able to stand on her own two feet in that department. She hadn't considered it a favor at the time, but it turned out to be exactly that.

Mandy had learned how important it was to tend to the care and feeding of board members. She remembered the same discussion she'd had with Rick before she left LaSalle. At Northwest, it had a whole new twist: namely, educating board members on what a public company needed from its directors. Before accepting the job, she hadn't considered that she would be teaching throughout the organization.

Mandy had to make sure her moves would not be perceived by Frank or Carl as an unwanted intrusion into their exclusive world. But it wouldn't be their private world much longer, especially since she was the corporate secretary and the general counsel in waiting. They better get used to it. If top management resisted her efforts, how would she accomplish everything? And why would they resist? Didn't they all have the same interests? She couldn't answer her own questions. She pondered the curious look she'd seen on Frank's face as she talked to the group earlier. She had a pretty good sense of resistance on the management team, and hoped Frank was not behind it.

Northwest had another important issue. The board was an old boys' club. There was a single woman on the board, and she happened to be a family member—Aunt Gretchen the troublemaker.

None of these directors had the depth of experience to counsel management on leading and operating a public company, or even assuring a careful offering process. Experienced directors were needed. If Frank wanted to get a board of directors with the right people in the least disruptive way, it would be best to do it before going public. If the company waited until after the offer, the new director would have to be voted in by public shareholders. She needed to find a way of getting at least one qualified director on the board without a shareholder vote.

Mandy wanted Northwest to present as slim a target as possible for anyone to take aim at its governance profile. She feared that Frank's hair would catch on fire once he had the combined attention of the Securities and Exchange Commission, the New York Stock Exchange, shareholder activists, Wall Steet analysts, and institutional investors, each having a hand on the Northwest steering wheel. He was about to cede control to a variety of agencies and constituencies who had professional and legal duties of their own, as well as their own agenda, and couldn't care less about a CEO's need for dominance.

The best way to assess Northwest's attitude might be to air her views with Carl first. It would test his sophistication with the concepts and his openness to make any changes, and would be a reminder of what she'd told him earlier at Gene and Georgetti's. Before this, she wanted to meet with the outside lawyers and investment bankers to give her some insights. Maybe they had already given advice on this.

Frank invited Mandy to lunch in his conference room with Carl and some of the other executives. The group was very energized when she got there, and Frank explained the reason.

"We got word today we've won the bid to upgrade the St. Lawrence Seaway."

Immediate applause erupted in the room. This was clearly a big deal for the company.

"This will be a big boost to our pre-launch pitch to the investment community. We can't announce it, so for now we're keeping a lid on it. The U.S. and Canadian governments control the release of the contract award news. Once they release the news, we can bring it out ourselves." Frank beamed with excitement, and added, "This takes us back to our roots. We've dug canals all over North America. I would say we've had a monopoly on canals."

"Except you don't really mean a *monopoly* literally, do you?" Carl quickly chimed in.

"Right," said Frank. "Carl's always quick to rap my knuckles if I use the 'M' word. Don't worry. This is all done by competitive bids."

After lunch Mandy followed Carl back to his office and asked, "How did the company win all those projects over the years?"

"We've always enjoyed a technological edge in construction methods, all the way back to the 1870s. Gus, the founder's son, had designed some improvements in steam shovels to achieve efficiency in excavation. He also invented tunneling innovations that allowed us to get some choice projects. They kept innovating along the way and kept winning deals.

"We cut our teeth on the Illinois and Michigan Canal in the 1840s, then did the Chicago Sanitary and Ship Canal and Cal-Sag Canal here at the end of the century. We changed the flows of the Chicago and Calumet Rivers, and it's been called one of the top civil engineering feats in the world. Then early in the twentieth century we did the granddaddy of all canals, the Panama Canal.

"We even did the original St. Lawrence Seaway work back in the mid-1950s. This new $5 billion improvement project will upgrade the locks and other infrastructure throughout the length of the whole St. Lawrence Seaway, raising bridges and dredging waterways wider and deeper to accommodate larger vessels."

Mandy found the new St. Lawrence Seaway project to be ironic. Rick Crawford had mentioned LaSalle winning the bid for the equipment. The award to Northwest for the construction work itself would put it into a transaction with LaSalle for equipment.

"You didn't construct the Suez Canal?"

"No. They missed out on that one. The French got that job."

Mandy and Carl went to a conference room to go over the offering process with the lawyers and investment bankers. Mandy saw that on the way into the conference room, Frank was nearby and pulled aside the junior attorney from the firm and had a conversation with her. She must have been acquainted with him from the prior work the firm was doing on the offering. Mandy soon was introduced to her as Ashley Tate.

Carl whispered to her that Frank was a little loose with his language, and sometimes it took a village to keep him on message. He even called Frank a *"rake stepper"* and told Mandy he needed her vigilance and help in spotting any misbehavior by senior officers. She suspected that it was Frank who he really meant, and not the senior officers plural. Carl was not sharing with Mandy that his source of information about his cousin was from his secret surveillance arrangement.

She was relieved to know this problem was recognized by Carl. If Frank was the face of the company with the investment community, the last thing Northwest needed was for him to turn out to be either an undisciplined blabbermouth or a source of worse problems. Someone who dropped news bombs with analysts or shareholders or abused female employees could only create big problems for a brand-new public company.

Strong leadership steps would be needed to make sure everyone deferred to the investor relations staff and avoid public speaking unless they were carefully managed and chaperoned. Senior officials of public companies were straitjacketed in their statements to the public.

After the meeting with the lawyers and bankers, Carl said, "I must admit I've been winging it so far. I want you to take this on and let me off the hook."

Mandy got out of her chair and went to the glass wall of the conference room, looking out and trying to decide how to answer Carl. Finally, she turned to him and replied in a very low tone of voice, "If Northwest is going to be a public company in a couple months, by then you need to learn the law and not rely exclusively on me. Even if you soon move out of the GC role, you still need to be getting control of things before that happens. Not only does Frank need to be careful, but you also, and both of you must serve as an example to the rest of the management team."

She was not thrilled to be lecturing her new boss, but she sensed it was necessary, so she kept going. "We have a duty to make sure the registration statement has accurate disclosures. You may be satisfied, but I'm not. I need some due diligence here, and if I find a disclosure needing change, it might require an amendment to the registration statement."

Carl had a stunned look on his face and meekly said, "I understood we were just waiting out the regulatory review to be over and we'd be ready to start trading. I wanted you to focus on how to operate." He looked very uncomfortable.

Mandy looked at him with concern and said, "I told you this before. Didn't you hear me?"

Carl just nodded and said nothing.

"I guess you didn't understand me then. I hope you understand now." The meeting with the bankers and outside lawyers was helpful and laid a good foundation for what had been done for the filing of the registration statement.

Later while meeting with Frank, Carl filled him in on the discussion with Mandy, and Frank exploded. He'd jumped up from the table, and throwing his hands in the air, screamed, "Goddamn it, Carl. First, I had Gretchen on my back, and now I've got your lawyer there too, and in her first week."

Carl put his hands out toward Frank but stayed in his chair, attempting a calming motion toward Frank's outburst. Frank needed an anchor for whatever was now going to take place to get them to the offering. Could Carl fill that role?

Frank poked his finger toward Carl repeatedly, and said, "We had no choice with Gretchen. She was here when we got here. But Mandy was your whole idea. You came under her spell. She's looking backward, instead of forward. If I don't get a better feeling about her soon, we might have to part company. I don't care how hot she is."

Carl was speechless. He feared another sexual harassment claim about Frank, who routinely trod right up to the brink of harassment with women and occasionally stepped over. When that happened, Carl had to iron things out with non-disclosure agreements and payments.

Frank looked at him and said, "Don't worry. I know what you're thinking. Maybe I'll check out Reggie. That should make you feel better." His last sentence had been a sneer.

Carl spat back, "She's FBI, Frank. Is that what you want? Sniffing around a cop?"

Frank stormed out of the room. He didn't have to let Carl know he now had Asian women on his mind, rather than the Doucette twins. Carl had seen that anyway from what he'd viewed on the secret camera. Frank headed back to his office and tried his best to calm down. He cooled down by watching internet videos of Asian women. He couldn't let his anger diminish what he'd achieved with the Canadians. The St. Lawrence Seaway project was helping with the recovery from Klaus Wagner's sabotage. After his uncle's death years ago, his father had coached him to take over the large capital projects management duties.

The disappointment from the loss of the Deep Tunnel bids to LaSalle was a scar in the Northwest story. Frank's father had been desperate to get back what he felt rightfully belonged to Northwest. It was a part of the business Frank knew well from his earlier position heading up engineering. Tunneling and blasting out excavation sites were in his DNA.

On his way in the hallway, Frank bumped into David Wilson, his direct report who now had the job of winning large capital projects. He gave him a big smile and said, "Great job on the Canadians. Let's take a walk." The two men rode down to the ground floor and left the building and walked along the Riverwalk talking, away from prying eyes and ears.

Outside Frank said, "I'm expecting you'll now turn your full attention to the Panamanians. What have you got in mind? Same thing as with the Canadians?"

Wilson told him, "I think so. My contact at the Panamanian embassy needs money. Why couldn't we have had this conversation in your office? Is there a problem?"

"No, no. Just being careful. No sense in having our conversation overheard."

"I hope you've got my back on this. I've done everything you asked me to do, but I don't feel too good about it."

Frank immediately convinced himself that Wilson was a possible liability that he couldn't afford. When he was done with his assignment, Frank would have to consider what he should do with him. This was the kind of thing that could sink Northwest if it got unearthed, and he was worried that the persistent redhead would get wind of it and blow him out of the water.

Frank said, "You've got nothing to worry about. I'll make sure of that. Let's go back separately. Just get busy on Panama." He felt confident he could control events.

They split up and returned by different routes. After turning away and walking up to street level and heading down Franklin Street, Wilson pulled out his phone and shut off the recorder.

C H A P T E R

10

FBI

THE FBI CONTACTED FRANK and requested that he come into the Bureau's office for a meeting. Wagner wanted to know the reason, and whether he should bring a lawyer. The Bureau assured him that neither he nor Northwest Engineering were the target of any investigation. The meeting was to discuss a crime discovered on an old Northwest jobsite. They agreed on a meeting and then Frank called Carl into his office, saying to him, "Carl, what is this about a crime at one of our old jobsites?"

"We would have tons of old jobsites, so I can't imagine. Do you want me to go with you, or have Mandy go with you?"

"You come. Not Mandy. She's got her hands full now as it is."

After going through FBI security, Frank and Carl were led to a conference room and offered bottles of water while they waited.

Steve Baker soon entered the room along with Reggie, and both Frank and Carl looked surprised to see Mandy's identical twin sister. They'd never met her and, like everyone else, were amazed by the resemblance.

Steve introduced her as Dr. Regina Doucette, Chief Forensic Pathologist of the Chicago FBI lab, and Reggie proceeded to report on what had been found.

"Human remains were discovered sealed inside a bridge abutment built by your company in 1871, according to Cook County records. The body showed evidence of fatal gunshot wounds, and we've been able to match the victim's DNA to the Carney family. We believe the victim to be Patrick Carney, the head of LaSalle Dredging and Excavation Company. Mr. Carney went missing the night of the Chicago fire, and his body was never found. He was presumed to be a fire victim and his body burned to ash, the intensity of the fire being what it was. The Cook County Sheriff's Office advised us that your company performed the bridgework. Then it was known as Northwest Drayage and Tunnel Company."

Frank leaned forward on his elbows and said, "OK, so what? That's over a century ago. What could we have to do with it?"

Steve Baker said, "We wanted your insights into your company history on this. We understand there was a contentious relationship between the two companies."

Frank said, "I'm sure every student of Chicago history has heard about the competition between the two companies, way back to the founders."

Steve said, "We wanted to have this discussion with you before we announced the discovery of the body. If you have any information relevant to this from your own files, we would appreciate your cooperation. But as it stands right now, we expect to soon announce the cause of death and the preliminary identification.

The site was a Northwest construction site 140 years ago, and today it's a LaSalle construction site. A little ironic, isn't it?"

Carl was clearly agitated, and said, "No. What's ironic is that we are actively preparing an initial public offering of Northwest Engineering. I hope there is nothing you announce that will reflect negatively on our company. Is there?"

"I'm in law enforcement, not investment banking. I can't answer the public offering question."

Frank said, "Are you insinuating Northwest was involved in a murder, just because a body was found on a Northwest construction site? Anybody could have dumped a body at a construction site. It doesn't mean the company had anything to do with it."

Steve said, "True. But the remains were found inside a barrel, intentionally covered with gravel and concrete. The barrel collapsed, but the wording on the barrel seems to carry the Northwest name. If a body is disposed of that way, it screams of a likely connection to Northwest . . . and murder."

Carl leaned in on the table and said, "If it's a murder, when did it occur?"

Reggie said, "Our analysis puts it around 140 years ago."

Frank asked, "How can you know that?"

She answered, "Carbon 14 dating of bones. The records of the bridge construction also correspond to that age."

Carl said, "How can you be sure it was a murder?"

Steve said, "I can't get into what we know at this point."

Frank said, "When are you planning to make this public?"

"As soon as we inform the Carney family."

Carl said, "I urge you to avoid making any associations with Northwest Engineering. We are on the brink of completing a big transaction and some unwarranted connection with murder would not be helpful."

Frank said, "We're happy to help in any way." Switching gears then, he said, "Dr. Doucette, I'll follow up with you and Mandy to have lunch." Frank pushed a business card to both Steve and Reggie, who took the cards and escorted them to the exit. When they left, she turned the card over, and a handwritten note was written on the reverse saying *Would love to have dinner with you. Please give me a call.* She laughed out loud.

Steve said, "What is it?"

"He's hitting on me," she said, looking at the card with a stunned look on her face.

Steve was finally coming around to Mandy's and Reggie's point of view on Frank. It had been a brilliant suggestion to pull in the Wagners for an interview. It was a legitimate inquiry for the Bureau and the U.S. Attorney to make, but it would shake them up and aggravate them. Mandy's old prosecutorial instincts were still sharp. Steve was uncomfortable doing this but had to admit they needed to do something to deal with the Patrick Carney murder investigation.

When the Wagners left, Reggie rushed back to the conference room they'd used. After letting some her thoughts marinate for a while, she had decided that getting the Wagner DNA would be useful. Just like the Carney connection had been made matching DNA, maybe the same thing was possible in the case of searching for the perpetrator. If it was possible for the victim, why not the murderer? But the opportunity was lost when Reggie returned to find that Steve's assistant had cleared the room of the detritus from the prior meeting, including anything that might have held Frank's and Carl's DNA. Reggie had not broadcast her suspicions about the perpetrator being a member of the Wagner family, but she was determined to see if there could be a connection.

In the Northwest Engineering offices, Mandy took a call from Reggie, who filled her in on the meeting at the FBI offices with the

Wagners. She made a mental note to speak with outside counsel and the bankers to see if this would have any impact on the offering and the registration statement. Her guess was that this was all history, and in the absence of anything currently relevant in whatever came out of the investigation, it would be a non-event.

Reggie said, "Frank and Carl were cooperative, but cagey. Frank invited you and me to lunch. Let's take him up on it. He's got a high opinion of himself, so he'd probably be talkative and overconfident. Oh, and he also gave me his card with a dinner invitation written on it. He sees no problem with hitting on his lawyer's sister."

"Are you going to tell Dan about this?"

"No! You're not the boss of me, Mandy. Butt out!"

————

Northwest's law firm did an exhaustive search for and description of all the company's litigation. A log of the cases was given to Mandy to study. The disclosure document only discussed current litigation, but Mandy wanted to get a feel for the history of their disputes. She also needed to see if there were any settlement agreements which Northwest had over the years, which might not have started with an actual lawsuit being filed. This wasn't within the scope of the firm's diligence. In fact, it had only done a five-year look-back, which to her mind was far too short. Five years was the disclosure law period for a securities registration filing, but seeing patterns was what Mandy wanted. A longer time frame was needed for that. She would have to find a way to get her question answered. A call to the partner about the litigation research was met with a referral to his associate on the deal, Ashley Tate, and she would be able to answer questions.

Instead of calling Ashley Tate, Mandy first gave Reggie a call, and they discussed the day's activities. Reggie said, "You sound like you're uneasy, or is the beginning of anything this big just naturally overwhelming?"

Mandy said, "Both. It's roughly what I expected. I can't hope to have a well-oiled operation in my area waiting for me. This just isn't a public company. Nobody knows what they're doing or what they've signed up for, including Carl."

Reggie said, "I thought your tidy corporate world had everything figured out. You sound to me like you have a bad case of buyer's remorse."

Mandy said, "It's just that it's not so tidy here. If you're new to the public company world, it takes awhile to ramp up. It doesn't matter how many *Wall Street Journal* articles you've read or who has talked with you about going public. Until you are neck deep in it, and looking at your own stuff, it's foreign to you. I've said it before—this place needs to learn to behave like a public company. But the feeling I'm getting from Frank is unsettling."

"You'll get it under control."

"And God, does he stare at me a lot."

"If it makes you feel any better, he was giving me the eye exam too," Reggie said. "Meanwhile, I've been daydreaming today about whether Dan is going to pop the big question to me."

"Huh? Where's this coming from?"

"Remember on the 4th of July when the folks were entertaining Dan and Patrick on the back porch and we snuck Patrick up to our room to look at our old headquarters? I have a sneaking suspicion Dan got traditional on me and seized a private moment with Dad to ask his permission. I caught them giving me side-eye at the fireworks. And Dan has been unusually attentive to me lately."

Mandy scrunched up her face and said, "Why have you waited over two weeks to tell me this?"

"I haven't waited. It just dawned on me what's been happening."

"I think he needs to ask my permission, too."

"What would you say?" Reggie said.

"I'm only pulling your ponytail. I like Dan for you. Would you accept?"

"Hell yes. This ponytail ain't getting any younger. Aren't you going to ask me if I love him?"

Mandy laughed loudly, which she rarely did. "Duh. I already know the answer."

"You should still ask me," she said, standing in a challenging pose with hands on her hips. That was her trademark when she was feisty.

"Objection, Your Honor. Asked and answered. How do you think he asked Dad, and what do you think he'd have answered?"

Reggie said, "I don't know, but I think Dad would have put him through some questioning before he gave his approval."

Mandy asked, "What kind of questioning?"

"Oh, you know, the usual stuff—love, security, et cetera."

"Ooh, look how romantic Reggie is all of a sudden. Why don't you just go with the flow instead of trying to dissect it like it's a dead bug?"

"Coming from you, that's rich. Aren't you the one who resisted her suitor and had to be coaxed into a date by a friend? Now you're interested in romance?" The comment made Mandy remember the connection she'd made with Patrick the year before when he had pursued her and she had leaned away at first.

The discussion had a much more serious undertone than the taunting exchange revealed. The sisters had been inseparable their whole lives. Only while Reggie had worked at Quantico had there been any real separation, and then the two had four to five phone calls each day. Mandy had steered clear of serious relationships, while Reggie had dated regularly. But that ended abruptly after Dan entered the picture. The marriage of one of the twins would be a seminal event in their lives.

Reggie was going to be the first to fall, so to speak, but Mandy was now seriously involved with Patrick. Since he'd made his intentions about a long-term relationship clear, she needn't worry that Patrick was just kicking the tires. Maybe she wouldn't be far behind her sister.

11

Meeting Gretchen

FOR MANDY'S INTERVIEWS with board members, she dressed in a plain dark blue suit, with hair pulled back tightly. A small conference room was used on the executive floor. She met Charles Winters, a longtime board member whose term extended back to Frank's father's time. He looked like a taciturn Will Geer from *The Waltons*, and he'd been around long enough to have the most knowledge of all the board members. He was dressed in a sports jacket without a tie. His demeanor was pleasant enough, but he looked like he lacked energy and enthusiasm for this process. There was no telling what he, or for that matter any of the other board members, would cough up.

Frank and Carl were present for the discussion, which rankled Mandy. She didn't like chaperones, especially when she wasn't sure of their motives. When Carl had told her that he and Frank would be present, she'd asked him why. He told her that the directors' memories might not be too sharp, and that Frank wanted to be present for any director's discussions. She sensed that she was being kept on a short leash.

Mandy said to him, "Mr. Winters, thank you for joining us. I see you've had some presentations in the lead-up to this process, and some have been done by the investment banker and our outside counsel. I hope I'm not duplicating their efforts, since I don't want to waste your valuable time."

Winters smiled and said, "I can't say I understand this whole process very well, but I trust you're doing what needs to be done. How can I help?"

"We have a business description in the preliminary registration statement. This includes the company's history, which also lays out the current litigation and describes the risk factors in the business. Those things need to be focused on by management and the board, with the understanding that you'll be signing the final registration statement. By signing it, you're endorsing it as complete and truthful. Since there can be liability for defective disclosures, I want to make sure we do the best job we can and that you're comfortable signing it."

"Defective?"

She said, "Either misleading, incomplete or inadequate."

Winters showed little body language that might signal discomfort. "Understood. Please continue."

Frank interrupted Mandy to say to Winters, "Charles, this is not to say that there is anything in the filing now that we're worried about, right, Mandy?"

Mandy nodded in response and then made random references to the draft business description and company history of Northwest. Winters nodded in agreement with her statements. She gave some standard description of what risk factors she'd learned from the disclosure documents of Northwest's competitors, given that companies in the same industries should have some common risks. LaSalle was one of them. She listed the litigation she was aware of, all of which was routine or insignificant, in her opinion.

"Mr. Winters, outside of the litigation matters I've mentioned, can you tell me if there is anything else you can remember that could be significant? Let's say going back further in time?"

Frank broke into the discussion again. "Mandy, this seems to be a wide-open question. Can you help Charles by narrowing it?"

Mandy got the feeling that Frank was behaving like an opposing counsel in a deposition, trying to interfere with the questions. It's what she feared. Instead of Frank supporting her with the process, he was hampering it. Like a runner feeling a pain in a critical leg muscle during a race, she fretted over it, half expecting it to suddenly disable her.

"By this question, I'm trying to find out if anything, even if not needed for the registration statement because it's older than five years, may indicate a risk to the company. The risk disclosure doesn't have a time element to it."

Frank said, "I don't want us speculating here. It could only cause trouble for us by raising questions without a basis. Let's move on."

Mandy said, "I'm not asking for speculation; I'm only asking if there is awareness of older litigation."

Winters saved her by interrupting and said, "Frank, I don't have anything to say anyway." By this point, so many years after Frank had ascended to the CEO position, his board membership had mostly changed. Charles Winters was the longest-serving director other than Aunt Gretchen.

Mandy said, "What about the risk factors I mentioned? Is there anything you would want to add that you might have seen in your years on the board?"

Winters shook his head, and Frank gave a meaningful look to Carl, who broke in. "I think we should be OK with the list as it exists."

The interview was over. Winters was averting his eyes from Mandy.

Mandy excused herself, and back in her own office called Reggie. "I just had one of the most choreographed interviews I've ever seen. This director might as well have had the puppeteer's crossbar hovering over him for anyone to see, with Frank the puppeteer pulling the strings."

Reggie replied, "You've seen others like that in the past?"

"Oh yeah. Last year I had a compliance meeting in another LaSalle office outside the U.S. I taped the meeting for repeat viewings. They didn't even know I'd done it. The division president was present, and in his native language commented to the group after I gave my compliance speech. It wasn't until I returned and had the tape translated that I found out he'd told them to ignore my comments."

Reggie said, "You've been holding back on me. I'd never heard that story before. What happened to the division president?"

She raised her eyebrows and with a little smile said, "He doesn't work at LaSalle anymore."

Three more mirror-image board interviews were done over the course of the week. But then came Gretchen Wagner, who had served for almost as long as Charles Winters. She was totally unhelpful and even cold during the interview. It was no surprise to Mandy, who by this time figured the board had been designed to protect the management team. She couldn't get the image of a combative aunt out of her mind from the telephone conversation she'd witnessed in Frank's office. Gretchen ended her interview and took Mandy's card when it was handed to her with the request to feel free to call Mandy if anything else later occurred to her.

Gretchen got up and turned toward Mandy to shake her hand. She showed a slight smile on her face, a mix of sincerity and sneer, and gave her a longer-than-necessary pressing handshake. The coldness had gone away, like a hand in January holding a pocket warmer. She'd only shown that momentary thaw to Mandy. Frank and Carl had gotten the full ice treatment. *There's more to come from this lady*, Mandy thought.

The last two board members she met were a banker and family lawyer, neither of whom had many years on the board and didn't even span the five-year period for the mandatory business history disclosures. She hated business-connected lawyers and bankers sitting on a board, conflicted by commercial relationships and guided by their own pecuniary interests. LaSalle had a strong policy to avoid conflicted board members and would never have allowed it. If she got her way, they would be jettisoned from the board, but that was another day's work. Despite Mandy's efforts to open up any directors' discussion, they were effectively shut down by the tag team of Frank and Carl. Mandy's attitude was that there could be no interference with due diligence in a securities law document, but that's what she was getting.

Frank called Carl to his office after the conversations with the directors. Sitting with his hands on the desk and an angry look on his face, Frank said in a sarcastic tone, "Your idea to hire a corporate securities lawyer was brilliant. She's throwing out the anchor. Don't tell me you can't see this happening."

Carl said, "No, I don't see what you're seeing. What are you concerned about?"

"Timing! We're on a schedule here. We have a whole investor relations program built around the timing of the effective date."

"I'll speak with the bankers about flexibility."

Frank pivoted and said, "What she said about changing the registration document is ominous. It's not what we want to see happening at this point. We've had outside lawyers prepare and file the registration statement, and she wants to tinker with it. I think she's on a fishing expedition. It was a mistake to bring her in."

Carl turned to Frank and said, "Look, we've had this conversation. Everyone was hounding us to staff up so we could hit the ground running and be prepared for the day we go public. The new constituencies will expect a smooth takeoff, and how could you blame them? We were in control of this process from the start, with no urgency unless we created it. How could I have held off?"

"That's your problem. She's getting directors excited and they're asking questions. Gretchen was already hostile; and now she's gone from docile to sullen. What's next?"

He gestured up at the wall toward the photo of their fathers together and said to Carl, "My father would not have let this get out of control. Figure out how to tame these women, for Christ's sake." He also looked over at the ominous glare from his father in the frame, knowing that he would have been inflicting a rebuke on him if he were still alive.

Later that night Mandy received a call from Gretchen Wagner. After apologizing for interfering with Mandy's evening, Gretchen came right to the point, saying, "Mandy, I wanted to speak to you without my family watchers. And please forgive my demeanor today in the meeting. It had nothing to do with you. I know you're just trying to do your job." She sounded sincere.

Mandy said, "I'm sorry, Mrs. Wagner. You call your son and nephew your *watchers*?"

"Yes, couldn't you tell? And please, call me Gretchen."

"To be honest, Gretchen, after all the director interviews, I haven't succeeded in getting much of anything. I'd consider them watchers of all the directors. What's going on?"

Gretchen said, "What I discuss with you, I'd appreciate you keeping to yourself. I don't want you to tell Frank or Carl that I called you."

"Of course not." She didn't even trust her own son. Talking to directors without their presence would not endear her to Frank and Carl, but she was doing it anyway. She sensed something important would happen.

"Can you please come to my condo in Marina City to discuss this? I'd better hang up anyway. This cell phone battery is dying. I'll feel more comfortable talking with you here, rather than over the phone anyway."

Mandy agreed and took the address down and promised to be right over. As she threw on some jeans and a casual top, with her hair down and loose, she got concerned about the woman's comments about her phone. She was very suspicious of cell phones with dying batteries, since she'd had an earlier experience with phones loaded with spyware. When she got to Marina City, Gretchen shook Mandy's hand and pulled her into a brief hug. Mandy was surprised by the gesture but preferred that to the frosty Gretchen she'd seen earlier.

"Thanks so much for coming over. I'm probably getting a little paranoid about who sees what I do. Please come in and let me give you a tour." She was being as pleasant and warm as she could. In fact, she was a completely different person from the one she presented in the interview.

The condo was on the fortieth floor and had a spectacular view of the river and the entire Chicago Loop. She gave Mandy a quick tour of the condo. The walls were filled with numerous family photos. Mandy studied them with great interest, particularly the shot of a boat with the two brothers on the sky bridge. From the balcony, Gretchen gave her a commentary on the panorama, finishing on the east view with a complaint about the new Trump

Tower monstrosity just next door. It now blocked her view of what had been open skies. The former low-slung Chicago Sun-Times building was now replaced by the ninety-two-story tower. She stayed well away from the railing of the balcony, telling Mandy that she was deathly afraid of heights. Mandy stepped to the railing and looked down. It was a long drop directly over the river, and she shivered thinking about a drop from that height. She was fine with heights, unlike her sister. Like Gretchen, Reggie could never have approached the railing like she'd just done.

Mandy looked over the balcony and said, "That's a long way down."

Gretchen said, "My husband Klaus used to love this balcony. I've lived here for decades and have never used it. I've only kept this place out of my memory of Klaus."

After getting her some tea, Gretchen got down to business. While she was getting the tea, Mandy picked up Gretchen's cell phone and it was hot to the touch. Another telltale sign.

"Sorry to be so mysterious, but I feel I can't speak freely around Carl and Frank. I've been on bad terms with them for some time, especially Frank. I was the one pushing the company to go public. I convinced the other family members to go along, though it didn't take much convincing. These days every financial planner warns against concentrating their wealth narrowly. The sermon is diversification. Frank never saw eye to eye with us, and he had to be dragged into it."

Mandy said, "What made you want the company to go public now?"

"Klaus always talked about it, saying it would make sense to diversify our investments. A few years after he died, I talked to my financial advisor, who simply asked me what exit arrangements I had with my Northwest holdings. I didn't understand everything, so my advisor got involved. My Northwest stock is valued at a certain level which is only theoretical, the advisor tells me, since there's no market for the shares. Without a market to liquidate it into, who knows what it would fetch? One thing led to another, though years passed, and we were finally talking about unlocking the value of the company by going public."

Mandy asked, "Why didn't you look for a buyer instead of going public?"

"We talked that through and Frank went ballistic. He couldn't stomach the idea that he would lose control. Once a majority of the family wanted to cash out and diversify, we worked as a bloc to change direction. We have no interest in participating in management and would rather have our value and not be subject to the whims of my nephew. If we were going to get our way and not have Frank trying to blow the idea up, going public was the only plausible route."

Mandy asked, "What about your tension with Carl?"

"Our relationship has been bad for some time. My son has harbored a grudge against me for years. I pushed Frank to bring in a seasoned general counsel years ago, before my son could take on the job after law school. I didn't think he was ready for it at the time. He's resented me for it ever since."

"And things are no better between you now?"

"Not really. Carl has never left any daylight between himself and Frank. Don't get me wrong. I love my son, but I'm disgusted by his mindless loyalty to Frank"

Mandy asked, "Is Carl like his father?"

"Klaus was principled. I don't know about Carl."

"You spoke of a seasoned general counsel. Was it John Booth, by any chance?"

Gretchen looked at Mandy as if she'd been stuck speechless, and finally whispered, "How on earth did you know that?"

"He told me so last year, while I was involved with him in another case. We didn't talk about it since I was concerned about different things at the time. All I can remember is asking him why he'd join another company after retiring. I recall him explaining he was doing someone a favor. Then he had some disagreement and he was gone."

Gretchen said, "Yes, he suspected some improper past business practices. The same thing had troubled Klaus. When Booth tried to raise the issues, he was unceremoniously dumped. It wasn't announced that way, but that's what really happened. If I were in your shoes, I wouldn't mention John Booth's name around Frank or Carl. John was a lovely man, and a dear friend. I've always regretted getting him involved in the company. His murder last year was a terrible loss."

Mandy felt guilt and was anxious to stop talking about John Booth. She said, "I gather that you have something to tell me?"

Gretchen said, "Yes. I understand you want the unvarnished history of the company, and Frank doesn't want to rehash old family history or secrets. But if you think it's important for what you need to do, I want to help you. Like I said before, this public offering was my initiative, and I want it to happen and be done right. So, tell me where you'd like me to start, and I'll be an open book."

Mandy said, "There's nothing like the beginning, so please start as far back as you can. I did the same thing with my boyfriend's mother. She publishes the *Chicago Business Journal* and was able to go back to the nineteenth century about my former company, LaSalle."

Gretchen sat erect with her hands on her knees, suddenly smiled and said, "You're talking about Beth, aren't you? I'm old friends with Beth Carney. We met while volunteering together at the Chicago History Museum years ago. Since I stopped the volunteering after Klaus died, we haven't seen each other. So, Patrick Carney is your boyfriend?"

Mandy said, "He is, and you have Chicago history in common with Beth Carney then?"

"We both married into these two families who had been historic enemies. We weren't burdened by the family feud and liked each other. We had plenty to discuss. We were friends, but we haven't seen each other for such a long time. That's my fault. I got upset over her magazine article about Klaus and his brother. I need to repair that friendship, I guess. The three of us should get together."

Mandy said, "What do you mean by a family feud?"

Gretchen said, "From the beginning in the 1830s there was trouble between Max Wagner and Seamus Carney, the founders of the two companies. Max had numerous run-ins with Seamus and his crews over the years, usually because of taunting the rowdy, hard-drinking Irish and unfairly criticizing their quality of work. The most toxic of the confrontations came when Max left the Delaware and Hudson Canal project. He worked for a while on that project and then headed to Erie, Pennsylvania. Max poached fifty of Seamus Carney's crew, and it enraged Carney and started a feud that continued for years."

Mandy said, "I'd love to hear about that sometime."

The older woman said, "It's a little late for a long story tonight. Maybe next time?"

Mandy said, "Sure, but can I change subjects and quickly ask you a question about the board before I leave?"

"Ah, the board. Surely a delicate topic to raise with Frank. Go ahead."

"I know what you mean. As soon as I raised board composition, I was in dangerous territory. The director interviews were stressful, with Frank and Carl looking over my shoulder and cutting off my questions. But I've made it clear to your son that once the company is public, the governance community will criticize the company for its board composition. And rightfully so. There aren't enough directors, and what few there are provide little diversity, except for you, and there are director conflicts of interest because of business ties. Please don't be offended, but the current board membership is inexperienced in public company matters. Frank would benefit by having directors with public company experience who can give him guidance. He doesn't appreciate this, I'm afraid."

Gretchen said, "No offense taken. I'm not suited for this anyway. And it's no surprise that Frank would do that. He doesn't like anyone questioning his actions. What do you suggest?"

"I'd like to recommend some new categories of directors, but to start with, I want to mention Ed Rosen. I worked for him when he was the general counsel of LaSalle and he's recently retired. He was a securities lawyer and served as the corporate secretary too. He'd be terrific, if only I could find a way to get his foot in the door."

"Why don't you feel him out about it, and if he's interested, I'd be happy to recommend him to Frank or Carl. But trust me. Frank won't like me poking my nose into it, especially after I butted my way in to get John Booth installed. But I agree that it should be done. I already had it out with Frank about participating in this whole process, so we're hostile with each other anyway. But I could always try to go through Charlie Winters."

"Perfect. Thank you."

"I've practically been gagged the whole time I've been a director since my husband's death. Frank is so controlling; I might as well not be on the board."

Mandy said, "Do you mean he doesn't let you speak at meetings, or that he disregards your input?"

"I don't get to give any input. Anything done at board meetings is so perfunctory that it's meaningless. I don't know what happened when Klaus was alive, and he was a board member. It would surprise me if he got treated differently, but then again he was also in management, so it might have been different. His brother Gus, Jr. was the CEO. Klaus ran a big part of the business involving large construction projects. Neither of them would tell you if anything was happening. You couldn't pry a word out of them. I think I was brought onto the board after Klaus died just to keep matters within the family."

"Did Carl or Frank advise you how to answer my questions?"

"Of course. They told me the less said the better, and they would make sure that what needed to be done for this offering, would get done."

"When did your husband die?"

"Over a decade ago, before Frank and Carl were in charge."

"You were brought on to the board by your brother-in-law, then?"

"Right, good old Gus, Jr. He was quite the character. When they weren't fishing, they went at it constantly."

"About what?"

"About how to do things. Gus was a ruthless dominator, and Klaus didn't want to be told what to do or be micromanaged on how to do things. He'd successfully built his end of the business and didn't like Gus's interference. They had big arguments, especially near the end before he died."

"May I ask what happened to your husband?"

Mandy could sense Gretchen deflate emotionally, like a balloon leaking air, even years after his death.

"It was tragic. He died from the very thing that had kept him alive his whole life—insulin. He was diabetic and sometimes was careless about his injections. Sometimes too little, and other times too much. He overdosed. Klaus had a history of needing medical attention because of that. He'd been out fishing on one of his regular trips with his brother on the lake. Gus, Jr. kept a boat downstairs at the marina. In fact, it's still down there. Frank inherited it when Gus died.

"The brothers fished a lot, and Klaus took his insulin shot while he was out on the boat on Lake Michigan. Gus didn't notice him missing for a while. He was found down in the cabin passed out, and by the time Gus got to him, he had been unconscious for some time and Gus couldn't revive him. Gus rushed back to the harbor to get medical attention. But by the time it arrived, Klaus had stopped breathing for some time. They couldn't revive him." Gretchen was crying now.

"I'm so sorry."

"Thank you. Klaus was too young to die, at sixty-three. I was ten years younger, and it left me very lonely. So, I guess I was kind of honored when Gus asked me to take Klaus's seat on the board. It took my mind off my own troubles. But then I got the same treatment from Gus, Jr. that I've been getting from his son Frank. Sometimes I think Gus brought me on the board just so he could keep an eye on me. I know that sounds paranoid. When this public company thing is over, I'm getting off that board. Let somebody else take a turn."

"Maybe this is none of my business, and feel free to say so, but what did you mean before when you said that Beth Carney had said something about Gus, Jr. and Klaus that angered you?"

She folded her arms in front of her, as if she was about to pout, but said, "I was probably overly protective of Klaus's memory. Beth is a journalist, and she'd written about disagreements between the brothers. I don't remember all the details now, but at the time I got upset and just shut down my contact with her."

Mandy had already been introduced to Beth's journalistic fervor. Hoping to pry out any more secrets, Mandy said, "Was there anything else you wanted to tell me about the board?"

"No, I was never kept informed except for superficial things. But I'm happy to speak to you privately again, and let you ask any questions you'd like. I'm not sure what I can answer about the past; the big things were handled by the brothers together. But I'm willing to try."

Mandy interrupted. "It's late and I should let you get some rest. If possible, I'd like to take you up on your suggestion and get together with Beth Carney and continue with both family stories. Would you be willing to do that?"

"Of course. I'd love to see Beth. Why don't you go ahead and set it up?"

At the door, another question popped into her head and she said, "Did your husband have an autopsy?"

"No, not with his history. It could have been a heart attack or stroke. There was no point in an autopsy, and the police said there was no suspicion of foul play."

Mandy said gently, "OK, so it wasn't a hard decision for you to make?"

"I didn't make it. I was too shaken up at the time. I relied on Gus to make the decision. The only thing I put my foot down about was that I didn't want Klaus to be cremated. Gus had urged me to go with cremation."

As Mandy left the condo, she pondered what she'd heard. The family had obviously run Northwest like the closely held family business that it was. That was to be expected. But, the apparent turbulence between the brothers piqued her curiosity. In addition, Klaus's death was mysterious. Before she pushed the elevator button she called Reggie and leaned up against the wall.

Mandy told her, "I've had a very unsettling discussion with one of the Northwest directors, Carl's mother Gretchen. She invited me over to her condo and didn't want anyone to hear about it."

"What did she tell you?"

"She was told not to say anything, so I better not go into it. She's not been treated well as a director. She's bitter about Northwest. Here's the big thing I got from her, though: her husband died from a sudden overdose of insulin. Is that common?"

Reggie said, "No. Diabetics are usually careful about their dosage."

"Supposedly he had an up and down history with his insulin injections."

"That's not unheard of, I guess. It's just rare. Let me pull up his death certificate details."

She hummed annoyingly while she typed and pulled up the death certificate on the Cook County system with the details Mandy gave her. While Reggie was working her database magic, Mandy was bouncing ideas off her, mainly to stop the humming.

"Gretchen told me that Gus wanted her to cremate Klaus, but she refused. I wonder why he'd want that."

Reggie said, "Not to sound paranoid, but cremation destroys evidence."

"Evidence of what?"

"Anything. Everything. But an autopsy might tell us a lot. If you can get her to sign a consent for disinterment and autopsy, we can find out. Now you've got me anxious to autopsy him right away."

They hung up and Mandy stood in the hallway wondering how to raise the autopsy topic with Gretchen. After a few minutes, she turned and walked back to Gretchen's door and knocked, and when she opened the door Mandy summarized the autopsy conversation with Reggie. Gretchen was looking horrified by what she was now hearing.

Gretchen was grief-stricken and had to sit down. She said, "Are you suggesting Klaus didn't die from the insulin?"

"I don't know. My sister said an autopsy could answer that question, if you consented to the process."

Gretchen asked, "Would anyone have to know about it?"

"I couldn't guarantee that with the permits we'd need, but we'd keep it as low key as we could."

Gretchen asked if she could sleep on it and let her know the next day, and with that Mandy finally did leave. Immediately after that conversation, Gretchen called her daughter and went through everything with her, especially the autopsy. Her daughter agreed to keep it to herself.

As she left Gretchen's building, Frank Wagner's spy Jack Greer was in his surveillance van parked outside the entrance to Marina City with his recording equipment. He had watched Mandy both arrive and leave. It was only when she left that he recognized her from the video feed he'd managed to get into Gretchen's condo.

Jack said aloud, as if he was with someone, "Who are you, lady?"

He'd earlier placed a video camera into Gretchen's condo using the key he'd gotten from Frank, and was able to start passing along some information to Frank. He wasn't going to pass along actual recordings, but the client would get the gist of things. After all, what he was doing was illegal, and he wasn't about to provide evidence of his wrongdoing to his client or anyone else. Clients should not be aware of means and methods, anyway. Jack had also installed spyware remotely onto Gretchen Wagner's cell phone, so he could track her movements. He sent a message to Frank telling him Gretchen was meeting with some young woman with red hair. Frank reacted badly to that news.

12

Minutes

MANDY RECEIVED TWO CALLS
the next morning. The first was from Gretchen approving the
autopsy, after discussing it with her daughter. Gretchen was still
upset over the idea, but she'd agreed to sign a consent. She had
also dug out her late husband's diary that she'd held on to after
his death, and she said she'd bring it to Mandy to read. Because
of her grief, she'd never had the nerve to read through it, and
still didn't.

The second call was from Sammy onboard *Bogie,* returning
from the lake voyage to Michigan with Ray. Sammy said, "I've got
some results from poking into the history of Northwest Drayage
and Tunnel Company for you. There's a lot here, but I can give
you the executive summary if you'd like."

Mandy said, "Yes, please."

Not one for soft-pedaling things, Sammy said, "Your people are crooks. I found a lot of articles from nineteenth-century newspapers. They reported litigation filed against the company by a variety of companies. The claims ranged from interference with contracts to attempts to cheat on competitive bidding. They conveniently all got dismissed without explanation and with confidentiality surrounding the settlements. My suspicion is that the plaintiffs were given inducements to back off."

"How do you know that?"

"Because the plaintiffs were all later listed as subcontractors to Northwest jobs. It was a pattern throughout everything I found."

Mandy asked, "What about any of them resulting in judgments against the company?"

"None. I think they were all resolved out of court."

"How long did this go on?"

Sammy replied, "About twenty-five years, or so. By then there were some antitrust laws passed and they must have adjusted their ways of working. I hope this has been helpful."

"It has. I'll let you know if I need more."

———

Next on Mandy's list was to examine the many years of Northwest board minutes. Then her next step after board minutes was to start digging through the law department files in search of settlement agreements. If there had been problems, and Northwest had bought its way out of them, there should be some trail. No lawsuits or prosecutions had proceeded to trial. Chicago businesses had a history of corruption, and it was anybody's guess how much money had passed hands over the years to make problems go away. The state had a less than stellar history itself. Look at what happened with the recent governor, now a federal prisoner, for attempting to sell former Senator Barack Obama's Senate seat after he'd been elected President.

As unappetizing an idea as it might be, reading all the old board minutes for newsworthy events was a necessary step. There was no telling how much history could be gleaned from reading the minutes. It was possible that once having been written, no one had ever read those minutes again.

She spent a couple days slogging through the minutes, and at the end of it, besides having dry hands, paper cuts and inhaling a lot of unwanted dust mites, there had been some interesting revelations. This was what due diligence was all about—99 percent boredom and 1 percent gold nuggets. Back home afterward, Mandy and Reggie discussed the highlights.

Reggie said to her, "That is not my idea of great entertainment. Maybe you should start by reminding me why board minutes are important."

Mandy said, "I know this is pretty unexciting for someone who dissects bodies, but in my world board minutes may be a gatekeeper for protecting the corporate status."

"You've got me on the edge of my chair."

"OK, I'll make this brief. You need a board of directors if you're a corporation. It must meet and receive information and then make decisions. There must be minutes kept of those meetings. Nothing is firm about what needs to be in the minutes, but if some activities need to be documented, it comes via the minutes.

"And if it doesn't keep minutes?" Reggie asked.

"If they don't respect the corporate form, then there's risk of what's called '*piercing the corporate veil.*'"

Reggie looked befuddled, and said, "I like the piercing part."

She continued, "It means individual shareholders can be liable, and their personal wealth is unprotected. If corporate requirements are met, the liability stays with the corporation, and if there are no assets beyond what it can produce, no one can reach the shareholders' assets," Mandy explained.

Reggie said, "This all sounds so boring. How can you stand this stuff?"

Mandy said, "It's not boring if you're being sued."

"It doesn't sound like respecting this corporate form thing is too hard to do though," Reggie said.

"No, but here's where lack of understanding, or worse—arrogance—comes in," Mandy said.

Mandy went on to explain that if nobody minds the store, and personal assets are exposed, it's a disaster. Potentially everyone gets hurt. Lots of owners of private companies, especially small ones, neglect or ignore things and invite a picture of the corporation as a sham. Then it's *game over* and the owners' assets can be reached.

She said, "I won't bore you with all the things I was looking for. I'll just tell you the good stuff."

She only got a hurry up motion from her twin, who was rolling her eyes.

"First, there was a chilling description of the Great Chicago Fire of 1871. Some of the Northwest employees had been burned out of their homes, since the fire incinerated all the buildings in its path in the two days it raged.

"The year after the fire, Gus Wagner was recognized for his accomplishments in designing steam shovel innovations and boring equipment. He'd gotten U.S. and foreign patent protection, and the board noted that these inventions would improve the company's competitive position."

"So, Gus was an inventor?"

"Apparently. Then the minutes noted that the company had successfully won the bid to construct a single-bore rail tunnel called the St. Gotthard Tunnel. Cutting through a mountain in

Switzerland, the job would take ten years to complete but would solidify Northwest's reputation and lead to further projects.

"Later on, there were successful awards for the Chicago Sanitary and Ship Canal, the Cal-Sag Channel and the rerouting of the Calumet River, the reversal of the Chicago River, and many other projects.

"Northwest had great success for a long time. As the century ended, they even moved their headquarters into the tallest building in the world, called the Monadnock Building. At the point of Gus Wagner's retirement, the board adopted a resolution of appreciation for his years of service. He'd led the firm for forty years after the death of his father, Max.

"Within the year he'd committed suicide, jumping off that building and splattering himself on the sidewalk."

Reggie scratched her head and said, "If everything had been going so well, why would he kill himself?"

"That's my question too, but there was no attempt to explain it in the minutes. I wouldn't expect them to. That's not the kind of thing that corporate secretaries write about. I'll have to ask Gretchen about it."

"Any other juicy stuff?"

Mandy continued, "There were vague references to agreements with various firms that were reviewed with and approved by the board. Normally a board-approved contract would be appended to board minutes, but there were no appendices."

"So, you're saying you found references to agreements without the agreements. Is that troubling?"

"It is in my protocols. If a board member wanted to understand what the company was contracting for and the board was being asked to approve, good practice would be to have the agreement in the record."

"And? Are you going to make me work for my dinner, or will you just tell me the '*so what*' of all that?"

"I had the list of the companies from the minutes and I called Sammy to compare to what she'd dug out of old newspaper reports. It was almost a perfect match."

"So Northwest was entering into contracts with the companies that had sued them?"

"Right. Sammy was very blunt about things. She said '*your guys are crooks*' and they had a track record of buying off competitors. Then in the twentieth-century minute books, the company was noted as the successful bidder for two mega-projects—the Panama Canal and the St. Lawrence Seaway Project. These were massive multi-year projects before and after the world wars. And now in the twenty-first century they talked about winning the deals for the widening of the Panama Canal and the improvements to the St. Lawrence Seaway. So those projects had been a clean sweep of victory."

"What does that tell you?"

"It's what isn't in the minutes that caught my attention. There was a deafening silence about the biggest project right here at home, that Northwest seems to have missed out on completely— the Deep Tunnel project."

"So, you win some and you lose some, right?"

"That would be uncharacteristic of the family. I'm suspicious that somebody dropped a ball. A big one. In any company there would be a high likelihood that the board would demand answers. There is zilch here about that."

Reggie said, "So what's your next step?"

"Reading Klaus's diary and seeing what he had been writing about, I think there's a connection between all these. I think it also might be useful to send Sammy in to hunt for the missing agreements. Northwest has a big warehouse where old records are kept. I learned they've been digitized, which will make it easier to research."

———————

Mandy endured an extensive day of executive interviews. Most of the officers had less than five years' service, so they weren't of much use to her. The company was divided into three operating groups: Bridges and Tunnels; Transportation Projects; and Ports and Canals. The leaders of the first two divisions were outgoing and proud of their activities, and nothing troubled Mandy about their discussions. The third division—Ports and Canals—was led by David Wilson. He had a much more muted reaction to being interviewed. When she asked him to describe the projects his division was involved in, he was either vague or reluctant to talk. He tended to refer to the company's press releases to answer her questions and did not volunteer anything else. Wilson clearly disliked the scrutiny; Mandy had developed a keen nose for that during her DOJ days. He'd said, "Why are we even having this discussion? I already went through everything with that law firm weeks ago. I have a busy division that I've got to run. Why don't you get what you need from Frank?"

Mandy said, "Yes, I imagine I could get what I want from Frank, but surely he doesn't have the insights his top division leaders have. I do appreciate your time and apologize for any redundancy. But because you've been here so long, I think of you as an old hand for this part of our work. If you could tell me whether any troubling practices were used in the division's past, that would be great."

"No. We keep our noses clean over here. We haven't done anything wrong and there's nothing to tell you. I need to get back to work." And with that dismissive announcement, Wilson got up and left.

Mandy had to think over what had just happened with Wilson, compared to easy discussions she'd had with the other division presidents. No one could possibly come away from that brief meeting with Wilson without thinking he was hiding something important. She decided that it was time to involve Ray to see what was going on with David Wilson.

First Autopsy

EARLY ONE MORNING a crew showed up at Graceland Cemetery on the north side of Chicago. With Gretchen's signed consent in hand, the crew efficiently exhumed Klaus Wagner's casket and transported it to the FBI lab on Roosevelt Road. Reggie supervised the autopsy of the body, which had deteriorated greatly after ten years underground. Her team worked on the body throughout the day, taking photos, tissue samples, checking all the organs, and finally starting all the chemical tests for substances. Puncture sites were found in the stomach area, which was undoubtedly where Klaus Wagner was used to injecting his life-sustaining insulin. Except that this final time might have been life-depriving.

Once all the tissue tests were completed, Reggie's team served up the results of the autopsy, and the remains were re-interred without fanfare. No news outlets had caught on. While the disinterment was possible with only the next-of-kin's consent, a probate court order was required for exhumation and the Bureau obtained it. The tissue samples had yielded some surprising results that could still be present after all this time using modern technology. New toxicological testing methods allowed for the detection of trace amounts of certain chemicals years after death, despite the replacement of bodily fluids with formaldehyde.

The amount of insulin evidenced in Klaus's tissues was within an acceptable range to what would have been expected from an injection. However, traces of potassium cyanide were found in the liver. Reggie's team explained that cyanide was rapidly absorbed in a person's system. It meant unconsciousness in seconds and oblivion in minutes.

When she was done writing the autopsy report with her conclusions, she called Mandy and gave her the highlights. "Klaus died from cyanide poisoning. He wouldn't have observed potassium cyanide mixed in with insulin from just looking at a filled syringe, if that's how it was done. Your man was murdered."

Mandy said, "If Gus Wagner had gotten hold of Klaus's insulin supply and prepared a syringe, Klaus could have administered his own death sentence. His brother probably was experienced with needles after a lifetime spent with a diabetic sibling."

"Preparing a syringe on a rocking boat in the middle of Lake Michigan might not be a happy prospect to a diabetic like Klaus, so he might have been a good Boy Scout and had it ready before leaving Marina Towers. Then he wouldn't have to fiddle with it while underway. Cyanide could be conveniently added to that prepared syringe."

"So do you think Klaus self-administered the fatal dose prepared by Gus?"

Reggie said, "That's what we think. I can easily imagine that once out on the lake, Gus asking his brother to take the helm while he went to the head. Gus was familiar with his brother's set-up for taking his insulin, so it would be no trouble to top off the syringe with cyanide, and Klaus would be none the wiser. It had to be something like that unless he had a co-conspirator."

"So, Klaus goes down belowdecks to take his shot and he carries out his own death sentence. What happens with cyanide?"

Reggie answered, "Once it entered the bloodstream, Klaus would be unconscious within seconds, and death would occur in minutes. The poison would spread instantly throughout the bloodstream, suffocating the red blood cells from oxygen. All someone would have to do was throw the spent syringe overboard, fill another with clean insulin and empty it into the water, and leave it to be found still sticking into the dead Klaus."

Mandy said, "According to Gretchen, Gus, Jr. said there was no need for an autopsy, and Gretchen had been too distraught to question it. Thank God Gretchen had refused his idea of cremation, and now the notion of giving Klaus an autopsy has paid off."

Mandy now understood why the brother wanted cremation. Reggie had immediately put her finger on it when she had earlier told Mandy on the phone that cremation would eliminate evidence.

When Klaus's autopsy was completed, Gretchen opted to have the body reburied, and that required a reburial permit. That permit, along with the exhumation probate order, became public and was picked up in the public documents sweep that Jack Greer had put in place for any mention of Gretchen, and he'd reported to Frank that the filings had popped up. Carl was shocked to find all this out from his cousin and volunteered to ask his mother what was going on. Frank had been very subdued upon hearing this news.

Even though the autopsy was controlled by Reggie, it was her boss Steve Baker who controlled the timing of the release of the results. He didn't want to bring Gretchen into the picture until he'd consulted with the U.S. Attorney, so the delivery of that bad news was deferred for a day or two.

C H A P T E R

14

Surveillance

MANDY INVITED BETH and
Gretchen to her apartment the next afternoon. She waited on her
balcony ten floors above ground level, looking east down Hubbard
Street through her binoculars. It was great people-watching in
River North. She and her sister routinely entertained themselves
watching the city from that balcony, when they weren't running
the streets of the city. As she watched, unexpectedly Gretchen
approached from three blocks away and Mandy noticed a van
creeping behind her, possibly stalking. It would either leapfrog
her or nearly reach her, then pull over and watch as Gretchen
walked on. It was repeated for the entire three blocks until she
entered Mandy's building, when the van pulled over and just
sat waiting a hundred feet away. While waiting for Gretchen to

arrive, she quickly called Ray Hanson and asked him to check on the van.

When Gretchen came, Mandy asked her about the conversation she'd had with Frank about bringing Ed Rosen on to the board.

Mandy said, "Did Frank ask you whether I'd been involved?"

"I spoke to Carl, not Frank, and told him it was my idea. He didn't question it, but I could tell he was suspicious. Of course, he's suspicious about everything where I'm concerned. Why, did he or Frank confront you?"

"No, but I brought up the director issue yesterday with Carl in an email, and he replied that he'd raise it with Frank. I'm sure I haven't heard the last of this."

Beth arrived and she and Gretchen had an emotional reunion. Mandy excused herself to get some drinks and snacks, leaving the two women some privacy. They hugged and Gretchen got a little teary-eyed after reminiscing with her old friend about Klaus. She gave what sounded like an apology for holding against Beth what she'd written about the brothers after Klaus's death.

From her kitchen she could hear Gretchen saying, "I wish I'd kept up with you after I left the museum, but I'd been struggling since Klaus died, I guess. I probably overreacted to the article you wrote about the brothers and their friction. At the time, I was hyper-sensitive to any criticism of Klaus. After all these years I now realize you were just doing your job." She heard Beth say, "Thank you for understanding that. Klaus's death was so tragic. I'm so sorry you had to go through that." Beth didn't mention her concern when Gretchen had failed to return her calls.

Both women admired the wall covered with mounted medals and photos. Scores of marathon and triathlon finishers' medals from the sisters' past races hung in the front hallway. Amid them were two distinctive framed Presidential Citizens Medals they'd received the year before at the White House for the role they played in a national security breach. Mandy joined them and explained how she and Reggie were dedicated long-distance runners with a goal to run a marathon in every state. Reggie was also a triathlete and would soon be participating in the Chicago Triathlon.

Mandy hadn't seen Gretchen as relaxed as she was now with Beth. Both women not only looked to be in good spirits but sounded like they were conspiring. Mandy suggested that they talk about the conflict between the families, going back to the earliest days.

Beth started off, saying, "I think we all know that the two immigrants, Seamus Carney and Max Wagner, had a combative relationship working together on the Erie Canal. Seamus moved on to the Delaware and Hudson Canal after completing the Erie Canal. He'd gotten experience in masonry and was able to command a total workforce, not just laborers. Then he moved to the Baltimore & Ohio Railroad, the first large-scale commercial railroad in the country. He'd learned of a rail line being planned in Chicago, and he jumped at the opportunity to bid on the project. By this time, his first son Patrick had arrived, and was soon joined by a sister. It was time to settle down.

"The Carneys settled in Chicago eventually, and Seamus established the LaSalle Dredging and Excavation Company. He built the floating swing bridges on the Chicago River, then the Galena and Chicago Union Railroad line between those two cities."

Mandy asked, "So from then on, the Wagner and Carney companies and families grew and competed for large-scale projects in Chicago?"

Beth said, "Yes, but along with the competition, resentment and hostility grew, and this did not bode well for the future. The mid-1800s were important in establishing Chicago's dominance among cities in the interior of the country, and strong competition between the companies drove strong emotions.

"When the Carneys began the Galena rail line construction in 1848, a project lasting until 1853, they began a process they were to repeat many times as railroads began to compete with shipping. The city became the site of the world's largest convergence of railroad lines, eventually eclipsing the waterway systems for the method of commerce. LaSalle was set to become the preeminent rail line builder in Chicago. The city was humming, not only from all the construction and the influx of immigrants, but also from the panic over death and sickness."

Mandy said, "What caused that?"

Beth answered, "Unbridled growth, mixed with rapid industrialization and inadequate infrastructure. It made for a toxic environment. Up until then, human and animal waste found its way into the streets and into the river. Every day in the warm months, the city experienced deaths from cholera. It hadn't been present in America before the Europeans showed up, but it soon came ashore with new faces. Then it showed up in Chicago when General Winfield Scott was sent with troops to protect it from attack by Chief Blackhawk of the Sauk tribe. Blackhawk never did attack, but *Old Fuss and Feather's* troops showed up infected with cholera. Every day the Chicago newspapers published the names of the cholera victims released by the Chicago Board of Health.

"Cholera is a waterborne disease. Once it found its way into the river, it rode the current into Lake Michigan. Once there, it went into barrels of fresh lake water by those providing water to the local population. Chicago was the fastest-growing city in the world by 1850, and by the late 1860s it had grown to over 300,000. The need for fresh water was important."

Mandy asked, "How did that problem get solved?"

Beth said, "The water contamination situation was dire, and the city eventually found a solution, or at least the beginning of one. An engineer by the name of Ellis Chesbrough was lured away from Boston. He became Chicago's Chief Engineer and its savior from cholera. His plan was first to raise all the buildings and streets in downtown Chicago, then install sewer pipes and connect them to the newly raised buildings and under the streets. Then he planned water pipes way out into the lake to pump in clean drinking water. The plan took more than twenty years to accomplish. By then, LaSalle was one of the city's favorite contractors, having built bridges and the first railroad. It won the entire lake tunnel project.

"Later, during the Civil War years, after the two founders, Seamus Carney and Max Wagner, had died, their firstborn sons took over their family businesses. Patrick was drawn more to the creative side, while Gus struggled to compete and yearned for the advantages LaSalle's business enjoyed. We think that Patrick's interests were focused on improving the construction and manufacturing processes used in tunnel construction and excavation. He relied on his brothers to run the operations.

"Patrick worked continuously on the solutions to problems from his little hideaway on the south side. This was how he countered being observed and spied upon by anyone in the company's main factory facility. Only a couple of people had ever known about this location.

"Up until 1871, Patrick was actively involved in designing certain concepts at his workshop for use in those types of projects LaSalle was doing. He was a self-taught draftsman who had become very skilled. Patrick kept his ideas to himself, though, not trusting the other workers. He had projects needing secrecy to keep their value and from piracy. According to my husband, the only protection for so-called trade secrets was simply keeping them secret. Once a trade secret became patented, he could rely on patent law protection. He wasn't there yet and couldn't stop some leakage of his activities entering the rumor mill.

He was in constant fear his competitor had placed spies in his operations."

Mandy was befuddled. She had heard now from Beth about Patrick Carney designing equipment, and the Northwest board minutes had praised Gus Wagner doing much the same thing. Were they both inventors? That sounded to her like an unlikely coincidence. Mandy was not a big believer in coincidences. She said to Gretchen, "Let's give Beth a breather and maybe you can give us the Wagner story."

Gretchen took over the story, explaining how Max Wagner had escaped the repressive Prussian Empire of the 1820s and found new opportunities in America on the Erie Canal. As an apprentice mason in Europe, he had skills to use to great advantage. He moved to other projects along the coast of Lake Erie and continued west to Chicago. He'd finally married along the way and started his family, with his young son Gus as the first of the new family to be born in America.

"By 1835, Max had established Northwest Drayage and Tunnel Company, and he'd set his sights on making a bid for the large Illinois & Michigan Canal project. He won that project and worked on it for over a decade. Along the way, it took the lives of many workers due to the harsh manual labor involved. Steam-powered shovels were new and would take some time to become widespread. Work was completed by pick and shovel, with the occasional black-powder explosion.

"Max introduced his son Gus to the business when they started on the Illinois & Michigan Canal, and by the time the canal was finished, Gus was a skilled mason and was also in control of the business. Max had put his son in charge of investigating and incorporating any promising new technology and techniques into the work plan. Eventually Gus was able to convince Max to buy a steam shovel. They used it to complete the canal.

"Competition between the Wagners and the Carneys was fierce, though, and when the advantage swung to LaSalle for the projects, it drove Max to take desperate measures. Klaus told me that Max had been suspected of offering bribes for the projects he won. But even if that was true, he said there were no laws broken since the legal system had yet to mature in terms of preventing corruption. It wouldn't take long though. The robber barons became dominant because they used anti-competitive means. The post-war period was still lawless, in some ways.

"Anyway, in the late summer of 1870, when Max's health forced him to cede control to Gus, the son was struggling. He proposed to Patrick Carney a combination of the two companies, arguing that both had significant advantages. Patrick gave an immediate and resounding rejection."

Beth said, "Patrick inherited his father Seamus's grudge against Max Wagner for stealing his workers. He wasn't about to help him out."

Gretchen added, "After Max died, the full weight of responsibility for Northwest rested heavily on Gus's shoulders."

Mandy said, "We've been at it for a long time today. I suggest we break it off here and resume another day. I don't want to wear you ladies out. I can't tell you how much I appreciate what you've told me."

Beth reminded Mandy that she had some old letters from Patrick's family going back to the time of the fire, and they could be of some value to Mandy. Gretchen had handed over Klaus's diary that she'd brought along. They agreed to meet again soon and continue.

Beth had a little sheepish grin on her face and turning to Mandy, said, "And I have a little confession to make. I want this to eventually be material for a series in the *Chicago History Journal*. Gretchen has agreed to collaborate with me on what she knows. So, let's not allow too much time to pass before we resume."

They all laughed. Gretchen confirmed that she would have lots of interesting material for her to include, and said, "I taunted that arrogant nephew of mine, telling him I was going to be a contributor to Beth's series."

After the women left, Mandy called Ray. "What have you got?"

"I know this guy. He does work for Frank Wagner. I'm following him now. Your guests are just leaving and he's following the one heading toward the river."

Mandy said, "That's Gretchen Wagner. Can you watch him for me?"

"He knows me, so I'll have to be very careful. It might be better if I asked Sammy to do the surveillance work from now on. He doesn't know her. Are you having more of these meetings?"

"We need to have more, so I'll schedule another one soon and let you know."

Jack Greer had spent two hours in his van outside Mandy's building, after having trailed Gretchen to the apartment. He positioned himself in the ideal vantage point so that he could use his close-up lens to get a photo of the tenant list next to the elevator, and the name Doucette was listed. It wasn't long before he saw Beth Carney go into the building. He recognized her from her reporting for the *Chicago History Journal*. He already reported to Frank that he'd seen the two older women entering the Doucette woman's apartment. He could tell his client was seething with anger at the news. Frank had taken it hard that his aunt was in private conversations with Beth Carney. He referred to her as the muckraker from the *Chicago History Journal*. It figured. Just at the time his public offering was nearing launch, Frank could ill afford his own aunt setting off an explosion to the deal. Frank needed to rein in his aunt until the offering was over, then extinguish her flame. Didn't Gretchen understand she was potentially throwing away a fortune?

Ray's new parabolic listening device, aimed from his discreet location at ground level, picked up the vibrations from Greer's van window. Hearing just Jack's side of the conversation was enough to reveal to Ray that Greer was spying for Frank Wagner. He let Mandy know and observed that if Greer was tailing Gretchen, he'd capture Mandy's and Beth Carney's involvement too. This should have made Mandy pause any more provocation, but she was convinced that she smelled something rotten and needed to get to the bottom of it. She asked Ray to see what he could find out about David Wilson, after his hostility in the recent interview. Mandy could hardly call it an interview. It was more like a master class in deflection and non-cooperation. From her DOJ days, she knew something was wrong when she started hearing the little voice inside her giving her whispered warnings. She was getting that now.

15

Plumbing Archives

PATRICK'S FAMILY OFFICE SUITE was in a nondescript building on Wabash Street in the Loop. The L tracks rumbled with the trains circling the Loop every couple of minutes, with the screeching and clickety-clack of the steel wheels playing like an urban soundtrack. Through one of the windows with a northeast view, he could just make out the stunning Chicago Tribune building, the 1925 neo-Gothic skyscraper with its gargoyles and flying buttresses. He had been keeping an eye out on the building's conversion to a residential tower, thinking it would be a fantastic place to live. It made him pause as he imagined the possibilities.

The treasure trove of information it held, though, was a gift from his mother. An historian, journalist, and now apparently genealogist as well, Beth Carney had protected the family story as best she could. There were cabinets and shelves crammed with binders and memorabilia.

His primary interest, of course, was the family history that the room held. He was excited for the chance to take a deep dive into it. Finding things to help Mandy in her project was energizing. Patrick had been forcefully introduced into Mandy's life the year before when they had barely avoided an intentional boat attack while kayaking the Chicago River. It soon became clear that it was attempted murder. He'd felt the need to protect Mandy then, and was feeling it again now.

He realized he was having a surge of emotions as he sat before the stacks of Carney materials. Foremost was his love for Mandy, and that he considered himself so fortunate to come across her path. And at the prospect of delving into family secrets, now knowing that his ancestor was murdered, gave him great fear. Both combined to put him on an adrenaline rush to begin. That said, he wasn't immune from thinking of his own self-interest. For a storyteller, particularly a historical fiction novelist, he needed to find a relic he could use to conjure up stories. Patrick wished he'd stumbled on to this idea before, since it would have spared him a lot of trial-and-error effort to conceive plots. It was here now, though, and he was burrowing into it like a hungry mole.

He started with the binders containing the Carney family genealogy. Some diligent ancestors had gone all out to document their quest. Besides family trees, the binders were replete with birth and death certificates, marriage records, U.S. census records, and even church registries of marriages. Fortunately for his genealogy pursuits, the family line had been pristinely Irish, without any dilution. He might be the one to initiate the mixture, given the French-Canadian/Italian beauty he loved. It made the tracing and tracking easier.

He wanted to get a good handle on his own line of ancestry, especially focusing on the first Patrick in his family line, who they now called P1. Page after page of information sheets and official records lay before him. He'd look for anything revealing about the fire and the disappearance. The first Carney in the country was Seamus, of course, who'd emigrated in the 1830s from the town of Tralee, in County Kerry. There were copies of birth and marriage records from a local parish he could examine. Afterward, everything was based in America. Seamus's marriage record from Pennsylvania was there, followed by the birth record for the eldest child, Patrick, also from Pennsylvania. Another two binders contained the family line through each "Patrick" and up to the present. His own records were included as well, including copies of his books. His mother had been busy keeping the collection updated.

Then he located some dusty boxes labeled Pinkerton investigation. Pinkertons was one of the oldest and most respected security firms. It became famous because one of its agents accompanied Abe Lincoln on his train ride to Washington, DC, after the 1860 election. She helped him avoid an assassination attempt in Baltimore, using disguises and special tactics. The firm's actions laid the groundwork for the establishment of the U.S. Secret Service, which happened only months after Lincoln's assassination.

According to the letters, suspicion had been rumored among Carney family members that the Wagners were behind some of the losses of LaSalle's business opportunities. Pinkertons tried to find a link with the fire and the disappearance of Patrick. They used spies inside Northwest and even the Wagner household. His mother had told him that Northwest used spies to learn what P1 was doing in his secret location. Spies were falling all over each other. Anyway, over the course of months, nothing could be found to help with the question of P1's fate. There was some evidence found, though, that Northwest had colluded to win construction projects from the Carney company, since they had routinely edged out LaSalle's bids.

Patrick was too impatient to wait out his investigation and decided to call Mandy right then.

"Calling in the middle of a workday?" she said.

He said, "I was reading through all the family records and wanted you to know what I found about your company."

"Uh oh. You sound pretty excited."

"Fasten your seatbelt. The reports I've read cover the decade after the fire. The family hired the Pinkertons detective agency to investigate, but Pinkertons didn't turn up enough for a lawsuit. Even so, they clearly found evidence of unethical business methods. The company was bid rigging."

Mandy asked, "What did the family do about it?"

"Nothing. A handwritten note in the file said they couldn't see a path of recourse without opening themselves up to huge expenses and maybe counterattacks. They chose to leave it to posterity."

Mandy said, "My dad told me that prior to the 1890s, those kinds of shenanigans were not actionable."

"There's a nice lawyer word for you—'*actionable.*' Anyway, does this help you with anything?"

"Maybe. It may show a pattern of behavior they'd rather not have on display, but I don't think it would disrupt the offering unless it was recent conduct. What are you going to do now?"

"There's still more here that I must look at. And I have yet to spot a relic I can use."

"Seems to me that bid rigging might have been their standard way of doing business. You could get a story from that. I'm hoping for corroboration of that from Sammy. She's doing some more investigating for me."

Patrick said, "I'm going to let the ideas marinate until a storyline comes out. I get to imagine things that might have happened. I only need a good starting point."

"Lots of material for a book there. Congratulations."

"It's here for you to use if you want."

"Well, remember that I work for their company, and I don't want to help undermine them. By the way, how are the accommodations there?"

"Charming. Lots of dust bunnies and drawn window shades."

"No bed?"

Patrick said, "Would you come over if there was?"

"No, I'm a working woman in the middle of a workday. Gotta get back to the grind."

Turning serious, Mandy said, "Sounds like your family was rabid. Hiring private investigators is not a step taken lightly. I should know, since I do it myself."

Patrick was fully aware of Mandy's habit of hiring private investigators. He hadn't caught on that she had an investigator working right now until she'd mentioned Ray and Sammy. It sounded like she had them operating together, which I'm sure suited them.

"You're doing it again, aren't you? Hiring investigators."

"Sometimes you have to make a move to get what you need."

Patrick smiled. "I get it. I guess the family got some solid info from Pinkertons but didn't have the fortitude to do anything on it."

They hung up and Patrick returned to the files, soon finding a bundle of letters tied with a ribbon. Enclosed in one envelope labeled "Patrick's" was a charred and twisted belt buckle. These were the letters his mother had remembered. He started reading them and was shocked by what he turned up. What he'd just found was the trail to Patrick Carney's invention process and a possible source of more information. He wished he'd waited to call Mandy so he could pass this along, but he would take advantage of the situation to get his father's help.

Mandy meanwhile had turned to text messages that had come in. She struggled to identify the name Ashley Tate and finally remembered her as the associate lawyer she'd tried reaching. She returned the text message offering to speak now, and soon got a call.

Ashley said, "I'm sorry about this, but I really needed to speak to you. I've been taken off the Northwest deal." She was clearly upset.

Mandy said, "What happened?"

"The partner reassigned me after he'd gotten a call from someone at the company. They claimed I'd been annoying Frank Wagner at Northwest. It was pure nonsense. Wagner actually made a pass at me, and I resisted him. Then somebody got spooked when I started asking questions about the St. Lawrence and Panama Canal deals."

"What was it you were after?"

"It was just routine due diligence for the filing. I was surprised by the reaction, and just wanted you to know."

"Who pulled you off the deal?"

"The senior partner, but he'd been ordered by Carl Wagner."

"Are you sure Frank Wagner had an interest in you?"

"Yes. He never tried to hide it. He made a comment on my body, and I avoided him like the plague after that. I don't think he likes being rebuffed. Isn't he smart enough to know that I can't be in relationships with clients? And doesn't he appreciate that we're in the twenty-first century and there's a thing called sexual harassment?"

Mandy said, "You realize I have a duty to protect the company, so it's a little uncomfortable for me to address this with you." What she had wanted to tell Ashley was that Frank was arrogant, regardless of what he appreciated.

After that call, Mandy now started to think about Carl's preoccupation with his cousin's behavior around women. She needed to be as concerned about sexual harassment as Carl did. Mandy had seen some corporate heads roll in her Justice Department days after the highest level of corporate wrongdoing, and that was where her anxiety rested. She worried much more about corruption issues, since it was her preoccupation during her DOJ days. Was the intense focus on the prurient side of Frank blinding Carl or her to other more serious issues that lay hidden? If Ashley Tate had stumbled into a risky area by asking about the St. Lawrence Seaway and Panama Canal deals, could Frank have purposely set her up to be taken out for the sexual harassment incident as a pretense to get her attention away from the deals?

C H A P T E R

16

Investigation

MANDY HAD ALREADY GIVEN
Ray her suspicions about Wilson and the means of securing new
business. He was now hard at work to see what he could find out.
The team was pursuing the same theory from both ends of the
time spectrum—Mandy through mining family resources and
Ray and Sammy through hacking and investigation.

Ray and Sammy were aboard the *Bogie* and were hacking
away. Being an expert hacker, Ray Hanson immediately set about
finding a way into Jack Greer's and Northwest Engineering's
systems to see what he could learn. He found his way in and
was floored to find video feeds from almost every inch of the
Northwest Engineering headquarters. After some tedious surfing
of the video feeds, he landed on some worthwhile clips. One had

captured a brief hallway conversation between Frank and another executive who he soon learned was David Wilson. Another one showed Frank Wagner in his own office talking to himself. Ray had found a hidden door into videos of Frank's office, accessible by only one user, Carl Wagner. That hadn't stopped him from opening it. The third one was a bizarre view of either Mandy or Reggie—he couldn't tell the difference between them—doing some kind of spasmodic dance in an elevator. He was excited by what he found, but since they lacked audio, he called Sammy up from below deck to do some lip-reading.

Sammy first lip-read the brief hallway conversation between Frank and David Wilson. She told Ray that Frank had asked Wilson to now turn his attention to the Panamanians, since he'd done so well with the Canadians. She couldn't tell what that meant but it was not lost on her that they were careful not to speak around others, and it looked like they were heading outside the building to talk. Next, she watched a video of Frank talking to himself in his office while he was watching a video of elevator passengers. One of those Ray had watched, with the gyrating Mandy or Reggie. And since there was no audio, Sammy lip-read his bizarre soliloquy about women. Finally, she said, "You know, I recognize his guy from some work I did making poker profiles for him. He never met me, since my online service carries no identification."

She stopped talking and said, "Did he just say he'd like some of that?"

They replayed it and Frank was watching video of an Asian woman in another elevator, and Ray said, "You're the lip-reader, but it looks like it to me."

Sammy drummed her fingers on the furniture and with a devious smile on her face said to him, "Maybe we should accommodate him." They called Mandy and discussed it with her. Mandy was in favor if Sammy was up for it. Reggie wanted some

DNA, to make a possible connection between the present Wagner family and any DNA in Pi's resting place. She wasn't sure how to go about it before, but now an idea came to her.

Mandy had said, "Ray, are you sure you're OK with this?"

"I'm not crazy about the idea, but if it sounds worthwhile I can go along with it if Sammy can. I'd have to be nearby in case the wheels came off."

That afternoon Frank came to his penthouse to find a note in his mailbox from the concierge with a message and phone number to call. It was from a person named Hannah Lee with Windy City Inspections. Intrigued, he called and she told him she had to perform a visual leak inspection on behalf of the condo owners' association, so he made an appointment with her for the next day. When she arrived, he realized what a beauty she was and turned on the charm. He ended up inviting her out for dinner.

She accepted, and they ate at Harry Caray's Steakhouse at Dearborn and Kinzie, just around the block from Marina City. They had a long conversation at dinner, mainly letting Frank brag about his company and his own importance, while very little was asked about or volunteered by Hannah. That was fine with her. It had been her goal to leave few footprints and maximize the window into Frank Wagner. After dinner Frank invited her upstairs to his penthouse, where he proceeded to seduce her. She let him make some preliminary moves for a while, even getting to first base, when his phone suddenly rang. He looked at the caller number and said he had to take it, not bothering to apologize.

Opting to take a phone call over what she had to offer didn't make sense to her. His intensity and aggravation levels skyrocketed as he listened to the caller. She made a split-second decision, based on her instincts and professional analytic skills, that she had to bail on this guy. That prompted her to motion toward the bathroom, and he nodded while taking the call. She quickly went into his master bathroom instead of the guest powder room and when the door was closed, she searched the medicine cabinet and found a hairbrush with some brown and gray hairs amongst the bristles. She pulled a small baggie from her purse to keep her memento of Frank and tucked it away. As she was leaving, Frank was in the living room facing the balcony shouting into the phone. Sammy silently left the condo without notice from Frank. As she exited the building, she also deftly avoided the unsuspecting Jack Greer. Ray had warned her that Greer was posted near the entrance to Marina City for his stake-out of Gretchen. There was no sense in giving the other side any free surveillance of them. She had texted Ray on the way out and they met and left.

Back at the *Bogie,* they called Mandy for a debrief on her assessment of Frank. Sammy said she wanted to do it in person, so the sisters rode over to Belmont Harbor and boarded. Sammy handed over a small baggie of hair labeled "Frank Wagner hair."

Reggie started laughing. She said, "How did you manage to get this?"

She said, "It's from Frank's hairbrush. Hannah Lee got it."

Reggie said, "I guess Hannah Lee must have been in his inner sanctum to get this. Who is Hannah Lee?"

Sammy looked at everyone and just winked.

Reggie looked at them all and slowly she turned back toward Sammy and asked, "You? And you got close enough to Frank Wagner to get his hair?"

"I was going to get a lot closer than that until I watched him go ballistic on a phone call and instantly change into Mr. Hyde."

Reggie said, "What were you doing there?"

"He took me out to dinner and then back to his condo."

"How did that come about?"

Sammy said, "Turns out that he likes Asian women."

"You went to dinner with him and then to his place, and you stopped . . . wait a minute. Were you gonna . . . ?"

Sammy cut her off. "We got interrupted when he got that phone call and he got into an argument. When I saw firsthand how he could morph into instant ugliness, I didn't want to go any further with him. He's dangerous. I grabbed the hair and got out of there."

Reggie inhaled and blew out a long breath and said, "Looks like I've got some DNA delivery to do. Thank God I didn't have to do that. Do you have any other observations about him?"

As Mandy watched this story unfold, she became convinced that Sammy was a valuable resource for a variety of reasons, and she should be recruited. Clearly Reggie was impressed, entertained even.

Mandy said, "So if he hadn't had gotten that phone call you would have slept with him?"

"I guess so."

Reggie said to Mandy, "And you blessed this plan?"

Needing a change of subject, Sammy wanted to throw out an irresistible temptation. She explained to them that she was a student of the enneagram analysis of personalities, which was a tool she'd picked up in her psychology training. She had used it to categorize Frank Wagner as a number 8, a controller type in the enneagram world.

Sammy said, "Let's talk about Frank Wagner in enneagram terms."

Mandy asked, "What's that?"

"It's another personality typing system. Anyway, he's a handful. Wagner is what we call a '*true challenger.*' He's dominating, self-confident, and confrontational. If you find yourself in conflict with him, he could easily be a force of vengeance and an intimidating and overwhelming figure. He took the lead with me, and I imagine that is typical for him. I acted submissively so I could allow him to reveal himself. My guess is that if he feels threatened, he will be belligerent and protective. Even tending to ignore risks to himself. What we might instinctively judge as forbidden territory, Frank Wagner would plunge ahead fearlessly without hesitation."

Reggie asked, "Is he rational?"

"Stieg Larsson had a character in one of his books who did not experience pain. I think Frank Wagner is like that, but in his version he does not recognize risk—and he'd do anything if he was driven."

Sammy said, "I did a body language evaluation too. That's what we call '*kinesics*.' His body language tells me he's a '*regulator*.' He steers the discussion or thinking in the way he wants it to go. He's not very subtle about it, so you know when you're being de-emphasized. He gives stubborn clues to his emotions, though he tries to subdue them. He strikes me as being a very angry individual and frequently near the boiling point."

Mandy said, "How does this help us?"

Sammy said, "That's for you to decide. Besides what he demonstrated to me just now, I can only add that I got insights into him from some poker profiling I'd done for him awhile ago. He hired my online service to do a poker profile of his players, using some video of his players at a game he must have sponsored at his office. Turns out he was one of the players."

Reggie said, "And what did you learn from that?"

"That he's good at bluffing. If you haven't had any experience with him, I think you could be finessed by him with ease. He's very good at disguising his intentions. You can't anticipate what he might do."

Deciding not to let her off the hook so easily, Reggie said, "Remind us again how your evening ended?"

She gave a sly look. "Back to that, huh? It ended by me walking away unnoticed. I imagine it went well enough for him. He was on his way to second base when he got the phone call, and that proved to be the deal breaker."

Mandy said, "I feel bad about sending you in there in the first place. In fact, I don't think you should be alone with him again. Just disappear for now. He's obviously too dangerous." Ray agreed, and they left it at that. They needn't have worried. Sammy was not about to go near Frank again.

The sisters left, and down on the pier Reggie immediately confronted Mandy. "You put her up to that? You and Ray, her new boyfriend?" Mandy said nothing for a few seconds and Reggie shook her head while laughing and said, "Of course you did."

"It was her own idea, not mine. I had just mentioned your idea that DNA from Frank might be useful. Sammy is very . . . versatile, and fearless about it."

"You can't get away with saying that. You're the boss, and if she proposes it and you go along with it, it's on you."

Mandy shrugged her shoulders and said, "I've done worse."

"If he hadn't gotten that phone call, do you think Sammy would have let him cross home plate?"

"Like I said, she's fearless."

Reggie said, "Maybe you should hire her, then."

"I tried, but she likes being part of the gig economy. She values independence."

Then Mandy changed her tack and asked, "The FBI has to invite Gretchen in and tell her what happened to her husband. She has to know this before it gets out somehow."

The sisters called Steve Baker and he agreed to talk immediately to Gretchen before the U.S. Attorney held a press conference. Mandy lost no time and immediately reached out to Gretchen.

She answered her call and quickly agreed to Mandy's mysterious request to take a ride with her.

Mandy caught a taxi and was at Marina City in a matter of minutes. Gretchen was standing at the entrance on her phone when Mandy pulled up. When she got in, Gretchen said that her son was calling her to find out if it was true that she had allowed his father's body to be exhumed and autopsied. He'd just heard it from Frank.

Mandy said, "What did you tell him?"

Gretchen said, "I didn't tell him anything. I said I'd call him back."

"Did you tell Frank?"

"No way. I didn't even tell Carl. I only told my daughter, but she wouldn't tell either of them. I asked her to keep it strictly to herself."

"Then how could Frank have known?"

Gretchen said, "I have no idea, but Carl did mention a reburial permit."

Mandy scratched her chin and said, "I know. I think Frank has you under surveillance. That's got to be it. The guy he's using probably has a system alert for anything involving the Wagner name. That would have caught it."

"He's watching me? My own nephew?" She was fuming now. How ironic it was that as that conversation was taking place in the back seat of the taxi, two cars behind them Jack Greer's van kept pace with them.

Gretchen asked what was so secret that Mandy couldn't tell her. Mandy said it was about her husband's autopsy, and that it was best to let the authorities handle it. At the FBI office, they were led to a conference room where Steve and Reggie were waiting. Like everyone who first encountered the twins, Gretchen was shocked to see Mandy's identical twin sister in person for the first time, but she recovered quickly.

Steve said he appreciated her coming in and told her they had the results of Klaus's autopsy.

Reggie said, "I'm so sorry to have to tell you this, Mrs. Wagner, but I'm afraid the cause of death was not related to insulin. We found potassium cyanide in his liver."

Gretchen furrowed her brow and tears began flowing. She whispered, "That's poison."

Reggie said, "I'm afraid so, and it means your husband was probably murdered. I'm so sorry." She'd said it as softly and delicately as she could, but Gretchen's face crumpled. She began to shake and moan. Mandy put her arm around her, trying to comfort her. As she sobbed, Gretchen attempted to ask questions.

She choked out, "His own brother killed him?"

Steve glanced at the sisters and said, "We can't say that yet. We are only now investigating this, and we wanted you to know first. You were the critical link in agreeing to the autopsy. We wanted to let you know the results as soon as we could and to express our sympathy to you for this shock, and we'll do whatever we can to investigate."

Gretchen said, "Thank you. I don't know that any of this would have been uncovered were it not for Mandy. I've been such a fool for all these years, thinking Klaus had been reckless and caused his own death. And here he was killed by his own brother." She took in their awkward looks and guessed what they were thinking. She added, "He went out fishing with his own brother and came back dead. Gus killed him. And then he tried to get me to cremate him. I suppose that was to remove all evidence of what had happened."

She looked over at Mandy and they met eyes. Gretchen was sobbing in earnest now. She managed to say, "I know you just said you can't say it was murder, but I can. I know how much they had against each other. I know in my heart it was murder."

As gently as he could, Steve said, "You're going to be our most important source of information. We'd like to go over some questions with you when you can manage it. If you need some time to absorb this shock we would understand, but until we can speak to you in depth, we won't make any real progress."

Mandy gave Gretchen some tissues, who said very quietly, "It is a big shock, but I want to help in any way I can. I'm happy to do it."

Steve said, "We'd like to talk privately with you, so I'll ask Dr. Doucette and Mandy to excuse themselves if you don't mind."

Gretchen appeared to grow stronger and said she just wanted to help in any way. Getting to the truth was what she wanted. Mandy collected Gretchen's cell phone to let Steve's techie check it out while they waited. It was no longer warm, though. Her experience with bugged phones taught her that a warm phone was one sign of spyware.

Once Gretchen had been sequestered by Steve, Reggie said, "That is such a despicable family, and it doesn't matter what generation you're talking about."

Mandy said, "Look, I'm just relieved Gretchen didn't bite my head off for not telling her she was under surveillance earlier."

"Yeah, you skated on that one."

After thirty more minutes of discussion, Gretchen emerged. When she was about to leave, Gretchen mentioned that it would be a comfort to speak to Carl. When Mandy insisted it was not yet possible, Gretchen said she would reach out to her daughter then. Mandy got her an Uber ride back home, then went back to huddle with Steve and Reggie.

Mandy said, "Steve, can you tell me anything, or would it be a problem for your investigation?"

"We need to treat it seriously. More so than the skeleton from 140 years ago. With Klaus Wagner, if it was murder, there could still possibly be a perpetrator alive. Maybe there was someone else on that boat with the brothers. For all we know, Gus brought Frank along with." He let that sink in and then said, "I asked her about who prepared her husband's doses. I needed to see if she should be a suspect. I think she's in the clear. I think her first reaction was right on target—the brother. Of course, he's dead, so there's not much we can do. There's nobody left to question. I do think we should open a murder file on this, though, and hold it to see what else may pop up."

Reggie said, "I think we should have his death certificate revised and reissued, indicating murder by poisoning."

Steve said, "Oh, and Gretchen's phone was clean of any spyware, but it looks like spyware had been on the phone and then recently removed."

Around the time they were speaking, Jack Greer was in his van following the Uber carrying Gretchen away from the FBI. Fearing his means would lead to the discovery of him, he'd removed the spyware from Gretchen's phone remotely earlier that day. He needed to get into her condo to remove his video equipment. He was still tailing her, and called Frank to alert him to his aunt visiting FBI headquarters.

"Was she with Mandy?" He sounded unhinged to Jack.

"Yes. Gretchen was crying and Mandy was hugging her and looking troubled." Greer needed to get out of the Frank Wagner drama as soon as he could.

17

Tipping Point

BACK AT HER APARTMENT after leaving the FBI office, Mandy checked her phone and found a text message from Gretchen to call.

She did so, and the call was answered on the first ring.

"I hope it isn't too late for you. How are you doing?"

Gretchen said, "I've been such a gullible fool. Finding out Klaus was murdered by his own brother and realizing that he tricked me into skipping an autopsy is devastating. And even worse, I've been duped by his son Frank. How should I feel? The only two things I can be happy about are finally finding out the truth and pushing for a public offering. Without that, I wouldn't have you in the picture, would I? I would have gone to my grave in ignorance."

"Maybe not," Mandy said, trying to soothe her.

"I can't sleep anyway, now that I know what happened."

Mandy said, "Maybe you should try to get some rest. You've had a terrible shock and need to take care of yourself."

"Not yet. I want to get everything out in the open and get Beth to publish the whole thing. If I couldn't catch the murderous bastard when he was alive, maybe I can take it out on his son."

"Well, if you're up to it, Beth and I want to continue the discussion about family histories. She suggested we go on the architectural boat tour on the river. Getting some air will be good for you. Are you up for it?"

"Absolutely."

Mandy added, "There's something I've been meaning to ask you. When Klaus went on his fishing trip with Gus, do you know if they were alone?"

Gretchen said, "Steve Baker asked me the same question. I don't know for sure. I'm pretty sure that when Gus reached me to tell me what had happened, he wasn't alone. But it was ten years ago, and I was really stressed out at the time, so I can't do better than that."

The three women met at the Wendella boat dock at the foot of the Wrigley Building for their discussion. Beth had coaxed her husband into going along. Mandy was anxious to discuss the letters from Beth and the diary from Gretchen that they'd been holding for so long. Patrick had already told her of the patent-related stuff they had contained, so that a strong possibility existed that Patrick Carney's work might exist in someone's files. Gretchen had a collection penned by her late husband from the early 1950s and beyond. Mandy had finally read them.

As the group on the boat got settled, others were busy. Ray had assigned Sammy to surveillance of Jack Greer from a safe distance, since they didn't want anyone recognizing the woman known as Hannah Lee. They couldn't risk Sammy being seen by Frank now. Greer trailed the group to the Wendella boat dock just below the northwest corner of the Michigan Avenue bridge. While he purchased a ticket and waited in line to follow the others on board, he called Frank to tell him what was happening.

Frank wanted to see these conspirators in action with his own eyes, so he rushed down to the marina from his condo to wait for the boat to begin its voyage. Sammy immediately picked him up from across the river and focused on him. She was located on the Riverwalk on the south bank of the river across from the Marina City west tower, in a spot handpicked by Ray. What a stroke of luck that he showed up. She had only been planning to watch Greer, but now she had the big dog to watch. He accommodated her by talking out loud to himself, unaware of being videoed. The seeming tourist just happened to be able to lip-read his self-speech. Sammy loved people who talked to themselves. She'd learned in school that many people did it as a way of processing things, not that it mattered to her why.

Sammy was on the phone with Ray, who said into her ear "What's the vibe you're getting?"

"Not sure," she said, then "but I think it's *storm's abrewin'* whenever Frank Wagner's involved. And he's popped up across the river and I recorded him. When I'm done here, I'll go back to the *Bogie* and translate the recording."

She hung up and waited for someone to make a move. Finally, the entourage moved and she had more than enough ranting from Frank that she should go lip-read. She couldn't afford to be seen by Frank, now that she was no longer Hannah Lee. When Frank left after the tour boat, Sammy returned to Belmont Harbor to do the translation.

The three women along with Patrick the elder sat on the upper deck of the tour boat, with Mandy deftly avoiding row thirteen. There was no reason to invite trouble. They settled in for a ride through the granite and steel canyon walls on either shore of the river. Each of the older women wore scarves to keep their hair under control in the Windy City. In contrast, Mandy's red hair blew wildly behind her, showcasing her blue-eyed, freckled face. She was wearing shorts and a tank top with her running shoes while the other two were fully dressed and even wore light jackets.

Beth said, "I think we left off after talking about the commercial story on LaSalle and Northwest, but I wanted to start with a big picture."

Sitting a few rows away from them and using his cell phone to video the entire conversation of the three women was Jack Greer, a person unknown to any of them. There were other passengers doing just as he was, taking a video of the entire voyage with their cell phones. So he didn't stand out from others onboard. What were the odds of capturing the audio of the recording with all the noises on the boat and the river?

Mandy and Gretchen nodded, so Beth began. "It's helpful to view the history with a wider lens. The Industrial Revolution had exploded with inventiveness. My dear husband has helped me with this perspective. As far as inventions went, Fulton's steamship, McCormick's reaper, Whitney's cotton gin and Singer's sewing machine were the high-fliers of the first half of that century. Later, of course, the light bulb, telegraph, phonograph, automobile, and telephone would come along and combine to change lives forever." She stopped talking and made a hand-off gesture to her husband.

Patrick said, "Our ancestor Patrick toiled in between the two grand stages of innovation. His specialty was focusing on secondary inventions, that is, the improvements. He wasn't making discoveries in basic science or inventing new history-making objects. He was improving on prior designs. The steam engine, which in and of itself was revolutionary, was channeled into use as the steam shovel, among many other things. He was a veteran of pick-and-shovel crews whose hard work had created the canals. He had a clear vision of what problems his ideas would cure."

Their rhythm was broken by the Wendella boat announcements that then led into a long tour guide session. The audio quality would only decline further with that blaring in the background, but it didn't seem to faze the women. The boat headed west and first passed the site of the *SS Eastland* disaster from 1915.

The tour guide said, "This is where the largest waterborne disaster on the Great Lakes occurred. Over eight hundred souls drowned due to mismanaged ballast as the *SS Eastland* suddenly capsized. As the search for bodies took place, the so-called '*Foolkiller Submarine*' was also found on the riverbed. A one-man submarine, it contained the body of a man and a dog. The sub could have been on the river bottom for half a century. It could have been there at the time of the Civil War. And just like the Great Fire, no one ever solved the mystery of the *Foolkiller*."

Patrick resumed. "Steam shovels operated from rail lines, which had to be laid down in the direction of the work. The steam shovel rode the rail down and back on a rail car in a straight alignment. Its rotation was limited, like a man with a stiff neck pain and limited flexibility. He might have devised a swivel base allowing bucket rotation completely."

The boat was now passing Trump Tower and nearing Gretchen's building. Frank was above them, as was Sammy on the south riverbank. As the boat quickly passed right by Marina City, Frank had his opportunity to spot the women on the top deck. They were locked in conversation and oblivious to his presence above them. He clearly recognized all three and began a marathon outburst of threats and promises. Sammy was able to capture on video the whole diatribe from the opposite shore and had left.

Patrick Senior said, "Then when it came to tunnels, it was back to pick-and-shovel work, with the work stopped periodically to load materials. There was a need for improvements that would work in tunneling."

Gretchen was clearly agitated and interrupted, saying, "Gus Wagner hired an engineering firm and a patent lawyer in late fall of 1871 after the Chicago fire. He'd eyed a project in the Swiss Alps involving a large tunnel. It would bore through thirty miles of mountain, with train tracks to cross between Switzerland and Italy and avoid the need to cross through mountain passes and negotiate switchbacks. The bid deadline was several months away, and he planned to be aggressive to win the job. But first he had to get an engineer to prepare his ideas for the model-making and fabrication phases. He protected his design for just the kind of equipment you're describing and got U.S. and European patents."

She said, "Gus was energized by his new competitive advantage. He wanted to propel his company into a dominant position in large-scale capital projects. As train travel exploded, projects became plentiful. Canals continued to be a source of business, despite the growth of railroads. As railroads proliferated and were destined to replace much of the canal traffic, tunnels could be expected to be a constant source of work. Gus planned to capitalize on it.

"He still resented the Carneys for winning the early Chicago-based projects that should have been an advantage for Northwest. After all, Northwest had been the trailblazer with the Illinois and Michigan Canal, but LaSalle had pulled off a sweep of the large-scale projects Gus Wagner salivated over. Then, of course, Patrick Carney spurned his merger offer and insulted him in the process.

"By 1875, Gus got patents for a number of inventions, and ironically sold equipment using those inventions to LaSalle for its use in the second lake tunnel project."

As they approached the junction of the river branches, looming over them was the once-largest commercial building in the world, the Merchandise Mart. The tour guide said, "This building has been through a few lifetimes and now is a center for design and corporate offices. It's got floor space approaching four million square feet. The Kennedys once owned the building and did much to make it a centerpiece of Chicago commerce."

Mandy said, "Pretty ironic that now LaSalle will supply Northwest on the St. Lawrence Seaway expansion project."

Gretchen said, "Frank must be gloating about that."

A big puzzle piece was falling into place. As for motive, Mandy thought that an unlikely inventor would have a lot to gain by striking out against the Carneys. She wished the real inventor would make himself known, but it was not so easy when all the contestants were long gone. Her boyfriend's discoveries in the Carney family files gave her hope that they were getting to the truth.

Gretchen continued. "Toward the end of the decade, the City of Chicago initiated the bidding process for the Chicago Sanitary and Ship Canal, a thirty-mile connector between the Chicago River and the Des Plaines River. Northwest won that project."

Beth then took a turn. "After the fire, LaSalle moved off into other directions and became quite successful. And that went on for decades. Finally, after World War II, the Carney family finally got out of management and the ownership of the LaSalle business.

It was one of the early families to exit and cash out after the war. They sold 90 percent of their shares in the company in an initial public offer in 1946."

Mandy turned to Gretchen and interjected, "From Klaus's diary, this sounds exactly like what he was talking about wanting to do with Northwest. He looked forward to an eventual family cash-out of the Northwest ownership."

Gretchen nodded. "It's why Klaus was worried about anything the company might be embarrassed to have come out. It would pound a silver stake in the heart of going public."

As if on cue, the tour guide then said, "Ladies and Gentlemen, you are riding down a river along with the current, but that is only because of the feat accomplished over one hundred years ago. That was when the course of the river was reversed, and now flows toward the Mississippi River. That's too long a story to cover on this short trip, but I recommend it to you to learn about. It was done by the company that is now headquartered in that building to your right." He was pointing to the stunning headquarters building of Northwest Engineering.

Soon the boat had turned around at the old Bubbly Creek and was headed north toward Goose Island on the north branch of the river. The women were admiring the newest buildings along either side of the river. Mandy shivered as they passed by the point where she and Patrick had been sideswiped and nearly capsized in their kayak by a speedboat the prior year. It had been her first date with Patrick, and she remembered it as the point where an attempted murder turned into a wet t-shirt contest.

Mandy asked, "Does the family know what Gus was really like?"

Gretchen said, "Klaus told me that old Gus became aloof, brooding and pensive in his later years. Like a tortured soul. People often avoided him."

Mandy said, "I read a brief statement in memoriam for Gus in the old Northwest board minutes, after he'd committed suicide. What do you know about that?"

Gretchen answered, "Klaus mentioned it from time to time, but nobody in the family really talked about it. I got the idea that the family was baffled by it and didn't know what was troubling him. He'd been a titan of industry who'd built a very successful business, yet they found him splattered on the sidewalk of the street outside the headquarters building. Such a sad tale. I mean, to do that to yourself . . . I can't see ever doing that. I don't care how bad things got, I could never see doing something that horrific as a way out." Gretchen was visibly shaken by the thought.

When the boat tour ended and the women left, Greer uploaded his video onto his network so he could update his client.

———————

Sammy finished lip-reading Frank's angry soliloquy that she'd filmed as he snooped on his aunt and lawyer on the boat tour. She had read him to be saying a litany of things, concluding with, "*. . . that goddamn lawyer, and now they're a fucking threesome. I'm going to put an end to this.*"

Sammy told all this to Ray along with some body language observations.

Meanwhile, Frank took a call from Jack Greer on Sunday morning. "What have you got for me?"

Greer said, "I made a video of the women talking on the river cruise, but with all the clatter I couldn't make out their words."

"Please send it over. Keep your eyes on Gretchen."

Later, Frank received a call telling him they'd been hacked, and what had been viewed and copied. He asked the IT guy to trace back the hacker, and soon he was provided an internet service provider number identified with an "RH." Frank looked over a set of newspaper photos from last year that showed Mandy and Reggie in Washington getting a big award at the White House. A photo showed them surrounded by a collection of people, and one of those in the group photo was identified as Ray Hanson.

"The bitch unleashed a hacker on me."

Frank tried to calm himself to think things through carefully. He'd hated the family pressure to put Northwest into a public offering. These idiots had no clue what a total conversion it was to go from a private company to public. A friend had whispered to him that once he was public, he could be gobbled up in a hostile takeover, and he could do nothing to make himself insulated from that risk. And regardless of what happened, he'd still be tied down like Gulliver on the beach by the Lilliputians, with a murder of crows pecking him until he was sightless and bloodless.

When they went public, everyone would be looking over their shoulders. There would be different constituencies and predators to worry about. This was more than a mere distraction. His advisors had tried to calm him down, and made it seem like it would all be worth it when the shares were priced. The family members stood to get rich overnight.

But what did he really care about that? He'd already accumulated vast amounts of wealth over the years, both from his Northwest compensation and his inheritance. Enough, in fact, that he was able to squirrel away offshore accounts and residences in case they ever became necessary. If the need ever arose, he could skip off to one of his overseas homes and live the good life indefinitely in a country having no extradition treaty with the U.S. He had a ton of assets hidden away in countries safely outside the reach of U.S. seizure power.

He was under no illusion that he was immune from attack. He tried to stay away from controversy and largely had been successful. He'd stayed away from marriage too. Children were of no concern to him either; let Carl keep the family line alive. He simply wanted no distractions and was unable to compromise for a wife and family.

Their troubles began when Carl told him he needed someone who could put the pieces in place for them to operate properly as a public company. Frank had wanted to use outside counsel and not increase the headcount. They'd had a heated argument over it, but Carl had prevailed based on economics.

Frank remembered what he'd said to his cousin. "Carl, why can't you handle this? What happens if we get someone here who's got an agenda? Is this the kind of life you want to have?"

Carl replied, "What are you worried about?"

"Nothing. But you know how my dad was, and if someone gets a whiff of what he'd done in the old days, it could get messy."

"You worry too much. What my dad and Uncle Gus did is ancient history."

Frank reflected on what had occurred. Why was Aunt Gretchen nosing around in the past? What did he have to do with her? Why is she with Beth Carney? Why is Mandy Doucette hacking our systems? She doesn't know when to quit. She's much worse than John Booth, who couldn't keep his nose out of things, either. It was time he had a heart-to-heart chat with Aunt Gretchen. Mandy must go, like Booth. But he had to keep her around a little while longer so he could unearth whatever she'd put in motion that would have to be dismantled. He also had the LaSalle retread, Ed Rosen, to contend with on his own board. He'd reluctantly agreed to Carl's initiative to bring him aboard. Maybe he'd turn out to be a crusader too.

As the intrigue swirled around the hack of the Northwest systems, Carl's IT friend let Carl know that the hacker had apparently found his way into the highly restricted area of the videos supposedly accessible only to Carl. Carl had never intended that anyone else have access to those videos. Now it looked like all the videos of Frank's office were being viewed.

————————

Later that day Frank decided to go out on an errand. After the two shocks he had just received—first that his aunt was in a conspiracy with his lawyer and the muckraker Carney woman, and second that that same lawyer had sicced her bloodhound on his systems—he was becoming unhinged and reaching a stage of frantic desperation to strike out at his threats. Several people now had critical information about him, and he had to decide what to do about them.

He waited out the day and when darkness came, he pulled his boat out of the Marina City dock. The route from the marina to the company's warehouse on the south branch of the river was a short thirty minutes. He docked in the wharf area in the inlet, entered the warehouse and quickly collected his needs: chain, scuba gear, explosives, tape, and detonators with remote controls. In his shirt pocket was a glass vial he'd taken from the hidden vault. It was a Saturday night, and he was able to tackle his errand without workers present. His training long ago in the capital projects side of the business meant he worked with the crews when he was young, and through that he had learned skills he was about to use. As he was gathering his equipment, he was secretly being observed by his own security system, but he wasn't worrying about such things now. What was foremost in his mind was that he had to retake control of events, after concluding that he had lost control and was now vulnerable. He persuaded himself that his earlier suggestion to take the sisters out to lunch was one to initiate now. He believed he could control his fury, and he might be able to get some insight into what they were planning. His comfort that he had everything under control was eroding. Now that it was clear that Klaus Wagner's body had been autopsied, his deepest fears were taking center stage. All the money and homes in the world might not insulate him from a murder investigation. He had a lot of work to do.

18

Reggie's Return

MANDY AND PATRICK SAT on his condo balcony watching the sun rise over Lake Michigan one morning with Lincoln Park below. She worked on *The New York Times* crossword puzzle, a daily ritual that satisfied her urge to solve mysteries. Solving crossword puzzles was a harmless endeavor compared to the other enigmas she frequently found herself figuring out. Patrick, meanwhile, mulled over the discoveries in the family files and concluded that they would be more useful to his father, the patent attorney. As the son read, he was impressed by the improvements his ancient ancestor had conceived. The machinery he concerned himself with included steam-powered shovels, fan systems, boring machines, tracked movement systems, metal processing equipment, and a range of other equipment.

Mandy then switched quietly to her other growing preoccupation on her computer, studying the course map for the upcoming Chicago Marathon. It was one of her pre-race rituals to memorize the course and then visualize her effort through the race, taking into account the terrain and anticipating difficulties. Chicago's course was nothing to worry about. It was about as flat as one could wish, thankfully. Sure, there were those runners who actually liked hills, but the sisters were not among them. The only real difficulty would be navigating the large crowd of runners. Runners who failed to follow marathon etiquette were maddening to experienced runners. Most annoying were the "*buddies*" who ran abreast of each other and prevented faster runners from passing. Some slower runners cheated on the race corral staging and inserted themselves in amongst faster runners. Mandy's simple take on it was that people cheated when they could, regardless of whether it really mattered. Was there any human endeavor free from cheating, she wondered.

Patrick came across a promising passage. His ancestor had written that he was paranoid of others learning of his inventions before he was ready to begin the patenting process. This was new information. What had begun as trade secrets, protected only by secrecy, was being actively prepared for patent applications. Then he came across a lawyer's name who he'd apparently hired to handle the legal process and hold copies of his drawings for safekeeping for proof of his creations. He'd wanted a secure safe harbor.

Patrick was so excited by this that he started telling Mandy that he'd just come across something big. She stopped looking at her computer and watched him, while he called his father immediately and asked, "I've read the letters Mom's been holding. Have you ever read them?"

His father answered, "Not all of them, and even then, it was decades ago. Have you found something?"

"It turns out he hired a lawyer to keep the drawings of what he'd invented to prepare patent applications."

His father said, "Who was it?"

"Robert Todd Lincoln."

Mandy silently mouthed a question to him. "Who's that?"

Patrick put his dad on speaker. "You're on speaker so Mandy can hear you."

Patrick Senior said, "Hi, Mandy. Robert Todd Lincoln was Abe Lincoln's son. Isham, Lincoln & Beale was his law firm."

"Is the firm still around?"

"No. It was dissolved years ago. I think Lincoln died in the 1920s. He must have left the law firm shortly after the fire. If I remember my history correctly, I think that by the 1880s he was Secretary of War in President Garfield's administration, then later he became ambassador to Great Britain. He was probably well beyond worrying about some dusty patent files of a dead client's inventions in storage from his earlier life."

"Why wouldn't Lincoln have pulled out the files and handled them once Patrick died in the fire?"

His father said, "I think there were a lot of personal difficulties for Lincoln going on back then. Not only was 1871 disastrous for Chicago, but for the Lincoln family too. Abe's widow had almost lost her mind after her husband's assassination, but then six years later in the summer of 1871, things got even darker for her. Her youngest son died that summer. Robert was her only remaining immediate family member, and he took her to Europe for a few years to try to help her recover. But by 1875 they were back, and she was no better. She spent a lot of time with a psychic in the little village of St. Charles in the Fox River Valley west of the city, trying to communicate with her dead sons and her husband."

"She had more than one dead son?"

"Three sons had died. She'd lost Edward as a baby, then Willie died in the White House, and finally Tad in Chicago. She finally pushed things too far by trying to sell her clothes, under some foggy idea that she was destitute. In fact, though, she was wealthy."

Patrick said, "Where did the money come from?"

"Not from Abe, that's for sure. He hadn't made any, but she inherited her father's fortune and would never experience need again. Anyway, that was enough for Robert. He committed her to an asylum out in suburban Batavia, Illinois. She eventually got discharged and stayed with her sister until she died in 1882."

His father continued. "To say that Robert was distracted would have been a massive understatement. After his government service, he became general counsel for the Pullman Company. It doesn't surprise me that the patent files got lost, amid everything else that was happening then."

Patrick asked, "So tending to the Carney files would have been the furthest thing from his mind. What would have happened to them?"

His father said, "A firm has to protect files for the client. If the firm dissolves, there must be a process to return the files to the client. You'd have to connect with the firm's receiver if it went bankrupt. That would be the only way to find out what happened to those files. Or if it merged, then the successor firm."

"What would happen if a client died?"

His father said, "They would return the files to the family, I suspect. But I don't think Patrick was declared dead by the courts until well into the 1880s. The files may have been in limbo, sitting in storage with nobody to pay attention. Some more work needs to be done to get our hands on the material, if it still exists."

"Can you help us, Dad?"

"Sure. I remember some people who were with Isham. I'll check into it."

Mandy said, "Maybe the files would have been given to the company." Then, directing her comment to neither Patrick, she said, "Our researcher Sammy picked up on some part of Wagner history that may be important. She said the family was never aware that the original Gus Wagner was an inventor. I found mention of it in the Northwest board minutes, as well as Gus's suicide, which had never been revealed. Why would he kill himself?"

Patrick Senior said, "I don't know, but I'll bet the Carneys shed no tears for him."

Mandy said, "I'm missing something here."

———

Monday morning at the office, Mandy called her old boss, Rick. He said, "Ah, are you ready to come back to us so soon?"

Mandy said, "You mean you'd really have me back?"

"Of course. We have a search underway for a replacement but haven't found anyone we like yet."

She had a moment of euphoria, as she saw a safety net suddenly strung below her, and it gave her a much-needed boost to her mood and some additional resolve. "Not yet, thanks, but I'll have to admit there are things going on here I don't like. I'm calling about something else, though."

"Good," he said, "I was just sitting around with nothing to do anyway."

Mandy said, "Very funny, but please tell me if you're able to check on some old files for me? Like files from over a hundred years ago."

He was still struck that she'd said, "*not yet.*" Maybe things weren't going that well at Northwest after all, he thought. Maybe she even had a case of buyer's remorse.

His answer about files that age, though, was that it would be iffy to find anything. A record retention system has a review period, after which if a "*destroy designation*" was specified, the files would be destroyed. But if there had been any activity with the files, the review cycle would be restarted. If it was deemed "*keep forever,*" a file could still exist somewhere in the bowels of the off-site warehouse. File retention procedures are fine if they're being followed, but usually they aren't. People hate to look at old things. Many people are packrats, and in the most extreme variety of that they're called "*hoarders.*" It's the last thing anyone wants to spend time on. With any company it was the same. Humans were very bad at throwing things away. The opposite end of the spectrum was being a "*purger.*" Some people loved to purge files and belongings, preferring to enjoy the uncluttered state that was the result of a good purge.

Mandy said, "Patrick Carney's inventions from the time before the Chicago fire may be in your files."

"*The* Patrick Carney of LaSalle? Why would you care about him?"

She said, "Remember before I left for Northwest, I told you our crew had uncovered a skeleton in an old bridge abutment? Reggie identified the remains, and it appears to be Patrick Carney's bones. She concluded he was shot to death and was buried before the big fire. Maybe he was murdered for his inventions."

Rick asked, "How are they sure it was him?"

She explained. "Reggie's boyfriend Dan did his anthropology magic along with a team of forensic anthropologists, working with Reggie's pathology unit. They rearticulated the skeleton and evaluated the bones. Dan proved it was a male, and figured out the age, race and height. It all fit with what was known about Patrick Carney. Then with the new DNA technologies, what he extracted from the bones matched his genes with those of the modern Carney family."

"Mysteries really follow you around, don't they? Can you meet me for lunch and go through all this?"

They met outside the Smith & Wollensky's, whose entrance was in the Marina City lobby, and came within Jack Greer's surveillance area from his stakeout. Frank should know who his lawyer is chumming around with, Greer thought. Greer had kept a running video of the entryway in case he needed to show evidence. Usually, it was romantic affairs he was investigating, where this kind of surveillance was done. Jack used the equipment in the van to make a clip and texted it to Frank with a question of who it was meeting Mandy. When Frank recognized Rick Crawford, he blew up. His own lawyer was agitating his aunt, the FBI and now his competitor. What was she doing? Did she have a death wish?

Inside the restaurant, Mandy said to Rick, "I'm sorry to drop this news on you. I suppose it's a bit of a bomb. And it isn't public yet. Steve Baker is still doing an investigation, and he wants to do his work first. This issue could play into that."

Rick said, "If there were files sent to LaSalle, do you have any idea when it would have happened? I'm not sure how long patent files would be kept."

She answered, "Sometime between 1871 and 1900, I suppose. It's unclear when he was declared dead. No remains were ever found until we uncovered them a few weeks ago."

Rick said, "What is Steve doing on this?"

"He's investigating the murder," she said.

Rick said, "What for? The FBI doesn't poke its nose into local crime, especially if it's from two centuries ago. And what about statutes of limitations?"

"There's no statute of limitations on murders, but you have to have a living perpetrator to prosecute, I'll admit. And he was invited into this by the Water District police."

He eyed her skeptically and said, "But . . . ?"

"But if Patrick Carney's inventions were stolen, someone might be able to do something about that."

Rick said, "Yeah, but let's remember that theft does have a statute of limitations. How do you get around that little problem?"

Mandy said, "Maybe for a criminal theft case. Instead they could file a civil theft action, and if they had failed to act they could be barred from a remedy.

"If I'm defending the guy suspected of the theft, I argue that the person sitting on files failed to act. The claim should go away.

"But what if they didn't know about the theft? Then they would not be expected to pursue a remedy they didn't know was needed. If they were in other businesses by then and had no duty to act. That would be my response if they brought a motion to dismiss."

Rick said, "Is this some kind of provocation on your part?"

Her cell phone chirped with an incoming text message from Patrick. She looked at it and then showed it to Rick. The message said "Isham transferred Patrick Carney's files to LaSalle in 1898."

Mandy gave him a stare and said, "Are you going to help me or not?"

He blew out a long breath and said, "What's in it for me?"

"Well, besides doing a favor for a friend, if your boss found out you'd uncovered a big infringement that could be worth hundreds of millions—found money—how would that be for you and your boss?"

With eyebrows raised and a big smile taking over his face, Rick said, "OK, I'm in. Let me get someone on it." He decided not to ask the question on the tip of his tongue when she got the text message. Why did it seem that Mandy was pursuing evidence against her own client?

"Please make it Susan Chambers. She's a great detective." Susan was the assistant secretary who had been of help countless times during her years with LaSalle.

That next weekend, Mandy, Patrick, and Dan stood on the edge of Lake Shore Drive above thousands of triathletes nervously awaiting the beginning of the annual Chicago Triathlon. The standing room was choked with spectators hoping to spot their athlete, and if they found a front-railing perch to watch, they were protective of it. The three had arrived early enough with Reggie to get a front-row spot. Now looking down on the field of athletes, it was anybody's guess which one was Reggie. They watched anxiously to see if Reggie would spot them and get their attention. It was commonly understood that spectators helped with the participant's sense of support, especially if they were dedicated to a specific racer. Reggie stood on the Monroe Harbor concrete embankment with her group of women in her 30–35-year-old age group. She scanned the overlooking railing and finally spotted her support group and frantically waved at them to get their attention. Once she had them, they had her for the moment the race started. After the start it was virtually impossible to keep track of your racer.

Starting in 1983, the Chicago Triathlon was now the preeminent short course triathlon in the country. It was called "*short course*" to distinguish it from the Ironman events, which were for total mileage of 70 or 140. The triathlon event was a three-sport race starting with a swim, followed by a bike ride and ending with a run. Transition periods divided the three stages, allowing for changing gear. Various distances were common in triathlons, with the ultimate being the Ironman at 140 miles. In Reggie's case, she would be competing in an Olympic-style event, starting with a 1.5-kilometer swim, followed by a 40-kilometer bike ride, and ending with a 10-kilometer run. The total mileage for the event was 32.

It was a time trial start to the swim in the Chicago Triathlon. Every ten seconds a group would pass over the swim timing mat and dive into a cold Lake Michigan and begin the mile swim. It was a down and back swim course and all she had to do between breaths was spot the large red buoy at the turnaround. Those buoys always reminded her of an oversized cartoonish kidney shape, bobbing in the water. But in the churning waters of the *combat swim* it was like a beacon for swimmers. She was barely able to tolerate the water temperature with the sleeveless wet-suit she wore, but she'd rather be cold than have her freedom of movement restricted by a full-body wetsuit. It was bad enough to be kicked, punched, and swam over, without also feeling like being wrapped in rubber bands. But that was exactly her sensation wearing a full-body wetsuit.

Her breathing on both sides had been working well for her so she plowed on ahead and pulled herself out of the water feeling good. She didn't care where she ranked in her age bracket. Since her recovery from the prior year's nerve gas attack, she only wanted to prove to herself that she could still finish. Forget about a podium finish for her age group, though she did still possess a subliminal urge to see her times. Since it was a time trial, no swimmer could know how they were doing until seeing the electronic board listing their bib number. A timing mat at the beginning and end of the stage would record the time. As Reggie passed over the timing mat as she crawled out of the lake, amid other aged-group racers, her pink swim cap identified her amongst all the swimmers as a female 30–35 age group member, and her dedicated spectators watched carefully to try to spot her coming out of the water. Swimmers typically ripped off their swim goggles and latex swim hats as soon as they could get their legs running on dry land. In Reggie's case, as soon as she emerged from the water and revealed her red hair, Mandy spotted her and pointed, jumping up and down for her.

Mandy's excitement was because she knew the swim segment was Reggie's least favorite, and her finish was an early positive sign that she was back in the swing. Dan was just as excited, since he'd acted as her lover-doctor ever since the scare of the prior year. He was conservative about her jumping back into competing, just because of his protectiveness. He had supported Reggie's re-entry, though, since he knew what motivated her and didn't want to impede her. She had to recover sometime, after all, and now might be just as good as anytime to test herself.

Then Reggie threw herself into a mad scramble to the transition area where her wetsuit was peeled off by the volunteers, leaving her in a one-piece bike and run suit, and off she was, scrambling to get on her clip-on bike shoes. She mounted her Cervélo carbon-fiber tri-bike, pushed herself off and clipped her feet into the pedals to begin the second stage. She had thought to tie a pink kite-tail style ribbon on her bike seat, thinking that her spectators would be able to spot her by it. As she'd hoped, Mandy and the guys did spot her crossing over the timing mat for the ride and could follow her out onto the bike course.

Mandy said, "She really looks strong. What a relief."

Dan and Patrick were smiling and Dan said, "Maybe I can retire now as her chief worrying officer."

Then began her fifteen-mile ride up and back north on Lake Shore Drive and another ten miles on lower Wacker Drive that avoided surface traffic. This was the easiest stage for her. She powered through it and roared into the transition zone again, changed into her running shoes and headed out on the six-mile run. She was relieved that she'd come off the bike without any chafing that would have made her run miserable. Her spectators spotted her coming in to finish the bike stage and start out on the run, then walked over to the finish line in Grant Park.

As she crossed the finish line after the run stage and collected her finisher's medal, her long recovery and return to form was at last over. She hadn't even had a whiff of not finishing at any part of the race. If she didn't finish, it would have been a crushing reality for her. In any racing event, participants dreaded the DNF—did not finish. Doing so might have meant that her tri career was over, and maybe even her marathoning career, as well. Reggie had finished in a respectable top third of her age group. She was back!

Mandy and the guys collected Reggie and her gear and they began the trek back to the north side of the river to celebrate. Mandy hadn't seen her sister this happy since they'd finished the Paris Marathon together. Dan was hugging Reggie all the way back, and Mandy could tell they were getting closer all the time.

19

Wacker Club

SAMMY SET ABOUT researching several things through Northwest's systems, thanks to Ray's hack. One item she was looking for was agreements and litigation settlements in the old Northwest files. Mandy had learned Northwest was digitizing the vast paper records it had stored for over a century in its warehouse. She had thought that might have been the way a lazy management would deal with the task of purging files. If you didn't want to take the time to do an evaluation but still wanted to get rid of things, these days you simply set some intern in front of a scanner and had them feed documents in and locate them on a thumb drive. It was the pragmatist's solution to file review, and possibly an unearned gift to plaintiffs. Anything not destroyed in a file maintenance review could be evidence.

Mandy had promised herself that when the dust settled from the IPO, she would have the files examined and destroyed if possible.

From her cozy nest in the *Bogie* on Sunday morning, Sammy was hard at work. She was now a stand-in for a plaintiff. She salivated over the vast number of files to search. Another nifty surveillance trick Ray had enabled was tapping into the various security cameras in the Northwest facilities. They'd been programmed to film only while some movement was taking place, which allowed one to view a large time frame just by skipping from clip to clip. It was tempting to look at locations which only had a modest number of clips so it wouldn't be a gut-wrenching bore to go through. One of those was in the warehouse, which had the connection with Sammy's assignment. Before plunging into the digital agreements available, she looked at the security footage and saw that her favorite villain, Frank Wagner, was starring in the clip playing. Just hours before Frank had been collecting dangerous items, it seemed. It looked to her like he was preparing to make a bomb. She struggled with the openness of his actions. Wouldn't he know that video security was operating 24/7? From her knowledge of kinesics, she instantly diagnosed him as frenzied. As a lip-reader, she was able to decipher his words, as he ranted during his brief video cameo appearances. Snippets of speech turned up the names Hanson, Wilson, Greer, Klaus. Klaus? To what end she could not pick up. He was probably pushing through a mental tunnel, driven by a mission only he knew, and oblivious to anything recognizable in peripheral vision. Like cameras.

The list of old lawsuits was the same as she had compiled on her own, and now Mandy had unleased her to find litigation files that might contain agreements. It didn't take long for the search to bear fruit, once she had deciphered the filing system. As she pulled one confidential file after another, thick with agreements slapped with a tape requiring approval for opening, she looked at them and started to update her list. It was not lost on her that the files all contained destroy dates decades past, and obviously went undestroyed. If the company had been minding its document controls properly, all the files she was now unearthing would probably have been destroyed without a second thought. Instead, they now fueled the machine Mandy had built to look for problems.

She quickly finished her research and called Ray into her compartment to view the clips of Frank arming up.

———————

Reggie met her sister and Frank for lunch, despite Mandy's fear of anything having to do with Frank. Reggie argued that they should accept Frank's invitation, since there had been enough happening that they would learn something useful. As painful it might be for Mandy, it could reveal more about Frank. The sisters just couldn't anticipate just how painful it would be.

The three met at the Wacker Club in the west Loop across the street from the Willis Tower. Over lunch, they talked about Chicago and their history growing up, schooling, hobbies and so on. Mandy was guarded compared to Reggie. She had no desire to spend more time with Frank.

Frank said at one point, "What is it about you two that gets you into high-profile situations?"

Reggie volunteered an answer, "Our curiosity. Our dad always drilled it into us to ask why something was the way it was, or how an object worked, or any number of other questions that would put us into detective mode."

Mandy said, "Bob Doucette has always been an adventurer and detective, and it's always led him to bigger and better things."

Frank nodded and said, "That's probably what I could have used all along. People who have curiosity, rather than people who want to get in close to the action and feed off it."

He could be quite a charmer when his interests weren't at stake. When lunch ended, Frank said he had to visit the facilities before heading out, and he excused himself. After waiting a few seconds, Mandy did the same and Reggie had some time to herself at the table. She quickly slipped on a plastic glove from her purse and grabbed Frank's empty water glass and utensils and discreetly slipped them into evidence bags she carried in her shoulder bag. She then replaced the items with those at her place at the table and peeled off the glove and shoved it into her bag. Once Frank returned, he noticed nothing awry at the table. They parted company on the street and he made apologies and took off north on Wacker Drive, while Mandy and Reggie stayed to talk on the street.

Frank's private thoughts as he walked briskly away from them was that they were a powerful team together and he should find a way to deal with them, but he first needed to get them sidelined and complete the offering. He was troubled as he walked away, and started to talk to himself and worked himself up into a frenzy.

Still standing on the corner where he'd left them, Reggie opened her purse and gave Mandy a peek.

"Why did you do that?" Mandy asked.

Reggie said, "He wasn't likely to willingly give up his own DNA, was he? Steve had the chance to get it the other day but didn't even try. He said he was worried it would put Frank on the defensive. I've got to run back in for the bathroom. I'm about ready to burst."

"Why didn't you go in the restaurant?"

Reggie said, "How could I have gotten the DNA then? Also, I didn't want to give Frank another chance to hit on me if we were walking to the bathroom together."

Mandy asked, "What's so important about getting DNA? I thought what Sammy collected satisfied that."

"Sammy's hair DNA test hasn't come back yet, and I don't know if what she collected included hair follicles. Besides, I worry a little about chain of custody with her sample. This way I'll have DNA and fingerprints, and I don't have proof problems. I am my own witness on custody. Besides, I couldn't be sure that it was his hair, even if it had the follicle. Now if Steve had just gotten the water bottles from his meeting with the Wagner cousins, I wouldn't have had to worry. But he didn't, and the ever-efficient assistant had removed them when I went back to check."

Mandy said, "What if you'd been caught stealing silverware from the club? Can you see the headline? 'FBI chief pathologist busted for shoplifting.'"

"Don't be a hypocrite. You did the same thing with that CIA creep last year and I just followed your lead. Steve would have figured it out if I'd been caught."

"Yeah, but what good would it be to have Frank's DNA?"

Reggie said, "When we pulled out Patrick Carney's DNA, look what we found out? You know I've been suspicious about the Wagner role in that murder." *Maybe the family could be tied to the old murder since they were feuding with each other*, Mandy thought. She knew it was wise to pay attention to her sister's hunches.

Mandy looked off in the distance and Reggie said to her, "What's the matter? You've got a strange look on your face."

She turned back to Reggie with a grim look and said, "I hate to admit this, but you were right. I should never have done this. Not because of disloyalty to LaSalle, but because of the despicable human being that Frank Wagner has turned out to be. I'm feeling much better now, actually."

"Why? Have you decided to do something?"

"No, but I've decided it was a mistake. Now I have to figure out what to do about it."

"I love it when you admit I'm right."

Mandy said, "Don't gloat. We need to talk it through tonight." The opposition from Reggie should have made more of an impression on her than her competitiveness. That was it, after all, the desire to get a big position had clouded her judgment. And to make matters worse, if that wasn't bad enough on its own, she once again had failed to hear her inner voice. It was one of life's mysteries that her truths would come to her in some fleeting fashion and then disperse like wisps of smoke, not to be grasped by her conscious self again until something brought them roaring back to her. Maybe the Oracle was exerting too much influence on her, after all.

Reggie gave her a quick hug and said, "Thank God. I was hoping you'd see the light." Then she ran off to the restaurant for the bathroom. Mandy gave herself a quick reality check and was happy with the result. Even though she didn't know the next step, at least she knew she needed one.

The feeling was short-lived. Standing there waiting, she was suddenly conscious of a person bearing down on her. She looked in that direction and was startled to see Frank rushing back toward her. He'd stopped to clear his mind and, in that moment, convinced himself to take the bull by the horns and confront her. He'd turned around and marched right back to Mandy.

Stopping six feet away from her on Wacker Drive with cars rushing past them, he spat out, "I found out your spy buddy Ray Hanson has hacked his way into my systems. I also know you've been meeting with Gretchen, even at the FBI. You're also scheming with Beth Carney and her journal, aren't you? Just what the hell are you up to?"

The ultimate confrontation with Frank was now upon her, like it or not. Like a sudden inner calm had descended upon her, Mandy felt unafraid of him. Anything he now did was sure to confirm to her what she needed to do. She said, "I've met people like you before. You're a bully and a predator, and now you're showing your true colors. What's next, will I be picked off by a car crossing Wacker Drive?"

He leaned closer toward her, hands on hips, and whispered, "I'm on a schedule and don't have time for your detective bullshit."

"Your company has the time."

Pointing to himself, Frank said, "I AM my company, and I'm telling you to back off."

This would have been the perfect time to unload on him with her best elevator speech about her duty to the corporation, and not to some wayward officer who'd gone rogue. Except she wasn't in an elevator. Going into that kind of legal nicety would have fallen on deaf ears with Frank, anyway.

Noticing out of the corner of his eye the twin sister coming out of the building they'd all just been in together, with a vicious look back at Mandy and a menacing finger pointed at her, he turned toward Northwest's headquarters and marched off shouting, "Stay away from Gretchen. I know you've matched her up with that Carney muckraker too."

From a distance, Reggie witnessed the end of the incident with Frank and yelled, "Hey, what's going on up there?" She signed the letters "O" and "K" to Mandy with a shoulder shrug to indicate a question. Mandy signaled back with the balled fist-nodding sign of *yes*.

Running back to rejoin Mandy where Frank had been standing, Reggie said, "What was that all about? Trying to get you to do a nooner? Or was it just garden variety threats?"

Mandy stared at her and said, "I think war has just been declared."

Reggie said, "I can't believe it. One long pee was all it took for you to decide you were wrong and then declare war."

"He'd been on good behavior at lunch, but then his dam must have burst and he was threatening me."

20

Game Over

FRANK CALLED CARL into his office and started yelling at him. "Mandy's acting like a vigilante. She needs to be cut loose."

"What's happened?"

He explained that she was working with the FBI and having secret meetings with Gretchen and Beth Carney. Frank had not shared that he'd hired an investigator, or what he'd concluded on his own. He told himself that going on boat trips with Gretchen and Beth Carney was probably not that worrisome. But huddling with the FBI and Gretchen was going too far.

"Mandy is behind everything. I want you to fire her immediately."

"If we get rid of Mandy, how am I supposed to finish the offering? And what reasons do I give for letting her go?"

Frank said, "Do whatever you have to do. Get the law firm to handle it and use them for anything else until you can replace her. Tell her Gretchen admitted to being in contact with Mandy and I refuse to have anything like that going on behind my back. Give her a generous severance package if she keeps her mouth shut, threaten her, or do whatever it takes; let's wipe the slate clean. Maybe she's some kind of crusader or Gretchen has lured her into her web, or both. We need to end this."

Carl was deflated but resigned to going with the flow. "I'll take care of it right away. What are you going to do about my mother? Do you want me to talk to her?"

Frank slumped a little and blew out a breath. "She's always been a mystery to me, and we should have never kept her on the board. She probably poured her venom out once she had Mandy's ear. There's no telling what she filled the redhead with. It's time for her to retire from the board. She'll be a billionaire once the company goes public, so she'll probably be relieved to see Northwest in her rearview mirror. Or at least me."

Carl said, "I'm worried about what's going on with her."

"Do what you think best. She seems unstable to me, but she's your mother."

"Do you want to inform the board?"

Frank ignored the question and waved him off. Carl gave out a big sigh and said, "OK, I'll get it rolling." Once Carl left, Frank concluded quietly to himself *Gretchen, you and that red-headed bitch are going to pay for undermining me.*

Mandy was back in her office after the shattering encounter with Frank on the street corner, and trying to get her wits together to figure out her next move. The things she'd learned about the Northwest activities in the years of the prior Wagner generations were chilling. Klaus Wagner's diary had laid out a roadmap to collusion and concerted activity with competitors, designed to secure business illegally. Unfortunately, there was no proof.

She was mentally ticking off all the disturbing things that she had learned, especially Frank's explosion on the street corner only hours ago. Her office phone rang, and she saw it was from Carl. He asked her to stop by his office, and as she did so she found that a senior person from human resources was already there. This was a very familiar type of triangular meeting Mandy had participated in many times before, but never as the third person to enter the room. The third person was always the target, she knew.

Mandy said, "What is this?"

With a cold expression, Carl said, "Mandy, I have been told by Frank that you've been having meetings and conversations with my mother, without his knowledge. Is that true?"

"Yes, she contacted me after her interview when we were all together. It was important to hear her out. She was not comfortable talking in the interview. What's wrong?"

"Frank asked you not to have conversations with directors without him present. He also tells me you and my mother have been visiting with the FBI. Is that also true?"

Carl was not making eye contact with her.

Mandy answered, "Yes, we have found out some information about your father's death that is significant and troubling."

That almost knocked him off his script, but he only hesitated a second and continued. "I'm afraid your disregard of Frank's instructions on this has caused him to terminate your employment immediately. Please accompany our HR representative back to your office, and she'll discuss with you the arrangements for your termination. You will then be escorted out of the building. I'm sorry it has come to this."

As shocking as Mandy's statement had been about his father's death, Carl was desperate to finish his part of the termination and hand off the mess to human resources. It was textbook protocol in terminations to have the firing person deliver the bad news and immediately leave the scene. The newly fired employee would be left in the hands of human resources, which was trained in handling such difficult situations.

He stood up and left without uttering another word, but he could hear Mandy's departing words. She was shouting at him from his office doorway, "You're making a big mistake, Carl. And you're about to face some real pain. Better get ready. You'll need a good lawyer." Heads turned throughout the floor and watched the spectacle taking place.

He just kept going as if nothing had been said. Mandy was led out of his office and down to human resources. Once there, she was told about the severance being offered in return for her confidentiality. Like many of the terminated employees she'd witnessed when a termination occurred, she struggled to take in the words being spoken by the HR person. It was all just going past her. She was handed a form of agreement and asked to look it over and get back to them within the week with a signature. Someone from security escorted back to her office to retrieve her purse and personal cell phone and then showed her to the exit, after taking her building pass and company cell phone.

Mandy was in shock. She moved numbly through the process, realizing now how it was being on the receiving end of a termination. This was coming on the heels of all the discoveries made, and without so much as a chance to explain herself and to lay out everything she'd learned. It was clear that Northwest was at serious risk. She was out of a job, but she was feeling suddenly light, as if she might float away once the Chicago wind caught ahold of her.

Mandy had never even been criticized before by her employers, much less terminated. She'd been involved in plenty of terminations, but this was a first. Her compliance work routinely involved disciplinary actions resulting in terminations. Problem executives would routinely be put into the hands of counselors who would do some coaching to save those who could be saved. She referred to that as *charm school*, but she was offered no such opportunity. Countless people were regularly escorted out of offices, toting severance packages, and now she was one of them. In truth, she'd known instantly in her gut what was happening when her boss invited her to a meeting with a senior human resources officer in attendance, but hadn't wanted to show any of her cards.

She had always anguished about the feelings a person might have for an abrupt firing. Now it was her turn. The initial feeling was shame and embarrassment, not unlike when unmasking the harbormaster fraud case as a teenager. After that feeling, anger would flow out of her like lava. Speaking of the harbormaster, she suddenly recalled that he had fired her back when she had blown the whistle on her co-worker. Now she had to recognize that this was her second firing. Silently she told herself that she would go after the Wagners just like she had gone after the harbormaster so many years ago.

As she trudged along Wacker Drive on the way to her apartment, she stopped in the middle of the Franklin Street bridge leading to River North and made quick calls to Patrick, Reggie, and Steve. After she got to her apartment, almost immediately Patrick showed up and held her for a few minutes. She was showing great self-control, given the sudden ouster. Before she could begin her story, Reggie showed up.

Mandy went through the whole thing with them. She feared she might break down as she told the story, but she felt instead a sense of righteous indignation at the Wagners and Northwest. In fact, the more she talked about it the better she felt, as if a skin of worry was being shed.

Reggie was irate. "We're going to take those bastards down for this. You don't owe them anything, so you better be OK with us being aggressive. I'm only a pathologist, but I think we can push Steve to turn up the heat to high. I'm getting that DNA checked right now."

Patrick said, "You can't feel guilty about this. This was not your fault."

She didn't answer him, but did take another hug.

Mandy said, "I'd been trying to sort out all the threads involved in this mess before they fired me. I'd already decided to leave the company on my own, I think, but Frank beat me to the punch. After I think it through and get past the shock, I actually think it's better to have been fired. Things will become a lot easier if I'm not conflicted by employment. And if I'd quit, I wouldn't have a claim for wrongful discharge either. Now I do."

Reggie said, "What's in the severance package they gave you? Are they trying to gag you with severance money?"

"Yeah, but they're out of their minds if they think I'm going to tie myself up in a non-disclosure agreement. I already have the attorney-client confidentiality rules to contend with. But if I can prove that Northwest is violating laws currently, that rule won't apply. I'm not signing anything."

Patrick squeezed her hand. "These guys have brought this on themselves. You were doing what you needed to do. It's not your fault."

Mandy said, "I pushed it too far, I suppose, but I feel OK with this. I suppose you're going to say 'I told you so?'"

Reggie said, "No. We're past that. The last thing I will let you do is beat yourself up about this."

Patrick said, "Frank Wagner will regret the day he messed with the Red Deuce."

At 9:00 a.m. the next morning, the U.S. Attorney for the Northern District of Illinois announced the investigations into the deaths of Patrick Carney in 1871 and Klaus Wagner ten years ago. The setting was a press conference in the lobby of the Everett Dirksen Federal Building on south Dearborn Street. The announcement identified both deaths as suspicious and were being treated as homicides, and the Chicago office of the FBI was leading investigations. Steve Baker had advised the Carneys of the event and Beth Carney made sure she was there in her capacity as the *Chicago History Journal's* reporter.

21

The Northwest Way

DAVID WILSON, Northwest's executive in charge of canal operations, was busy. His movements had been tracked by the team of Ray and Sammy with an intensity that produced results. Panamanians were to be Wilson's next efforts, they knew. Ray succeeded in getting access to Wilson's online calendar and could see his meetings and travel arrangements. It showed his approach to the Panamanians was going to be through its embassy in DC. His meeting attendees were revealed by email copies. One name stood out amongst the others.

Roberto Perez was a commercial attaché, and that triggered a complete investigation carried out by Ray. Perez was mid-level at the embassy, fortyish with a couple of kids and no obvious source of excess disposable income. Perez had not been ostentatious in his use of resources; he had set up some tax-free education accounts for his children, purchased annuities to carry him for twenty years, and bought some development property that would intentionally sit untouched until a flip sale was possible. These were the investments the careful Señor Perez made with his new financial resources. But despite that low profile, Wilson's careless actions made Perez visible to Ray and Sammy, and with it the Northwest scheme. Eventually Sammy was able to make a direct connection between the Panama Canal Expansion oversight committee and Roberto Perez as a key person in the Panamanian government. After Ray succeeded in tracing a financial flow between financial intermediaries and Perez, the money trail had been established. Ray reported back to Mandy, and her reaction was to package it up and put it in the FBI's hands for building a case.

The files of the original Patrick Carney had gathered dust in LaSalle's patent department for over a hundred years. After Carney's death, his files had been sitting in the files of Isham, Lincoln & Beale for decades, long after Robert Todd Lincoln had moved on to government service. Once Susan Chambers unearthed them, Mandy alerted her FBI friend Steve Baker. Multiple copies existed, but by agreement, it was left to Patrick Carney, the patent lawyer, to examine them and make sense of what had happened.

Everyone awaited his conclusions, and he would not disappoint. Resting inside were handwritten memoranda signed by his ancestor Patrick Carney, along with many drawings of mechanical devices and draft patent applications. Once his review was completed, he'd come to a stunning conclusion—Gus Wagner had stolen the inventions and patented them as his own after the original Patrick Carney's death. Mandy had been warned by her boyfriend and his mother that the elder Patrick Carney kept the flame of the family feud alive and strong. Now that flame was like a blue flame on a welder's torch. Until this point in his life, Patrick Carney the Fifth had nurtured his hatred of the Wagner brothers Gus, Jr. and Klaus, but with this discovery he expanded his appreciation of the feud back many generations.

Next, he studied how Robert Todd Lincoln went to great pains to address the lack of anything comparable in industry—so-called *prior art*. The files were a gift for anyone building a patent claim, and he thought it was highly likely that LaSalle could have successfully obtained patents for the inventions. Lincoln had also documented the steps Patrick Carney had taken to establish his claim of a trade secret. An expansive record of valuable intellectual property to keep secret and then patent, and ultimately profit from, resided in combined files of Isham, Lincoln and Beale and LaSalle Enterprises for over 140 years. That record never had a chance to be used because of his murder.

He'd searched for patented objects which had used technology and mechanical approaches like those found in the files. Fortunately, he was able to use the modern digital searchable files of the Patent Office. Beginning in 1875, a steady stream of patent filings for the devices mirroring those contained in the Carney files appeared. They contained handwritten drawings which were duplicates of those found in LaSalle's files. These had conveniently omitted the original ownership notations at the bottoms of the pages and now included inventor information naming Augustus Wagner. If Patrick had lived and filed his applications, his lawyers would be able to assert that there was no *prior art* that would cause his applications to be denied.

In his excitement, he called his son to report on his conclusions, and to arrange to bring the others involved into the full picture.

"Son, I've concluded from these files that P1 was probably murdered for his inventions, and I think the murderer was most likely Gus Wagner. Surely Wagner was a thief and infringer of Pi's trade secrets."

"Dad, I hope you've taken your blood pressure meds."

"Don't worry about me. This justifies my grudge against that family more than ever."

The next challenge would be establishing the damages LaSalle had sustained, and Mandy's use of Sammy would pay off, she bet. Before her firing, she'd had Sammy dig out old invoices and sales records as well as the litigation and settlement files from Northwest's warehouse. It seems they'd never got rid of anything. The result was that LaSalle probably could prove damages.

Both Patricks allowed themselves to imagine how life would have been different for the Carney family and the LaSalle business. Fortunately, the LaSalle business had been able to pivot into new directions and thrive, but the question of what might have been hovered over all of them. Patrick's dad was very pleased with himself.

———————

Mandy and Reggie took to the streets on the first weekend of October for a long marathon training run with their running group, most of whom were also running the Chicago Marathon at the end of the month. They were winding down from the training distances, so it was easy going for them to be ready for the race but avoid injury. While running, Mandy floated a trial balloon with Reggie.

"I'm thinking of calling Rick."

They looked at each other and Reggie said, "To get back into LaSalle?"

"Why not? Rick said before that I would be welcome back."

Reggie stopped running and pulled her sister in front of her and said, "I didn't know that. Why didn't you tell me?"

Mandy said, "I was afraid you'd have pushed me to change my mind and go back."

"Of course I would have. Are you sure he was serious?"

"Pretty sure, but there's only one way to find out. I can't imagine he would mislead me on something that significant."

"Do whatever makes you comfortable. I can't imagine being fired. Must be a terrible feeling, especially if you're not at fault for anything. You're lucky to be out of there. Are you worried about money?"

"No, I've been pretty good about saving. I'm ignoring their one-sided severance offer with handcuffs attached. If it means no money from them, then so be it."

22

Rebound

FRANK WAGNER had not gotten to be CEO by being indecisive. He was daring, impulsive, and aggressive. His father Gus, Jr. had passed along those characteristics. It didn't mean he was infallible, though. Mandy Doucette was one of his few mistakes, but she was a big one. Choosing employees, especially executives, was a roll of the dice any time. Replacing a key employee was just another hurdle for Frank to clear, and he would persist.

The original Gus, Max's son, had pulled the company out of a tailspin. LaSalle had topped them in the race for the early Chicago capital projects. Frank couldn't be certain about what precise steps Gus had taken in the 1870s, but Frank's own father had bragged about the comeback engineered by his nineteenth-century namesake ancestor. Out of the literal ashes of Chicago after the Great Fire, the Northwest string of successes was a set of miracles unequaled by any other company. His own grandfather had pulled off similar feats in the mid-twentieth century and kept Northwest in a competitive position. It was Frank's turn to pull off a magic trick now by launching the public company.

The turmoil wrought by Mandy Doucette in the going-public process had to be undone and put behind them. Her ouster was step one, and he would lean on his cousin to pick up the pieces so no ground was lost. Next was Aunt Gretchen's disloyalty and treachery. She needed to learn a hard lesson. Long ago his father made sure she was neutralized by being on the board, where he could outmaneuver her, living Sun Tsu's saying of *keep your friends close and your enemies closer.*

If there was another inheritance from his ancestors, it was his taste for revenge. He couldn't rely on Carl to do what was necessary. The guy was timid and weak, not to mention that his own mother was the problem. Carl couldn't even spy on Frank without Frank catching him at it. Gretchen was conspiring with the Doucette women and the FBI, and this was worth taking executive action to disrupt. This was consorting with the enemy of the highest level.

Gretchen had been docile for years following Klaus's death, and she'd been brought onto the board by his father. She was suddenly infused with some animus which could prove harmful. He attributed this to Mandy. Since he was in the final leg of the stock offering which Carl said was imminent, he couldn't take any chances. It was entirely appropriate for his aunt to retire from the board as the company went public. He had to make sure she was not a festering boil waiting to be lanced. Though he was unlikely to get it, what he wanted was the reason she had gone to the FBI. What had driven Mandy to poke her nose so far into his business?

Among several residences he had, Frank continued to maintain the penthouse unit his father owned at Marina City. It was a spectacular space overlooking the Chicago River and the Loop. Sitting there now, just floors above Gretchen, he called her.

"Aunt Gretchen, I wanted to see what is bothering you. I'm told you've been speaking to Mandy Doucette and visiting the FBI offices. What's going on?"

Gretchen said, "I shouldn't be talking to you. I was told we should not speak." She was as cold to him as she had ever been, if not more so.

"What are you talking about?"

"Whatever you did is under investigation," she hissed.

"What have you told them?"

Gretchen said, "Nothing. How would I know anything to tell them? You've as good as shut me out of any information. I might as well not be a board member."

As calmly as he could, Frank said, "I think you've come to the right conclusion. I'll have Carl get you a resignation form to sign."

"Fine. Then I can let the world know how Klaus really died, now that I know he was murdered and who did it."

"I would be very careful if I were you," he whispered.

She said, "I also think it's time to get all of Klaus's written accounts of Northwest's business practices. That could complicate things for you."

Frank said, "What are you talking about? What have you gotten your hands on?"

"I think I have a couple things to discuss with Mandy about that FBI business, too. I think I'll give her a call."

Frank shouted, "Mandy Doucette doesn't work here anymore."

He heard her gasp, and she hung up abruptly.

He called Carl to come down to his office. "I've had a very disturbing call with your mother. She refused to talk to me and wanted Mandy. When I told her Mandy was gone, she hung up on me. She sounded frantic to me. I'm worried about her. Can you get over there and talk to her?"

"Yes, I'll go over, but I'm not sure she'll talk to me either. What do you want me to do?"

Frank said, "If she tells you what's going on, it would be best. If not, I think you need to get her resignation. She agreed to resign. If she resists, tell her she'll be off the board soon anyway once the company goes public, so why stay on if it's difficult for her? If you can at least get her to communicate constructively instead of flinging threats, it would help."

Carl said, "I'll do what I can."

"Call me tonight when you're done with her."

Gretchen called Mandy to tell her about the tense conversation with Frank and hear directly from her about being fired.

After the call with Gretchen Frank sat impatiently awaiting Carl's call, which came at nine o'clock.

Carl said, "I met with her, and she's a mess. I've never seen her so distraught. I was afraid to leave her alone after what she told me. She seems to be convinced my dad was murdered and who did it."

Playing dumb, Frank said, "What? Who does she think murdered him then?"

"She wouldn't say. It's crazy. And I've never seen her like that. I had it out with her about letting them dig up my father's body. She said they found cyanide. She said she wasn't supposed to talk to us."

"She must mean my dad. Is she accusing him of murdering his own brother with cyanide, just because they went fishing together? That's preposterous."

"She didn't say who. Maybe the feds are feeding that line to her. She threw me out, screaming that she can't trust anyone."

"Did you get to talk to her about resigning?"

Exasperated by the question, Carl pulled out a piece of paper and looking at it, said, "That's the only thing that went well. She signed it. Do you know anything about my father's murder?"

Frank said, "Of course not. And this is the first time I'm hearing anything about murder. I'm as shocked by this as I was by that skeleton in the barrel. Let's huddle tomorrow in the office in the morning and decide what to do. Are you worried that she would harm herself?"

"I'm not sure. I've never seen her like this."

———

Tuesday morning Mandy called Rick and asked if she could visit, and they agreed to meet at his office. When Mandy showed up in casual clothes, Rick was surprised.

"What? Are they casual every day at Northwest?

Mandy said, "I don't work there anymore. They fired me."

Rick looked at her, speechless, and motioned for her to sit.

He quietly said, "What happened?"

She said, "Maybe I got too aggressive. I was pursuing routine due diligence, and it led to some very ugly stuff. They recognized I was going down a path they didn't want me to go down, and they pulled the plug. Lying, cheating, and stealing . . . always. These guys and their ancestors may be the epitome of it. And here they are blundering into a public offering, with all their baggage ready to be opened and shown to the world."

"They got what they paid for, I guess. They bought your vigilante expertise and got a full dose of it."

She glared at him without speaking.

He said, "It's a good thing! That's what I'm saying." Rick tilted his head and looked at her. "You want back in? I've still got your spot open. I can pay you more, though I can't match what you got at Northwest."

"You don't have any concerns about Northwest?"

"Such as?"

Mandy said, "They could try disrupting my return. Maybe even sue to block me from returning to LaSalle. Mess with my bar admission."

Rick said, "Nope. I trust you. Period."

"God bless you. Thank you. And yes, I'd love to come back."

"Take a week off. I'm putting you on the payroll as of today."

Back at the apartment, Mandy was counting her blessings. She had been guilt-free about refusing to sign the Northwest non-disclosure agreement, but she hadn't been unemployed since leaving law school. It was a weird feeling. Mandy wanted a place to go each day. It was great that LaSalle wanted her back, and she looked forward to getting back to working for a respectable company.

A visit with the Oracle was in order, so she traveled up to his Evanston office and explained what had happened. She got a supportive reception, which she expected.

Then she said, "I've been thinking a lot about Reggie's point about loyalty—not to LaSalle, but to Northwest—am I at fault for being disloyal to Northwest right out of the gate?"

Her dad said, "Only true character attracts allegiance. The Wagners didn't have what it takes to earn it."

She was quiet for a few long seconds, then said, "I have another one for you. There's an attorney-client issue I need your opinion on. What do you think of my risk on the canon of ethics if I were to go the whistleblower route?" Mandy had been struggling with whether her code of ethics requirement to maintain client confidences would prevent her from blowing the whistle.

"Look, if you were only concerned with old crimes, you'd probably be stuck. But if current or future crimes are involved, I think the crime-fraud exception to the attorney-client privilege is available to you."

A lawyer was barred by the code of ethics from disclosing confidential information protected by an attorney-client privilege. Only the client could waive that privilege. But there was no privilege for the commission of a current or future crime. The law had concluded that as a matter of public policy, it was for the greater good of society that an attorney could inform on a client to prevent a crime.

Mandy said, "What if it's a little of both?"

"You're golden. Besides, if you're going to bring down a criminal activity and they get prosecuted for it, I don't see them getting far trying to bring disciplinary actions against you."

"Looks like I'm going to take a run at bringing them down, then. I think Ray and Sammy have got solid proof of bribery of Panamanian government officials," she said.

23

The Launch

EARLY IN OCTOBER, a celebration took place at Northwest Engineering's offices. The occasion was the Panamanian government's announcement of the award of the multi-billion dollar widening and improvement of the Panama Canal. Frank Wagner shook David Wilson's hand in front of all the employees at the company's headquarters. He praised him for completing the successful bid of the Panama Canal expansion project as well as the St. Lawrence Seaway upgrade. Wagner hyped up the significance of the win to Northwest and said that these wins made up for the loss of their bids for the Deep Tunnel project. The celebration was brief, though, as the executive officers had to head out to New York for the next day's stock exchange opening, but Frank promised Wilson that he'd celebrate with him later. Wagner would take the occasion of tomorrow's stock exchange launch to stress the importance of the contract award to Northwest.

Northwest's senior officers were riding high the morning of the second Tuesday in October. The SEC had declared the Northwest registration statement final, and the offering was imminent. With Mandy Doucette and Aunt Gretchen out of the game, Frank had pushed the process to a conclusion with no further resistance. He'd finally done it, and he hoped his father would look on with pride over his son's accomplishment. It had required him to transform his company into something he no longer recognized. But on the other hand, he could return to the big leagues using his family's approaches to success.

Few people had experienced an initial public offering and a New York Stock Exchange listing, yet here they were. After breakfast in a large stock exchange conference room, they gathered on the balcony overlooking the trading floor. At the magic moment they pulled on the opening bell to ring open the trading day. Trading officially opened for Northwest Engineering common stock, and its life as a public company officially began. After the bell, stock exchange officials handed out a heavy bronze medallion with the symbol of the bull and bear in relief on one side, and the other stamped **NORTHWEST ENGINEERING** and bearing the trading symbol **NE**—their own personal mementos of the day.

After the opening, Frank had interviews with stock analysts, as was typical. The Northwest financial relations staff attracted at least a half dozen firms to pick up coverage of the company and issue reports. Those reports would be based largely on what the company's spokespersons disclosed, and Frank intended to lead them to positive expectations.

Public company handcuffs were now upon them, so they had to take special care to deal with them. Limitations on speech were now a daily reality. Frank relied on Carl and their new chief financial officer to be the guardians and protectors of those risks. Naturally, since he was the CEO, everyone wanted to have his point of view. He couldn't talk about certain things unless they were already publicly disclosed, and he found this suffocating. Anything provoking a public company's anxiety, be it Wall Street analysts, institutional shareholders, shareholder activists, the stock exchange or regulators, would be risky to a company.

Before the offering, his greatest fear besides Mandy was Gretchen popping up out of nowhere to cause trouble. Shortly before the company went public, Gretchen's resignation had been received by Frank like a gift. She'd gone out like a lamb. Without Mandy in management or Gretchen on the board, there were no impediments to the offering. But Gretchen still held great risk to Frank personally, and he didn't know what she was doing with Mandy and Beth Wagner in the shadows. He feared that she'd learned too much over the years, whether through her husband or otherwise. She was tight with the muckraker Beth Carney. Now that she was convinced Klaus had been murdered, she could publicize her accusations through the Carney woman's *Chicago History Journal*. But would she accuse him?

24

Old Theft

MANDY TOOK ADVANTAGE of her week off to get in some good long runs with her sister as the marathon race date loomed. As they started out early one morning, heading north on Franklin under the El tracks, Reggie said, "I want you to explain some things to me."

Mandy said, "Fire away."

"OK, first I need to tell you something. We've been able to make a connection to the DNA from the hairs with the skeleton. The connection is with Frank Wagner, or rather with his ancestor."

Mandy stopped running and said, "That's fantastic! Why didn't you call me right away to tell me?"

"Because you'd just been fired and I didn't want to put any more anxiety on you. St. Dymphna can only hold off so much bad juju."

"What are you talking about? That's good juju."

"How so? What can you do with that?"

"I think it would be strong circumstantial evidence that a Wagner ancestor could have been involved in Patrick Carney's death."

"Enough to conclude it was the murderer?"

"No. But it's a good start. I have to admit it was a good move to steal Frank's utensils at lunch."

Reggie said, "Will you tell Patrick and his family? I can't imagine their reaction."

"I can guess. Partick will be inspired for a story, his mother will salivate over a multi-edition series, and his father will feel justified in his feud."

"Speaking of Patrick, how's it going with him?"

"You know, I just feel safe with him."

"Is that all you feel—safe?"

"Are we really having this conversation?"

"Yes, now cough up the goods."

"I'm sure I feel the same about Patrick as you do about Dan."

"Good. I like Patrick a lot. He's good for you."

They had reached Chicago Avenue and turned east to reach Michigan Avenue, then north past the Water Tower and onto the path along Oak Street Beach. They continued their discussion about their boyfriends until there was no more left to say. It was early enough in the day to have mirrorlike lake water, before the winds picked up with dawn and the waves started. The sun was peaking above the horizon. This was why they lived in Chicago. The temperature was in the low 50s and humidity comfortably low, and if it held that way it would be ideal for the marathon in a couple weeks. It had only been several years since the infamous 90-degree Chicago marathon that had been canceled mid-race. Race officials had acted quickly once all the heat exhaustion casualties started piling up and the aid stations ran out of water. One young runner had collapsed and died right in front of the sisters around mile nineteen, and plenty others had been taken to emergency rooms.

Reggie asked, "What are you thinking of doing about Northwest?"

"Steve urged me to file a whistleblower claim against them."

"Is that a big deal?"

Mandy said, "Could be. Remember that they threatened me over confidentiality issues and reminded me of the attorney-client privilege."

"So, what about that?"

"I talked to Dad about it. He thinks if there's current crimes taking place, or they're planning a future crime, that privilege falls away for them."

Reggie said, "What does that mean?"

"I can go the whistleblower route and sue them. They can't get my license revoked. Steve told me the U.S. Attorney would support me about coming forward to report the crime."

They ended their run and returned to the apartment, and later Mandy headed up to Patrick's condo on Lakeview to spend the day with him. They walked down to Lincoln Park and crossed under Lake Shore Drive to the lakeshore and sat watching the lake and talking about everything.

Mandy asked him, "You haven't filled me in on your dad's conclusions after looking at all the files from Rick. What did he say?"

"He went through everything in our family records and then through all the LaSalle files that Rick produced. After that he pulled up the Patent Office files on Gus Wagner's patents. The short answer is that he thinks those files can be used to prove that Gus Wagner's patents from the 1870s should be invalidated. They should never have been granted because Carney's files prove he was the first inventor."

"Fantastic."

Patrick said, "But wait. It gets better. Dad found that the Wagner patent case had copied the materials from Patrick Carney. Dad says if we can show the damage LaSalle suffered we can sue Northwest for theft and patent infringement."

"Sounds too easy. I'm sure it wouldn't be."

He said, "We'd need to show the sales that Northwest had from the stolen inventions. Got any ideas on how we could do that?"

"Sammy can help with that. She located the sales accounting records long buried in that big warehouse. They've all been digitized, so they can be searched easily. When I was there I learned that they kept everything. That bad habit could be their undoing."

"Can you ask her to look?"

"Ask her yourself," she said, pointing across to Belmont Harbor. They'd been walking north along the running path and were in sight of the *Bogie* in the harbor. They smiled at each other and headed down to the dock, calling Ray along the way. When they got to his slip he welcomed them aboard and after the small talk, Ray said, "Is there something we can do for you?"

Mandy told them what was needed and asked for their help. Sammy said, "All I need is the equipment you want sales records about, and I'm off to the races."

Patrick said, "I'll get a list from my dad for you."

He asked Ray when he had to head back to Florida and the answer was soon. The Belmont Harbor Marina rules called for the removal of all boats for winter by the end of October. It was the same for all the marinas on the lakefront. Ray, in fact, had started preparing *Bogie* for its southern voyage.

Mandy and Patrick left to return to Patrick's condo and on the way, Mandy asked, "Have you told your parents about matching Wagner DNA to the hairs in the cloth in the skeleton barrel?"

"Yes, and they wanted to know how were you able to make that match?"

Mandy said, "You told them we had Frank Wagner's DNA from a couple of sources, right?"

"It brought a smile to my dad's face. I think he's getting ahead of himself and maybe thinking all this will change the family history we've been told our whole lives."

"What about your mom?"

"She said the family has suffered for over a century with this mystery, and now it's turned out worse than thought. It's one thing to think Patrick Carney died and was incinerated in the fire, but it's another thing to hear he was robbed and murdered. Both my parents want the death investigated."

Mandy said, "They know there can't be murder charges brought, right?"

"Yes, but they could sue for wrongful death even if criminal charges couldn't be brought. Then they could be looking at damages from Northwest."

"Did you tell them about Klaus's autopsy and finding potassium cyanide?"

"My mother was torn up over that one, I think mainly because of what it would do to Gretchen. I know she's tried calling her."

"What about your dad?"

"He was giddy about being able to blame Gus, Jr. for his brother Klaus's death. He's convinced Klaus was murdered," Patrick said, slamming his hand down on an imaginary table as they walked down Lakeview Terrace.

"Wait until he hears that the FBI is considering whether Gus, Jr. was acting alone."

25

Cleaning Up

IN AN OLD PARKING LOT at one of the idle and long-abandoned industrial sites along the Cal-Sag Channel on the far south side of the City of Chicago, a burning van without license plates was found early one morning. It had been some kind of activity center, fire investigators reasoned. It contained internal dish receivers and numerous communications devices that were now burned and twisted metal. The van was not fitted for comfort, but rather as a stakeout vehicle. Its VIN numbers had been removed or obliterated everywhere that was reachable, including the frame, the body, the engine and transmission. Only one place remained. The searchers located it in the engine compartment and were ultimately able to tie the number to a Steven Greer from Erie, Pennsylvania. Mr. Greer received a visit from Pennsylvania State Police, and he informed them that he'd sold the vehicle to his younger brother Jack. He had not heard from Jack, but gave all his brother's contact information to the police. They passed it through to the FBI immediately and even before leaving Steven Greer's home, they had gotten word that Jack Greer was missing.

Steven Greer had been warned by the state police not to try reaching his brother, but even if he had it would have been futile. Jack's body was presently wrapped in a heavy chain and resting in three feet of water on the bottom of a cove off the Cal-Sag Channel, not far from where his van had been torched. His absence was no impediment to the FBI's activities, though, since Ray Hanson had cracked the code on any surveillance data Greer had gathered anyway. His mortal remains were of no immediate consequence. He had never had a chance to remove the device he'd placed in Gretchen Wagner's condo, which was still operating.

Jack had been surprised when the passenger door of his van swung open as it sat parked outside Gretchen's building. After momentary relief hit him that it was just his client Frank hopping in the front seat, he lost consciousness as he was tased. He never felt the needle he'd then been stuck with.

On a routine check after the burning van had been found, a Calumet police boat patrolling the Cal-Sag Channel spotted a committee of vultures poised in a nearby tree to the shoreline. The patrol boat then found and pulled a body out of the water, bound by tape. The report found its way to Steve Baker's attention due to its proximity to the van. The body was transported to the FBI autopsy suite, where Reggie was able to establish that the cause of death was a large dose of potassium cyanide accompanied by taser markings on the neck. No water was found in the lungs. It was dead when it went into the water. The body was soon connected to the burned van, and the identification turned out to be that of Jack Greer. Steve Baker added another murder to his list of Wagner-connected victims, since Mandy had informed him of Frank's use of Greer. Greer might have been a witness against him that Frank wanted to take out of the game. But they didn't have enough to point in Frank Wagner's direction.

While the Pennsylvania police were visiting Steven Greer, hundreds of miles away Frank was meeting David Wilson at the Marina City dock. They boarded Frank's boat and headed out through the locks for a fishing trip to celebrate the Panamanian award. They had waited on the fly bridge while the locks from the river to Lake Michigan opened, and a handful of boats proceeded to enter and rise up to the lake level. It was a beautiful mid-October day, and the lake was calm. Wilson admitted to being less of a fisherman than Frank might be, but Frank told him that if the fish weren't biting, then the ice-cold Grey Goose would be enough of a reward.

They motored due east for a while and got out of sight of the skyline. No other boats were within sight either. Frank suggested that he whip them up their first cocktail. He left Wilson at the helm and reappeared after a few minutes with two glasses of vodka tonics, and they toasted to the great success and tilted them back. Within seconds, Wilson's whole body clenched and he collapsed onto the fly bridge deck and writhed for a minute, then lay still as a white froth bubbled out of his mouth. The potassium cyanide, Frank's weapon of choice, had been undetectable to the naked eye. Frank stood off to the side and pulled his binoculars up to do a 360-degree scan of the lake. When Wilson had fallen, his glass had dropped out of his hand and crashed on the teak deck and shards of glass spread everywhere.

While Frank was certain they were still alone, he dragged the body down to the lower deck, and made sure everything belonging to Wilson was in his pockets. Next he pulled out the heavy chain he'd taken from the warehouse and wrapped it around the body and fastened it. He opened the dock gate and edged the body over the side. His former colleague slipped quickly into the two-hundred-feet deep lake for his permanent watery grave. Just to be safe Frank powered up and started back, and while on autopilot he swept up the glass fragments and tossed them overboard. Then he mopped up the spilled liquid and tossed the rag over as well. With that done, he drained his glass and made a second for himself as he planned out his next steps. The first thing he would do back at the office would be to say he'd given Wilson a couple of weeks off and understood he was taking a trip to the Caribbean. A second witness was now eliminated.

26

Second Autopsy

FRANK HAD KEPT his hands off Gretchen, biding his time after the stock started trading. At the approach of the opening, he hadn't wanted to introduce any drama to upend things. He waited patiently but was as intent as ever on neutralizing Gretchen. She was a landmine waiting for a misplaced step. Her words to him the last time they spoke, warning that she knew who had murdered her husband, were what drove him now.

Carl had told him his mother was extremely distraught that she had lost her husband to murder. For many years she'd suffered the loss of her mate, and only now found out she had been led around with a blindfold, compliments of Gus, Jr. and then Frank. Now she had learned she'd been under surveillance. His mother had been taking sleeping pills as the only way to be able to sleep at night in her grief-stricken condition. Her association with Beth Carney and the risk of a magazine article full of accusations was too much for Frank to take. He had been alarmed at the *Chicago History Journal's* announcement of an upcoming story on a Hatfield-McCoy-style business feud that ran through most of Chicago's history.

A couple weeks after trading in Northwest stock had started, Frank had a frantic message from Carl. The cleaning lady had found his mother's condo empty with the balcony door wide open and the drapes blowing out. Carl had rushed over to Marina City and met the cleaning lady at the condo. Gretchen was nowhere to be found. The concierge had not seen her go out. Immediately he called the Chicago Police to report her as missing. A search then took place and by three o'clock that same afternoon a body was found floating in the marina dock area. Carl was asked to come to the scene to make an identification. When he arrived, a sheet covered the corpse. The coroner's man pulled back the sheet, and his mother lay in an open body bag. Her skin was unnaturally white and puckered from floating in the Chicago River for hours. She had visible trauma to the head, the only part of her that was visible in the body bag. Carl identified her and had to be helped to a chair. The Chicago Police told him that she had apparently fallen from her condo balcony forty floors above. The police said their working theory was that Gretchen Wagner had taken her own life.

An autopsy would be conducted. There would be no repeat of the Klaus Wagner episode. The police concluded that with one exception, nothing suspicious was found at the condo. A video device was found in her unit, but since it only recorded and passed along what it captured via an unknown link, there was nothing on the physical surveillance equipment to review. Without the link, nothing could be viewed by the police.

Carl told the police his mother had been agitated and had been distraught over her husband. He'd been worried about her, but she had become distant from him, so there was no meaningful contact. No suicide note had been found in the condo. Once the Chicago Police learned about the murder of Klaus, they connected it to the FBI involvement and brought Steve Baker into the picture. He in turn called Reggie to his office and they called Mandy to tell her what had happened.

The sisters were devastated by the news. Both felt guilty for different reasons. Mandy regretted being the person who had drawn out the information from Gretchen and then invariably led to her mental state. Would Gretchen have been as agitated had she never learned of her husband's murder? Reggie cringed at the news and thought that her autopsy of Klaus Wagner could have been a fatal blow to Gretchen. It occurred to Mandy that she had repeated the prior year's tragedy when she had pulled John Booth into another situation and he'd been murdered. Mandy worried about anyone else she had used in her efforts—Ray Hanson and Sammy Wong maybe? Even Beth Carney? Did they all have reason to fear for their safety?

Steve had also mentioned the discovery of Jack Greer's death and eventually connected him to Frank Wagner. He speculated that video surveillance equipment found in Gretchen's condo could have been Greer's. When Mandy learned that Greer had been found wrapped in a heavy chain, she immediately recalled the report she'd gotten from Sammy awhile back about the video of the Northwest warehouse. Frank Wagner had been seen collecting a variety of threatening items, one of which was large chains.

Gretchen's death made the news, since it wasn't every day that a person jumped off a fortieth-floor balcony. It was reported as a suspected suicide. Mandy knew that Gretchen had emphatically said that she would never take that way out. She'd made a point of saying that when the story of Gus Wagner's plunge to his own death in 1910 came out. Beth and Patrick Carney had heard her say it. It had been on the boat tour they all took together. Mandy's little voice told her that Frank had to have been involved somehow.

Given the FBI's involvement, the Cook County Medical Examiner was only too happy for the FBI's forensic pathologist to conduct the autopsy. The body was transported to the FBI lab, where it awaited the scalpel and saw. Reggie was too shaken up to do it herself and would only supervise.

Mandy was slumped in a chair in their apartment, unable to move, speak or look away from the TV screen as she watched the news coverage. Her hand covered her mouth, and she was crying. This was her doing. She was sure of it.

She called Reggie about it and said, "I didn't see this coming. She was such a brave woman for reaching out to me, and I let her in for this. If she jumped off that building, I can only imagine what agony she must have been in. Her husband murdered, her son co-opted by Frank, the pressured resignation from the Northwest board—those could have been too much for anyone to cope with. She was living in a Wagner family horror show, and anything could happen. Frank was a terrifying and combative menace to Gretchen."

Reggie said, "I feel awful too. I had a hand in this, suggesting the autopsy of her husband." At least Reggie was sharing some of the guilt with her sister. But the fact remained that Mandy provoked danger. It didn't matter that she'd had a noble purpose for doing so. Nothing would console her.

Mandy said, "Remember, though, that without that autopsy no one would ever have discovered Klaus's murder."

Mandy fretted over what she was about to do but nevertheless had to move ahead and take the whistleblower plunge. She'd consulted those close to her and got no resistance to the idea. She was on autopilot writing the letter, and it took her three hours to complete. When she was finally done, she called Reggie to check in with her.

Reggie asked, "Are you feeling better about Gretchen?"

Mandy told her, "No, but right now I'm putting that aside. I'm concentrating on this whistleblower letter. I don't have enough bandwidth to cope with Gretchen's tragedy. It's in your hands."

"Let me at her. I'll figure it out, and I better head down to the autopsy suite to start. About the letter, how's it coming?"

Mandy said, "It's done. I need to run it by a lawyer, and then speak to Rick about it."

Reggie was pumped up to do an autopsy and headed out to the lab.

The next morning, Mandy got busy. She'd met some whistleblower lawyers from her days in the Justice Department and she picked one to use. Ever since a recent series of high-profile financial frauds and a market collapse occurred, Congress had protected whistleblowers. Naturally that led to the growth of whistleblower lawyers. After a call to explain the circumstances, Mandy and her lawyer came up with a plan.

Patrick spent the night at Mandy's apartment. They had a light dinner with Reggie and went over the latest developments. Patrick described how crushed his mother had been at the news of Gretchen's death, and she was unsure what to do. She was preparing to break the story in the *Chicago History Journal*. She wanted to have it all written up so she could rush it into print when she had a green light. She intended to do it as a serial, spread out over several weeks.

Mandy held up her hands with her palms facing out and said, "She should hold off as long as she can. I think Gretchen is owed some respect here."

Patrick nodded in agreement and turned to Reggie, saying, "What about the autopsy?"

Reggie said, "We did it last night. She drowned. I can also tell you that she had blunt force trauma to the head. But not visible were bruises under the arms from being treated roughly prior to her death, like being dragged. It was not trauma from the fall, and I don't think the fall would have taken her into a collision with the building anyway. The head trauma was from a blunt instrument, like a truncheon. It wouldn't break the skin. If she had hit the building, the injuries would have been much more severe than what I found, and skin would have been broken and bloody. She'd taken sleeping pills. Not enough to kill her, but enough to keep her unconscious if someone was handling her. In my opinion, a person with that many drugs in her system couldn't have gotten herself over a balcony railing either."

Patrick said, "Drugged, bludgeoned, dragged, and dropped from a skyscraper?"

Nodding, Reggie said, "Murdered." She and Mandy were both crying by now.

———

Steve Baker's agents had been working closely with their counterparts in Canada and Panama after being pulled into the case by Ray Hanson. He'd supplied the name Roberto Perez, and the Panamanians had taken it from there. On the Canadian side, the Royal Mounted Police investigators soon identified a financial trail leading to a St. Lawrence Seaway employee who had been one of the team working on the awards of the Seaway Expansion project. The Canadians had been happy to share what they had learned about his recent improved lifestyle. Steve believed there was enough to warrant Wilson's arrest on charges of corruption and bribery, as well as a search, so armed with the warrants, an FBI arrest team descended on his Gold Coast condominium home early one morning while neighborhood children were on street corners awaiting school buses.

When they got no answer to their knocks, they forced open the door. Nothing was amiss and the bachelor was not at home. After visiting his office and being told that he had left for a visit to the Caribbean, they were put into a holding pattern. But when news of the missing David Wilson found its way to Mandy, she knew her chances of avoiding any problems from the attorney-client privilege problem had soared. She had clung to the idea that a present or future crime would come out, and now it had. She knew they would not find Wilson in the Caribbean or anywhere else.

27

Time Capsule

FRANK INSISTED on a huge media presence for the opening of the time capsule of the Monadnock Building on its one-hundred-year anniversary. His new role in life was to be the chief cheerleader for Northwest Engineering. Northwest's public relations chief urged him to look for opportunities like this one. He liked these events, but they presented risks. If the warnings he'd received in the preparation to go public were to become reality, things could turn perilous at some point with the external constituencies. He hated to give any credit to Mandy Doucette for influencing how he thought about the things, but in truth the same warnings had come from the lawyers and investment bankers who preceded her. Anyway, his takeaway now was to milk this one for all he could. The press always sought scandals and tragedies, so this one might be boring for them. That was too bad, he thought. The event took place on a Saturday morning, with decent media coverage for the live event. Local and national press were invited, and a local media personality was the master of ceremonies. Frank and Carl were serving as co-hosts.

The Monadnock Building was reputed to be the first skyscraper in the world, at sixteen stories. It led to larger and grander-scale buildings worldwide. Its architect was Daniel Burnham's firm, Burnham & Root. He was the famous architect responsible for the Chicago Plan and the 1893 Chicago Columbia Exposition. Northwest Drayage and Tunnel Company, the predecessor to Northwest Engineering, occupied the building at the Jackson Boulevard and Dearborn Street intersection in 1910 as its corporate headquarters.

Steve Baker and two of his agents were there. Ongoing investigations involving Northwest and the Wagners were underway, and he made sure he was well-represented. Frank Wagner, after all, was at least a person of interest and at worst a suspect. If Mandy still worked there, she would have attended. Beth Carney was on the sidewalk, since her *Chicago History Journal* series about the Wagner-Carney competition was ready to go. Beth was accompanied by her husband and son. Mandy and Reggie stayed away, watching together on television from their apartment. Mandy recognized this as a grand public relations stunt. It had Frank's fingerprints all over it. Thinking that a board presence was in order, Ed Rosen and Charles Winters also stood in that congregation on the sidewalk on Dearborn Street.

The lobby was jammed with press, politicians and others. It was open to the public. The event began promptly at 10:00 a.m. The emcee made introductions and turned to Frank to make the ceremonial removal of the cornerstone of the building. Masons were present to extricate the time capsule. It sat inside a large cavity. TV cameras were permitted to view the inside before anything was removed.

Once the space was opened, there was an immediate sense of relief. Fortunately, there were items inside to be inspected and revealed to the crowd. Carl had urged that the capsule be opened beforehand to avoid any surprises, such as an empty space, but the TV station insisted it be done live. Carl had dreaded a Geraldo Rivera-like surprise of an empty space, which had happened much to that reporter's embarrassment years ago. A suspected Al Capone storeroom was opened on live TV and found empty. Even though there was a risk that this cavity would be empty and a potential media bust, the network didn't want to run the risk of a fraud charge by having opened it beforehand and having staged contents.

The emcee brought out the items one by one, while Frank and Carl identified and announced them to the crowd. Frank was first handed a roll of plans which were described as the original layout by Burnham & Root for the building. Next, Carl held up a Chicago Loop street plan for that year. Then came a series of old photos of the most significant Northwest capital projects in Chicago, including the Illinois and Michigan Canal, the Chicago Sanitation and Shipping Canal, the Chicago River and Calumet River projects, and other items. Frank and Carl took turns identifying these photos.

Finally, an envelope was taken out as the last item. The emcee looked to Frank and Carl for direction, and they motioned for him to proceed. He opened the envelope and read its contents. The outside of the envelope bore the notation

From Augustus Wagner, 1910.

The envelope was opened, and the emcee began to read its handwritten contents:

My name is Augustus Wagner, and I submit this letter as a true and honest account of events during my tenure at Northwest Drayage and Tunneling Company. By the time this letter is read, I'll be long dead and forgotten. But my wish is that it be known that I take full responsibility for the events described below.

Frank turned to Carl and made a closed-mouth desperate whisper, "What the fuck is this? What did that old bastard do?" Carl merely gave him a befuddled look and shrugged.

The emcee took his eyes off the letter to look up at the crowd to see what kind of reaction he was getting from the live coverage and continued. Excitement had suddenly infected the audience, and the emcee hoped for a ratings grand slam in the making.

For many years I struggled with what my sons and I have done. But there is nothing to be done about it now except what I do here with these words. My father Max started this company, and he was a builder. But he was no innovator. He was losing business hand over fist to his main competitor, LaSalle Dredging and Excavation Company.

Once my father died, the delicate condition of the company became clear. I concluded that the best answer was to combine with a more successful company. Many families depended on Northwest to survive, and I was driven to succeed for them. So I swallowed my pride and made a proposal to Patrick Carney, the head of LaSalle. His company was the natural partner to pursue. He angrily rebuffed my proposal, though, not even hearing me out. It left me desperate.

I had learned through my sources of his secret inventions that could help save my business. I found them one night in 1871, when I broke into LaSalle's workshop and found his drawings. He surprised me in the act, and I shot and killed him to save myself from discovery. I took his drawings and the body and set fire to his workshop and to a barn a couple of streets away. I've regretted my actions my whole life. What I had started went on to burn down the City of Chicago. I stuffed his body in a barrel and buried it in a bridge abutment under construction. That fire spread to a three-square-mile section of the city, killing over three hundred innocent souls. For these things I have just described, I burn eternally in Hell.

After making Carney's inventions my own and securing patents, I used these machines to win construction projects around the world. Any means necessary were used to win contracts, and I trained my sons in the methods I'd used for years. By now these business practices have been outlawed, but I never stopped using them.

I ask for God's forgiveness. I also ask for forgiveness from the Carney and O'Leary families and the families of all those whose loved ones perished in the Great Fire.

With regret and remorse,
Augustus Wagner

Just as the emcee finished reading, Frank and Carl Wagner rushed off the rear of the podium to avoid the press. A cacophony of voices erupted once the letter reading was done. The Wagners had abandoned their public relations staff to react to the feverish bombardment now being leveled by the media. Not wishing to be cornered and pressed for comments, board members Rosen and Winters also quietly retreated. Steve Baker and his FBI companions, on the other hand, pushed their way to the front and took custody of the letter as evidence. The scene in the assembled crowd was bedlam.

Beth Carney captured the thirty minutes on video, as had every other journalist there, and all the news people made their way to the front to try to interview anyone remaining. None remained except for public relations staff attempting damage control. Media anchors scrambled to comment on what had just occurred on live TV. Normally anchors would turn to panels of talking heads for analysis, but there were none present because the event was not deemed newsworthy enough to stage them. They were left to repeat what had been read aloud. Steve instructed his team that all media recordings of the entire crowd were to be obtained and searched for anything important. The FBI agents left with the letter.

The Carney family members huddled together, incredulous about what had taken place. A public reading of a confession to all the crimes Wagner and his company committed. Beth went off by herself to call her office to get the press rolling on the first installment of her story. There was no time to reflect.

28

Fire
October 1871

AUGUSTUS WAGNER brooded at a corner table, tormented by what he was about to do. His rival, Patrick Carney, had entered Chicago's Wolf Point Tavern and walked deep into its smoky and poorly lit interior until he found Wagner waiting. Carney was a dark-complected, red-haired man, with an excitable personality. Wagner was black-haired and had a full beard, and his demeanor was that of a supplicant. Carney ignored the outstretched hand in front of him, sat down at the table, and said, "Ya got me here, so what do ya want?"

Gus said, "I'll be happy to explain myself, but I invited you for dinner. Can I get you a drink and some food first?"

"I have no intention of breaking bread with the likes of you."

By that autumn, Gus Wagner had become a desperate man, willing to take extreme measures to save his company and the three hundred employees who depended on him. The company, Northwest Drayage and Tunnel Company, was one of the first commercial enterprises in the 1830s. After a successful start, though, Northwest now routinely lost lucrative building projects to its main competitor, LaSalle Dredging and Excavation Company. Gus had swallowed his pride and invited LaSalle's president to dinner to make a proposal.

Gus had selected a casual setting, the Wolf Point Tavern on the north side of the main branch of the Chicago River, at the point of confluence with the south and north branches of the river. Carney had grudgingly accepted the invitation, thinking that Wagner probably wished to make peace. But the Irishman was unwilling to engage with the first-generation German owner of the Northwest business. He was skeptical of anything coming from the Wagner family. Patrick's late father, Seamus, had a history of conflict with Gus Wagner's father Maximillian.

Both fathers had immigrated to the United States— Maximillian Wagner from the Prussian empire and Seamus Carney from Ireland—in the early 1830s. They worked together on the Erie Canal in New York, developing a contentious relationship in the process. As the Erie Canal project wound down, they went their separate ways. Wagner eventually poached a number of Carney's workers and moved on to start his own company in Chicago after picking up jobs at a few points in between. That poaching ensured that when Seamus Carney followed west to Chicago himself, he would bring the bitter memory of his competitor's actions, and it would make for a volatile situation. While both founders had passed away by 1871, their two sons inherited their fathers' hostility toward each other.

Gus sighed and said, "Alright, if you can't be civil with me, at least hear me out. I'm going to level with you. My company and its employees are at great risk if our business fails, and I'm searching for a way to save both. LaSalle has been fortunate to win all the recent projects, and I don't begrudge you your success. It's true that Northwest has lagged behind. But we still have a lot of expertise and assets to offer. As much as I find it hard to do, I want to propose a combination of our companies. Together we could be a powerful force."

Carney glared at him and said, "Join up with you, after your father stole our workforce? Even without your father's poaching, you sit here with me as if you're without sin, conveniently ignoring the spies you've placed inside LaSalle. You think I am so naïve that I don't know that? It would bring me great pleasure to see you fail."

Gus was stunned by the spy comment, taken by surprise that it had been discovered. Though he was aware of Max Wagner's infiltration of LaSalle, he'd given it little thought and took it for granted. Carney was obviously livid about it.

Patrick Carney pushed back from the table, his chair tumbling behind him, and stormed out of the tavern. Stinging from that rejection, Gus brooded over his drink and finally left himself, determined to find another solution. He could now add public humiliation to his growing profile of setbacks.

After struggling for a few days, he'd elected a course of action. As he reasoned, he could only see two options: shut down the business and liquidate or do whatever it took to be able to better compete. Shutting the business down was inconceivable to him. His alternative to that was to gather the intelligence his father's spies had collected and use it to his advantage. One of those nuggets was the secret workshop Patrick Carney used. A reconnaissance mission there was necessary to see what tricks his competitor had planned. That might make him see how to counter LaSalle. The spies' reports about this workshop might just be wishful thinking or guesswork, but he needed to explore it in person. Carney's habit of staying away from his secret office on Sundays meant that a Sunday night trip to the LaSalle workshop should be possible without detection. The inconspicuous workshop in an industrial section of the city was empty on weekend nights. He only needed to pick the right Sunday night to strike. He found what he needed in early October, during a strong windstorm. These were good conditions for such a step. People would be inside and avoiding the windstorm and its dust.

No rain had fallen in Chicago in months, and the heat was also unseasonably high. Quite literally the city was a tinderbox. Angry winds whipped out of the southwest. Late on Saturday evening before Gus's planned visit, a major fire had raged in a lumber facility west of the Chicago River near the downtown business district. The fire had burned through the night, consuming four city blocks of industrial buildings in the process. Firemen eventually brought the blaze under control in the early morning hours on Sunday. With the wooden buildings and streets filled with sawdust, it had been a rich buffet of fuel. It was only through heroic efforts that the Chicago Fire Department had tamed the blaze, but it had paid dearly in terms of human cost and equipment failures for the effort. Its readiness for anything else was questionable.

Gus was armed in case he ran into any surprises. The last time he'd fired his pistol was in the Civil War. He carried that same weapon now in his belt, a tiny Smith & Wesson Model One revolver. About four o'clock in the afternoon he set out from home, ostensibly to check his own company facility to make sure everything was safe from the fire. Instead, he headed to the LaSalle workshop on the near southwest side of the city where

Patrick Carney conducted his secret activities. The office was a nondescript storefront without identification. At least the spies were right about that. Gus parked his buckboard a block away and walked to the LaSalle building. It looked empty and he broke in through a back door. He quickly searched the building, finding a large drafting table with design projects spread out.

Not long into his efforts, he hit paydirt. Carney had taken no special measures to protect his handiwork, other than hanging drapes over the front windows to prevent prying eyes. He must have been lulled into believing that an inconspicuous and unmarked space tucked into a nook in the neighborhood would keep him safe from prying eyes. What looked like a series of drawings of possible mechanical improvements to steam shovel equipment could prove invaluable. This had made the foray into the enemy camp lucrative, even though he hadn't even been sure what he was looking for in the first place. The drawings were plentiful, and without discerning what he should separate and give greater scrutiny, he opted to merely take any duplicates he found. He also found patent applications with the drawings, which he considered a bonus. By taking duplicates or even earlier drafts, he hoped to slip out undetected and have the missing copies go unnoticed as well.

Patrick Carney's day of rest was interrupted by the city's widespread fear of fire risk. The nearby Saturday night fire had rattled him and his brother, and they decided to split up and check on their properties. The brother headed west to their warehouse and office, well away from the downtown business district. Patrick broke the sanctity of his family Sunday and headed out to his secret workshop to protect it. Not discovering the break-in to his warehouse through the rear door, he used his key to enter the front. Daylight was dying fast, and Carney had stopped outside to ignite his lantern. Through the thin drapes, Gus caught the sudden flare of a match and a blaze of lamplight. As he heard a key being inserted into the front office door lock, he panicked. The roaring wind overcame any other sounds, and the blowing dust mostly obscured any shapes through the windows. Gus dropped to his haunches and prepared for a confrontation, cocking his pistol.

He swiveled around frantically looking for a path of escape but judged he'd be easily seen in the lamplight. Gus was trapped, and if he wasn't aggressive about it immediately, he could find himself identified or even captured. He couldn't let that happen. But he wasn't sure who held the lamp, since the face was obscured by a kerchief against the dust. It probably didn't matter. Whoever it was, he had to be eliminated. Once Patrick came in, he set the lamp on a front desk and started moving deeper into the space, unaware of the intruder. Acting quickly, choosing to use the advantage of surprise, Gus sprang into action. With Patrick no more than six feet away, Gus fired the Smith & Wesson into his chest, putting him down immediately on his back, moaning and gurgling on the floor.

Carney had only been inside for ten seconds, and yet now he was dying. Gus had no choice but to finish what he'd started. He might have been recognized, and he couldn't take any chances. He wasted no time and instinctively delivered a second shot to the head. Carney made no further movement or sound. When he was sure the body was lifeless, he moved toward him, pulled the kerchief down, and realized he'd killed his nemesis. Where the left eye had been, now there was only an oozing pool of blood and gray matter.

Adrenaline propelled him into action. He now needed to get the drawings gathered up and get out and away from there. But what about the body? If he didn't remove the body, it might lead to his capture. Gus swooped up all the plans and stuffed them into a canvas bag he found. Beneath the corpse of Patrick Carney lay a tattered rug, a good means to hide the body for transport. An idea suddenly popped into his mind. He pulled off Carney's belt and left it on the floor. Then he rolled up Carney's lifeless body and dragged it to the back. Slipping out of the shop with the bag of plans, he placed it in his buckboard then pulled it up to the rear entrance. Once confident he would not be observed, Gus dragged the body-laden carpet roll and wrestled it up into the back of his buckboard and covered it up with a tarp. He entered the shop one last time and toppled the lamp over, setting fire to the shop.

He well knew that if the fire department identified the point of ignition, it could be strong evidence of arson. Another fire would be needed to disguise what Gus had started. He unhitched Carney's horse from the hitching post in front and swatted it. The horse tore off with the empty buckboard trailing behind. As he scrambled away upwind of the shop, he passed nearby Dekoven Street and stopped, taking a few seconds to run to a nearby barn and set fire to the brush against its wall. That wall ignited immediately, and he was confident that the upwind fire ignition point would be found, instead of at the shop. Once the barn wall caught fire, he raced away in complete darkness, counting on it to subsume the first fire.

The fires he'd set quickly grew into a menacing blaze, spreading northeast and being fed by a strong southwest wind. A large lumberyard sat between the barn and the Carney workshop, and when it eventually ignited, it would end up burning fiercely for over two days and blow to the northeast, consuming the workshop and racing well beyond. It was as if the LaSalle shop stood directly in the path of a 2,000-degree torch until it was reduced to cinders, along with everything inside it except for some stray bits of metal, like a belt buckle. With any luck, survivors would conclude that Patrick Carney had been incinerated to ash in the conflagration. He couldn't take the risk that it would, though, and that was the reason that Patrick quietly accompanied Gus in the racing buckboard.

The Chicago Fire Department was in tatters after dealing with the recent inferno. By the end of the Saturday night fire-fight, much of the city's equipment was inoperable. Its firefighters were exhausted and recovering from smoke inhalation after the night's exertions. Sunday had dawned as another dry, hot, windy day, though. Any repeat of the Saturday night fire could leave the city open to widespread destruction. Fire was a frequent event throughout the world, in an era when wooden buildings were commonplace. That same night, a mere two hundred miles to the north, a massive forest fire of well over one million acres destroyed Peshtigo, Wisconsin, and another fifteen towns. Over twelve hundred deaths occurred in that inferno.

Gus hightailed it away from the blaze as fast as he could push his horse, desperate to escape the vicinity. The streets were filled with people scattering like squirrels in traffic. Into this chaos he moved without drawing any attention. It was every man for himself, especially now that another large blaze was upon the city.

He rode to Northwest's own warehouse building, and while on the way racked his brain about what to do next with the body. As he approached his warehouse, he passed rows of large, empty barrels, stacked and ready for use in shipping some of his goods. He hid the canvas bag full of plans in a safe location and dragged the body into the warehouse. He doubled it over and wrestled it into one of the large barrels and sealed it.

Gus loaded the barrel into the back of the buckboard and headed southwest to one of his construction sites less than a mile away. Northwest was building a series of bridges spanning the nearby Illinois and Michigan Canal, the same canal he and his father had built as Northwest's earliest project. One of the partially built bridge abutments was ideal for hiding the barrel.

He chose a pit that would serve as ballast for the bridge structure and then filled the hole with gravel to cover the barrel entirely. The hole would be filled with concrete this next week in a normal operation, permeating the gravel bed and the barrel buried under it. He would make sure to be on-site to personally conduct the completion of the abutment, and assure the barrel was concealed, hopefully forever.

In less than two hours, Gus Wagner had caused the greatest calamity in the young history of the City of Chicago, while successfully casting blame on a poor Irish family who would live with the undeserved public stain for the rest of their lives. The point he chose to start the second fire was a modest barn used by the O'Leary family to house a cow. The authorities initially concluded that the fire had started in the O'Leary barn. A stubborn myth arose that Mrs. O'Leary's cow had knocked over a kerosene lantern during a milking.

Gus had delivered a crushing blow to two Irish families—the Carneys and the O'Learys. In the same horrific act, the fortunes of the two companies were reversed. Gus Wagner had become a thief, an arsonist and a mass murderer, in the process saving his company and spurring the LaSalle company to regenerate itself and move off into other directions.

C   H   A   P   T   E   R

29

Turmoil
October 2010

ON THE WAY BACK to FBI headquarters, Steve Baker got a call from Mandy and Reggie.

Mandy said, "Steve, Reggie and I were watching Augustus Wagner's murder confession. That's our skeleton!" She was up on her feet now jumping up and down, shouting, "Gus's army pistol is framed and hanging on the wall of Frank Wagner's office. He showed it to me. It's even labeled."

Reggie screamed at Steve, "You've got to go get that weapon. If it's the murder weapon, we can match ballistics."

Steve said, "I'll get a search warrant signed and be there soon."

Mandy said, "OK. Beth Carney texted me to alert you she's releasing her story immediately."

"I don't blame her," he said.

Mandy and Reggie watched events unfolding across the river from their apartment balcony. The Northwest headquarters building was not close enough to see inside any windows, even with binoculars, but they waited and soon two black SUVs with blue flashing lights approached the building entrance, and a half dozen agents entered. The FBI was pouncing.

A call came in from Patrick from in front of the Monadnock Building. "Mandy, you should have been here. This place broke into pandemonium a little while ago. We're all ecstatic. A murder confession. I've got the best raw material for a book I've ever had, and it's my own family history."

Mandy said, "You think you've got pandemonium there? We watched the whole thing on TV and when I heard Gus's confession, I remembered Frank showing me his Civil War pistol hanging on his wall in a frame. The FBI is raiding Frank's office to seize it. Reggie is panting to do ballistics testing right away. And your mother texted me that she's releasing her story. Speaking of your mother, where is she?"

"Right here. Let me put you on speaker."

"Beth, have you got a reporter and film crew handy? There's a developing story at Northwest's headquarters. You better get over there."

Beth said, "What's it about?"

"The murder weapon!" Beth made no sound and sprang into action, pushing past Patrick's phone as she bolted.

Patrick yelled at her as she was running off, "Let's all get some lunch. Meet us at Eataly in an hour."

She'd better reach out to alert the public relations staff at LaSalle, because come Monday morning, if not before, they would be inundated with interview requests. Mandy then called Rick and urged him to pull his public relations folks into the picture and alert the CEO. She recommended he turn on the local news.

Northwest headquarters was sleepy on that Saturday morning, until the black FBI SUVs arrived. Steve and his agents stormed into the building and the security guards were overwhelmed upon being shown a search warrant. They were immediately allowed access and ordered the guards not to alert the Northwest office staff. One agent remained with the guards to make sure they obeyed. The agents barged their way into the office and passed a weekend receptionist. The Wagners were holed up in Frank's office licking their wounds when the agents suddenly burst into the office with a warrant.

They immediately took possession of all the firearms on the wall, after photographing the entire wall. No one had tinkered with the Civil War pistol in its frame. The agents took the whole frame. Frank and Carl were blindsided by the agents appearing with a search and seizure warrant, but were unable to resist, and turned over the framed gun as authorized by the warrant. They also took custody of the uniform, which doubtless had hair that could be put through DNA testing.

Frank made a feeble attempt to stop what was happening. "You stormtroopers can't do this. I have rights. Carl, get this stopped."

Carl looked at Frank and just shook his head, saying, "They've got a warrant signed by a federal judge."

Steve Baker sent the photos to Mandy and Reggie, and as Mandy looked them over, she had her epiphany about Frank's wall. It had bothered her when she first saw it, and now she could name it for what it was—a shrine to the Wagner empire and to its leaders—in Frank's case the visualization of his narcissism.

———

Lunch at Eataly was a boisterous, celebratory event which went on for hours. Patrick's father first asked for a moment of silence for those who died in 1871, then raised his glass in a toast.

"Imagine how history would have been different without Augustus Wagner—no murder of an inventor or horrible death by fire to hundreds of other people, families spared grief and ruin; a city intact; a pathological criminal enterprise trodden into the dirt."

They all clinked glasses and drank. As much as she was celebrating with the others, Mandy was deeply troubled by the lying, cheating and stealing by one family for a century and a half.

Mandy thought back on the initial visit she'd had with Frank Wagner in his office. She saw in her mind's eye the historical photos and memorabilia festooning his walls, including Augustus Wagner's pistol. The same one now suspected of being the murder weapon, and his uniform hanging in a sealed glass case. These could be the keys to unraveling the true story of what happened in 1871.

Beth totaled up the body count at the hands of the Wagner family. Including the people lost in the Great Chicago Fire, Patrick Carney, and probably Klaus and Gretchen Wagner, the combined total was over three hundred. Maybe the body count wasn't over yet.

Mandy said, "No wonder Gus killed himself. He even said he had trained his sons in his methods. I'll bet they, in turn, trained the next generation. Maybe right until the present."

"Augustus killed himself?" Patrick asked. The entire group sat speechless.

Finally, Beth broke the silence. "Yes. Gretchen told me years ago, but I'd forgotten."

Mandy said, "I stumbled across it myself recently in the musty old board minutes of Northwest. It was a closely kept family secret,

I guess. If I'd been responsible for all that, and then did what he did in the business, I'd feel guilty too."

Reggie said, "The old man must have been a tortured soul, but he deserved it."

Shaking her head, Mandy concluded, "Now I understand its significance, explained in Gus's own words. We've just watched a business and family shown for what it was—a crime organization. It's in a death spiral now, and Frank Wagner is a one-man wrecking crew."

Beth asked, "What happens at the bottom of the spiral?"

"He goes down the big drain. Shareholder class action suits over securities fraud, government and stock exchange investigations, criminal charges, bankruptcy, liquidation. And that doesn't include actions against individual executives. Then if it's still breathing and has any value left, the company could be picked apart and devoured."

Patrick said, "How would it start?"

Mandy said, "Class action suits will be filed immediately in a rush to become the lead firm. The lawyers are always poised to jump in, as the fees depend on who strikes first."

Beth asked, "What's next?"

"Investigations will be triggered. Criminal prosecutions will follow, if warranted. And this is just the legal side of it. Watch for some big market reaction Monday on Northwest stock."

Beth said, "A legendary family enterprise with its camouflage stripped away to reveal a crime skeleton." She was practicing some of her intended zinger lines before putting them in her story, and they were landing well.

———

In the days after the time capsule opening, nonstop unfavorable events beset Northwest Engineering. Its stock plummeted

20 percent in pre-market trading on Monday morning as the news reports spread nationwide and internationally, and the stock exchange halted trading of the Northwest stock until it stabilized. Another 5-percent decrease took place by the market's close of business. The investor relations staff was on the phone all day trying to calm stock analysts and its institutional shareholders.

No one could understand how the company allowed a letter to be read in public without a preview. It was an amateur's stumble in the world of public relations and certainly devastating legally for Northwest. The sponsoring network had scored a major news coup due to keeping the opening a surprise, so there was at least one winner in the mix.

This was what happened when an inexperienced CEO craving drama got what he wanted. Northwest's investment bankers and lawyers fumed. Frank had avoided or failed the effort to test the strength of its disclosures in the registration statement. Soon securities law class actions would start, and things would heat up.

As soon as the Everett Dirksen Federal Building opened for business Monday morning, Mandy's attorney filed suit against Northwest Engineering Company. It claimed that Mandy's termination of employment was illegal retaliation for her efforts to make proper disclosures in the stock offering. Accompanying that filing was the delivery of a whistleblower letter by Mandy into the hands of the local Securities and Exchange Commission and Department of Justice offices. It alleged fraud in the securities offering and corrupt actions in federal contracting.

In the Chicago office of the FBI, Reggie took custody of the Smith & Wesson pistol seized from the Northwest office, and her team was mapping out a procedure to test the ballistics from the barrel in Quantico.

The City of Chicago was reviewing all connections it had with the company where tax benefits or other inducements and incentives had been given to the company to stay located in the city. The Cook County State Attorney's Office announced a re-opening of the investigation into the cause of the Great Fire and the role Augustus Wagner had played. There was no telling how many families in Chicago were considering filing wrongful death lawsuits against the company. Class action lawyers were swing-ing into gear to recruit plaintiffs for wrongful death actions and securities fraud.

Several government entities, domestic and foreign, were open-ing investigations into the capital projects awarded to Northwest Engineering to look for illegal antitrust actions, including bribery and bid rigging. Governmental agencies managing current projects for which Northwest was bidding or seeking to bid announced a suspension of Northwest's qualifications to bid, leaving it tempo-rarily unable to secure new business or proceed with new awards.

Steve Baker had warned, "Don't be misled about this flurry of legal actions. Northwest has strong defenses to these charges, and it will not take this lying down. Just think about statutes of limitation, and how the attackers will have to get past them."

Mandy said right back to that, "If I'm thinking with my cor-porate hat on, the iffy claims and charges are not the immediate risks. It's the regulators and the market who'll inflict the first penalties. They don't have to worry about proof. They just need to shout FIRE!"

Sunday morning had also brought an onslaught of media attention to the unwanted events throughout the day. The *Chicago Tribune* headline that morning was:

NORTHWEST ENGINEERING—A TALE OF MURDER, ARSON AND FRAUD—GREAT FIRE CAUSE SOLVED

The time capsule story, complete with a verbatim copy of Augustus Wagner's confession, appeared on the front page above the fold. Another article recounted the often-told tale of the Great Chicago Fire of 1871, with the blame and later exoneration of the O'Leary family. The new villain, Augustus Wagner—murderer, thief, bid rigger, and arsonist—was featured. Yet a third article was an exhaustive story of the beginnings and explosive growth of Northwest Engineering, from its humble start as Northwest Drayage and Tunnel Company to its international dominance of capital infrastructure projects. The story grabbed the page one headline on all newspapers throughout the country.

Beth's first installment appeared in the *Chicago History Journal* that week, with further installments to follow on a weekly basis. Beth calculated that she would have enough material to last for over a month. Two stray subjects were promising to Beth as installments, but they were still without clarity. The first was the possibility that Klaus Wagner was murdered by his own brother. Next was the chance that illegal bidding permeated the company's success with the St. Lawrence Seaway and Panama Canal projects. Beth was sponsoring a series of on-air interviews in the days ahead. Also piquing her interest were rumors of more dead and missing persons—Jack Greer and David Wilson.

Following Mandy's alert to Rick Crawford, LaSalle was beset with questions about the explosive Northwest news. The media asked if LaSalle had reacted against Northwest for the historic theft of intellectual property. To buy time, the public relations staff said LaSalle was investigating the matter and would come up with recommendations on appropriate responses.

Rick pondered whether the statute of limitations barred his company's suit. It would have to be shown that LaSalle had a duty to pursue its remedy. In LaSalle's case, maybe nothing had triggered a duty. By the time it got the files over a hundred years ago, the business had already changed anyway. An entire generation had gone by since it had been involved with the equipment Patrick Carney had used and worked on. It was hard to see how a duty could arise decades after the events occurred, especially when LaSalle was by then in different businesses and the intellectual property was stale. The company would say its policy was not to comment on litigation. Rick had asked his staff to work with outside counsel to investigate a range of possible legal actions.

That response may have worked for LaSalle, but did nothing to alleviate the focus on Mandy. Her lawsuit and whistleblower letter had come out into the open. Considering her previous prominence, the media camped out in front of LaSalle and her apartment to get her on camera. Mandy reverted to extreme introversion when it came to media attention. She refused any interviews due to pending claims. But a better escape was the literal one. She took the underground exit to go out of the building on lower Michigan Avenue and blew past the original Billy Goat's Tavern, dodging the reporters clustered in Pioneer Court. She'd arranged with the doorman at her apartment to slip in and out the back entrance until the news cycle moved on. So far, she'd been successful at avoiding the onslaught.

LaSalle's attitude was that it was a good problem to have. Rick made a mental calculation that the company could only come out ahead. Northwest Engineering's board of directors, meanwhile, was down to a small number given the resignation and death of Gretchen Wagner and Frank's avoidance of Mandy's recommendation to bring new board members aboard. Charles Winters, the longest-serving director, called Frank and insisted on a board meeting. The board met on Tuesday and Charles took the lead in demanding answers to tough questions. It was clear to Frank that the board members had discussed matters the day before in a secret session.

Winters lost no time in criticizing Frank, saying, "We're shocked at what happened over the weekend. We're now looking at a serious situation with the stock exchange, the SEC and the courts. It's our understanding that numerous suits have been filed against the company, including one by Mandy Doucette. What can you tell us to give us confidence this storm can be weathered?"

Frank said, "We were blindsided by that time capsule. There's no evidence that any of it was true. And Doucette is just a bitter ex-employee."

Ed Rosen knew better. He went on to hammer Frank about taking such a risk and exposing the company the way he had. Frank was throwing out scattered incoherent comments. One of them was to repeat that no one could prove it was Augustus Wagner's letter in the first place. Rosen made sure he threw in a question about the new allegations that Northwest had obtained its most recent contract awards through corruption.

Charles said, "If you challenge the pieces of paper, I'm sure the FBI will authenticate them for you. If you're challenging the substance of the letter, do you believe that a suicidal Augustus Wagner would write lies about such matters? We know he committed suicide. What conclusion will the media draw from that once it becomes known? Would he intentionally bring harm to his company and disrepute to himself and his family, and then go on to jump off a building, unless he was guilty and truly repentant? What would be in it for him to do that?"

Frank had nothing to say to any of those points.

Ed Rosen asked a question. "How do you know there's no evidence? I understand the FBI has been investigating this company, and you even met with them."

"We did, but they made it clear to us we were not suspected of anything. They were pursuing the skeleton issue."

Ed followed up with another question. "We also understand our late board member Gretchen Wagner, your own aunt, was involved with the FBI. What do you know about that?"

Frank didn't answer. He had instinctively clammed up.

Ed said, "Why didn't you inform the board of the FBI involvement?"

Charles cut the discussion short and said, "Frank, we've had enough of this. You've been evasive with us. You've hidden things from us and you continue to do so. We fear that every stone that gets turned over will reveal another thing we'd rather not see. The board has discussed the situation and requires your resignation and immediate departure from the board and management of this company. We have prepared a short letter of resignation, and I am asking you to sign it."

Charles Winters put the one-sentence letter of resignation in front of Frank.

Frank stood stiffly before the paper just passed over the table to him. For a brief moment, he was carried back to the prior year when he had accepted the family's desire to go public, and what a ruin it could be. Then he said, "You won't even give me a chance to right the ship?"

Charles said, "If you don't sign the letter, we will remove you from the company and the board for cause. It's your choice how we proceed from here."

Frank glanced at it and said, "This is one sentence. How do you propose to compensate me for this resignation?"

Charles said, "We're not. If you don't sign, we will remove you and you'll be finished here."

Frank looked each board member in the eye and saw that he had no support. He breathed a sigh, picked up the resignation letter and tore it up. He stormed out and was met by security, who escorted him off the premises. He was offered the opportunity to sit with the head of human resources but waved it away. As he was led out the door, his car had been brought to the front. A quick execution. In Frank's mind, as he closed the door and put the car into drive, he imagined his father laughing at him and sneering at the nightmare Frank had created. By the time the board meeting ended, they'd terminated Frank for cause, suspended Carl Wagner, and appointed Ed Rosen as interim CEO.

During the discussion about Carl, the board members questioned him closely about his installation of surveillance equipment throughout the headquarters. An anonymous source had advised the board that Frank was using Wilson to corruptly win the project awards. Efforts to reach Wilson to appear before the board had proved fruitless. The board agreed to meet later in the week once Ed was able to achieve some stability, assess the situation without Frank's interference, and continue the review of the mess.

As a newly minted public company, Northwest's second filing with the SEC, ironically, was to report the departure of its chief executive officer and appointment of an interim CEO. The first was the resignation of board member Gretchen Wagner. The odor created by the collapse of Northwest Engineering as a public company resembled the old Bubbly Creek. And the fear inside the boardroom was that this was only the beginning.

Gretchen's condo had been sealed off as a crime scene. Steve had dispatched his evidence techs to the apartment to collect anything useful. What was found was being examined for any possible connection to potential suspects. One of the items found by the techs was different strands of hair to be examined and matched to DNA. The evidence techs already had the spy camera. Within a day, the U.S. Attorney issued a release informing the public of the suspected murder of Gretchen. Adding Patrick Carney and Klaus Wagner, there were now three deaths being actively investigated.

Gretchen's funeral was held shortly after the release of her body to the family. The event was sparsely attended. Notable by his absence at the funeral was Frank Wagner. Not a soul had seen or heard from him since his unplanned exit from Northwest Engineering. At the gravesite, Carl stood with his grieving sister and their families. The FBI approached him and asked him to answer some questions. Carl agreed to come to headquarters that afternoon. Beth and Mandy stood off at a distance from the meager gathering. Both women were crying over the loss of their friend. Mandy's guilt was a constant pressure on her.

Later after the funeral and at Carl's FBI interview, among the many questions covered, he was asked, "Mr. Wagner, when was the last time you visited your mother?"

Carl answered, "It was some time earlier that day before she died. I was there to try to understand what she was doing, and to ask her to resign from the board."

"How did she react?"

Carl was looking as earnest as he could when he said, "She was irate. She'd been to the FBI, as you know, and was cooperating. She signed the resignation, but then she threw me out. My own mother threw me out."

"Was it your last contact with her?"

"Yes, and it was very unpleasant. It was horrific what happened to her."

The detective asked, "Did your cousin Frank speak to her?"

Carl said, "He'd spoken to her earlier, and she'd hung up on him."

"Do you know if he tried to see her?"

"No, I don't. He could have, though, because he has a condo in the same tower that he inherited from his father, so I guess it was possible. The two units shared each other's keys, in case of emergency."

The detective asked, "Is there anything else you want to tell us?"

Carl swallowed and said, "There's probably some more that I can remember."

The detective said, "Like what?"

Carl said, "I think I need to get a lawyer involved now."

The Bureau decided that it would let Carl blow in the wind for a while, and that Frank Wagner was the prime suspect, anyway. A search for Frank was initiated to carry out an arrest for murder. His condo was searched, and the video feed from the Marina City cameras of the express elevator and parking deck cameras was reviewed. His boat was missing from the Marina City pier. As a precaution, Carl was advised to remain in town and be in contact if he intended to travel.

30

Race

EARLY ON SUNDAY, OCTOBER 21ST, Mandy and Reggie took an Uber with Patrick and Dan south on Michigan Avenue to the Conrad Hilton and Towers, once the largest hotel in the world. It was headquarters for the Bank of America Chicago Marathon, and just across Michigan Avenue from the race corrals. The day dawned clear with the temperature in the low 50s and no wind. In other words, it was perfect race weather.

As the sisters found their race corral to await the start, they had the usual observations—costumed runners here and there, groups of runners tackling the race together, runners from every imaginable country, etc. Chicago was one of the Marathon Majors cities, so it was a natural attraction for runners from all over the globe. Because it was one of the flattest courses in the world, it was also a huge draw for elite marathoners attempting to set world records, and many had been made there. As the starting time inched closer, the national anthem played, the wheelchair race started, and finally the forty thousand runners started to push over the starting line. It would take awhile for the entire group to start.

Race conditions remained ideal, and the course took racers north to Belmont Avenue and back down to the Loop, followed by a spur out west, returning to finish the final thirteen miles on the south side of the city. Along the way, the runners were passing some of the Doucette sisters' prominent spots—LaSalle's head-quarters, Marina City, the Chicago History Museum, Patrick's condo in Lincoln Park, the sisters' apartment, and the Northwest headquarters building. Mandy and Reggie thought they would be in a four-hour distraction from their recent ordeal, but in fact it was the opposite because of all the scenes they were passing. Each of them prompted another discussion of some part of the feud. At last, they made the final turn onto Columbus Drive, crossed the finish line, and received their finisher medals. They were thrilled with a sub-four-hour finish time, and happy to see arms waving at them outside the finishing chute. Reggie was especially buoyant. It was barely a year and a half since she had been near death from a nerve agent attack, and here she was pulling off a marathon finish after an earlier triathlon finish. Her year-plus journey from injury to marathon finisher was truly some kind of miracle.

Standing next to Dan with the thousands of spectators fencing off the finish line, Patrick was startled when Dan elbowed him and said, "Watch this," and then slipped away. Patrick looked on as Dan entered the finishers' chute through a gate in the fence opened by a videographer by prearrangement. The other side of the fence held the runners in the finish line corral area milling around after crossing the finish line timing mat. The runners who finished a marathon were in a high state of relief and happiness over their accomplishment. This was especially true of the sisters, after the long recovery of Reggie. Before anyone could stop him, Dan ran up to the be-medaled Reggie and dropped down on one knee. Reggie was tingling with what was happening, and Dan proceeded to profess his love for her and pulled out a ring as he proposed to her. The surprise proposal was enthusiastically accepted, followed by a hug and a long kiss. Applause broke out among the onlookers. The videographer took it all in.

Mandy quickly caught on to what was happening and had her own shivers as she witnessed the proposal. Reggie had a big smile and kissed Dan amid the other finishers continuing to pour in behind them. Photographers took shots of finishers clustered around Reggie and Dan to capture the moment, which would end up on the cover of the *Chicago Tribune* sports section the next morning.

After making it out of the finishers' area and meeting up outside the fence, Mandy asked Patrick, "Did you know that was going to happen?"

"Not a clue."

Mandy said, "Good thing Dan picked the right sister."

Patrick said, "Well, yeah, it helps you don't dress the same, and he did have her race number." Mandy laughed for a change. She hadn't had much occasion to laugh lately except for the time capsule opening. She had a happy expression as she hugged and congratulated Reggie, but next felt an overwhelming sadness that her best friend was now engaged, and she inwardly mourned the loss she was feeling already. It was important for Reggie's happiness that she kept her feelings to herself and didn't selfishly dampen the joy. Before leaving the finish line corral Reggie reached out to her and hugged her tightly, whispering in her ear that nothing would come between them.

A post-race, post-engagement celebration was in order, and after the sisters showered and changed, they all headed off to the Signature Room on the top of the John Hancock Center for lunch. This showed Dan's sentimental side, from the time a year before when he'd first met Mandy there with Reggie. Reggie was still glowing from both events that day. She would have to spend some substantial phone time later filling in her parents and siblings on the news.

Dan was finally getting what he wanted. For years as a colleague of Reggie at the FBI lab in Quantico, he'd struggled with his attraction to her. He had fallen in love with her quickly but was hamstrung by Bureau rules against relationships with co-workers. When he had finally left the Bureau when she moved back to Chicago, and taken up his teaching post at Northwestern's medical school, he hadn't wasted any time in taking the next steps. After getting Bob Doucette's blessing and waiting out Reggie's return to health, he seized the moment at the finish line. Patrick complimented him on his sense of drama and was envious of Dan's move. Everybody would have their eyes on him now.

The techs found the Smith & Wesson pistol seized from Wagner's office wall to be free of fingerprints and DNA. No surprise there. Their challenge on the ballistics test was finding usable ammunition for an 1860s vintage Smith & Wesson Model One seven-shot, a .22-caliber rimfire pistol. Cartridges only came into use in the Civil War, replacing black powder and lead balls. The FBI lab worked with the Bureau of Alcohol, Tobacco and Firearms, which maintained an exhaustive collection of weapons and ammunition. Through them, the right cartridges were located for a ballistics test. The next challenge was to fire a weapon that would not blow up in someone's face.

All went well, however, and within a week of getting the pistol out to Quantico, they had their ballistics test. A match was found between the bullets found below Patrick Carney's skull, and those fired from the handgun framed on Frank Wagner's office wall. The FBI could now say conclusively that the bullets that killed Patrick Carney were fired from the handgun found in Frank Wagner's office. As it was labeled as being the weapon owned by Augustus Wagner, and one of the hairs found with the body was DNA-typed to be an ancestor of Frank Wagner, Steve Baker had enough circumstantial evidence to connect the murder weapon to the murderer, who in any event had confessed to the crime in his time capsule letter. The FBI was most appreciative of Reggie's and Sammy's assistance by collecting Frank's DNA, which had been the link needed to show the hairs found in the barrel mess to be from an ancestor of Frank.

The suspected murder of Klaus Wagner by his brother Gus Wagner, Jr. would be a difficult matter to establish. It was beyond doubt that Klaus was killed by potassium cyanide, given the autopsy results. Steve focused on the death occurring on a fishing trip on Lake Michigan, in which the only two known participants were the brothers. If Gus, Jr. had nothing to do with the death, why would he influence Gretchen Wagner to forego an autopsy? The next point was the motivation for murder. Steve's team concluded that Klaus Wagner's diary, supplemented by the statements from Gretchen, established that Gus blamed his brother Klaus for the company's misfortunes. By refusing to use their father's methods during the 1950s and 1960s to win competitive bids, they had stumbled. They employed bribery and collusion liberally, as Augustus Wagner had confessed to in his time capsule letter, and to teaching his descendants these tactics. But Klaus Wagner had drawn a line in the sand with Gus, Jr. It was a sign to Gus that the company's streak of successes would not return with Klaus at the head of that unit.

Steve said, "Now we focus on Gretchen Wagner's death."

The next day, Steve met at FBI headquarters with Reggie and their old friend Ray Hanson, who claimed to have important information. Ray brought Sammy along.

Ray said, "When Mandy hired us to look into the man in the van trailing Gretchen Wagner, I stumbled across a surveillance program against her to include video recordings. I've been able to hack the program in place and pull up videos of the inside of Gretchen's condo."

With a curious look on his face, Steve said, "How did that get there?"

Ray said, "It was through Jack Greer."

"When we interviewed Gretchen, we discovered that spyware had been installed on her cell phone and then removed. Do you know who installed it?"

Ray said, "Jack Greer also."

Steve said, "Can we pull up videos right now?"

Ray worked his magic, and they were soon viewing a darkly lit video from inside Gretchen's condo. With the faint glow from a nightlight in the entryway, it showed a woman's body being dragged by the armpits through the apartment and onto the balcony off the living room. From there, the sliding glass door opened, and the body was dragged out and flipped over the railing. The ambient lighting outside from the Loop was sufficient to make out Frank Wagner's profile and face.

Mandy was horrified and she ran out of the room looking for a place to vomit. Reggie went and tried to give her comfort. "Keep your head down. Let's get you cleaned up and try to finish this. What happened to her wasn't your fault. It's all on Frank Wagner."

"I know. It's not guilt I'm feeling. It's revulsion over this monster. He's got to get what he deserves."

When they came back, Mandy said, "That's Frank. Gretchen told me Frank's father and uncle shared condo unit keys for a situation when one needed to get into the other's unit. That has to be how Jack installed the electronics. Frank must have loaned him Gretchen's key."

Sammy said, "But why would Greer have left his equipment there?"

Steve said, "He might have been killed before he could remove it. If Frank killed him, it might have been premature on his part. He should have waited until the stuff was removed. Otherwise, we might never have this gift."

Sammy asked, "Why do you think he didn't wait?"

"I'm sure Greer wouldn't have let Frank know what was in the condo anyway."

Steve asked, "That's why you don't let your clients know your means and methods?"

Ray nodded and asked Sammy, "Do you think you can read his lips? I see his mouth moving, he's talking." Sammy looked at the screen and asked that it be replayed. She had to do it a few times and finally said,

"He's saying *You witch! I made you a fucking billionaire. Now you'll be fish food. What we did to Klaus, I now do to you.*"

Mandy put her hand up to cover her mouth and gasped, while Steve slapped his hands together and said, "Gotcha!"

Steve had his hand out to Ray and said, "I'm going to need that laptop please."

Ray said, "Happy to oblige. Now that this is over, Sammy and I can head out for Florida."

Steve said, "If Frank considers you a threat, you could be at some risk. Be careful."

Ray said, "What kind of risk?"

Mandy said, "If he killed his own aunt, and you were a risk to him, why would he hesitate to harm you? You just heard him confessing to killing his uncle, and he apparently killed his own investigator too. We don't know where he is now, but he's being hunted. Frank is a resourceful enemy with lots of options."

Sammy said, "Remember also that I saw him on the security cameras gathering explosives and scuba equipment at his warehouse. Why would he be doing that unless he's planning something ominous? I think Steve's right."

———————

Reggie's work on Gretchen's condo came back with some fingerprint partials that she was able to match with that coming from the glass and utensils Reggie had swiped from lunch with Frank. In addition, the cameras at Marina City captured Frank entering the private express elevator to the penthouse at eleven o'clock but never showing a departure. One way that could have happened was if he'd left by boat from the marina below.

With the pending charges against Frank, his photo was on every television news program. They identified him as the prime suspect in the murder of his aunt. A multi-agency law enforcement task force now launched a manhunt for Frank.

Frank's penthouse in Marina City was searched. It had been stripped of things he needed. There was no doubt he was on the run. His boat was missing from its berth in the marina under the building, the same area where Gretchen's body had been found. It could be anywhere in the river system, or out on Lake Michigan. In fact, the narrow inlet on the north side of the Chicago Sanitary and Ship Canal was where it was now, in the spot belonging to Northwest Engineering. Frank Wagner lurked here in his boat hiding. Years before Frank had built a water-level structure into his Northwest warehouse and it was completely concealed. It allowed his boat access and shelter for his preparations. Frank was an explosives expert from his earlier days in the company's tunneling operations. He'd taken the supplies from the warehouse for a big surprise for Ray, rigging the boat in Belmont Harbor and setting it to explode in the early morning. He had spent his time changing his boat's name and registration number. He should be able to move undetected.

Since Gretchen's death, he had been sought by law enforcement. He needed desperately to take care of business and disappear. The sooner the better. But he wasn't sure what he was up against, so after he was done with his handiwork in the dark in Belmont Harbor, he lingered in his boat discreetly from a distance just outside the harbor. By this point in the season, many boats were gone and the rest were preparing to leave, as the harbor would close for the winter. As the time approached for the timed detonation, he suddenly saw the *Bogie* motoring out of the harbor. This was unexpected, and he decided to lay back a bit since the detonator was timed to go off soon. He started to trail Ray's boat at a safe distance and was getting excited that he would be an eyewitness to his own handiwork. He could hear the sound and feel the shockwaves of the explosion when the bomb triggered automatically at the set time. That was no surprise, but the fact that the sound and feel came from behind him did take him by surprise. He looked behind him and saw a fireball just outside Belmont Harbor. How in hell could the boat have exploded outside the harbor berth, he wondered. Steve's crew had deftly towed the bomb-rigged decoy boat just outside the harbor so the explosion didn't affect the berth area the *Bogie* had occupied nor the surrounding boats.

The *Bogie* motored on without hesitating after the explosion. He kept trailing at a distance. Later he read an online report on the explosion, fire and supposed death of Ray Hanson, an article obviously planted for his benefit. Frank wondered if he'd wired the wrong boat, and after thinking about it for a few seconds concluded that a decoy boat must have been used. Whatever it was, Frank admitted to himself that it was a very agile defense he'd just witnessed, but he laughed to himself that he was one step ahead of them.

31

Chase

FRANK KNEW EXACTLY where to find Ray, since he'd tailed him from Belmont Harbor the night before. He was moored close by and had a direct line of sight of the *Bogie* docked in Burnam Harbor, behind Soldier Field. The online *Chicago Tribune* pictured the hull of what was said to be the *Bogie*, burned almost to the water line but still afloat. The related article also reported that a body was found in the cabin, burned beyond recognition. According to the article, the body was presumed to be the boat's owner, Raymond Hanson. Frank was able to view the newspaper article on his burner phone and would have crossed the Ray Hanson name off his list, were he not on top of his game.

That morning, Steve collected Mandy and Reggie and took them for a drive south to Burnham Harbor, promising them a surprise. He wouldn't tell them where they were headed but turned off Lake Shore Drive into Burnam Harbor and went down to a half-filled dock. They talked only of Ray and the boat, and were so in shock, as they walked down the dock, that they were stunned by the sight of a navy-blue boat bearing the name *Bogie*. Steve yelled out, "Ahoy. Anybody aboard?"

Ray Hanson popped out of the cabin and said, "Welcome aboard."

Reggie said, "The walking dead?"

Ray said back, "Thanks to Steve, I've cheated the Grim Reaper."

They boarded and got comfortable, after the sisters hugged Ray. Suddenly Sammy popped up the stairs from belowdecks and joined them.

Mandy held up a copy of the *Chicago Tribune* front page with a burning boat at Belmont Harbor and shrugged at him.

Ray said, "Steve was a clairvoyant. He predicted Wagner would try to take me out, and what better way to do so than by boat?"

Stave said, "It didn't take any clairvoyance after Sammy spotted Wagner collecting explosives and scuba gear in those surveillance tapes. All we had to do was connect the dots."

Several hundred yards away, Frank was on his top deck with his binoculars, watching the joyous gathering on the *Bogie*. At one point he sneered out loud to himself, "How about that? Hello, Hannah Lee."

Onboard *Bogie,* Mandy pointed to the paper and said, "Wait a minute. What boat exploded then?"

Steve said, "It was a retired Cook County cruiser, compliments of the sheriff's office. We had a solid hunch he would try to take out Ray. Once we learned from Sammy that Frank had acquired explosives and timers from his warehouse, it wasn't too hard to imagine what Frank would do with them. When you added scuba gear, that could possibly mean an underwater demolition target. We cooked up the decoy to use. Frank is no slouch when it comes to setting up detonations, so he rigged up a little welcome on the *Bogie*. We didn't catch him in the act, but we did discover his setup and arranged for a transfer to the county boat. Then we awaited the trigger. After the explosion, we planted a story, including a non-existent body. Frank is probably quite proud of himself. And he's still out there somewhere."

Ray said, "I owe you guys. How can I help?"

"You've already helped us out by providing an attempted murder charge. But I recommend you get the hell out of here and make your risk profile as thin as possible. This maniac is still on the loose."

Frank waited them out and was up before dawn the next day. He prepared his rifle, just in case. He'd already used an alias vessel name and registration number from another boat, so he couldn't be easily seen. The forecast was for thunderstorms, and he wanted to get this done without battling Mother Nature too. Once done, he would find a way to deal with the redheads. They had been his undoing.

He followed Ray's boat discreetly. Several boat owners were preparing to leave the harbor, all intent on getting their boats out of the water and in storage for winter, since that harbor was closing for the season as well. The sky was threatening, and the rain came on intermittently, helping to shield Frank from Ray's view. The process first involved waiting in line to enter through the lock separating the lake from the river. Frank's challenge was staying close enough to Ray not to lose his tail, yet not be spotted. If he missed being included in the same grouping accepted into the lock, he could lose him. As the procession of pleasure boats made their way from Burnham Harbor to line up to enter the lock, Frank deftly slipped his boat into the crowd, so he was included in Ray's group, but safely back away from Ray's view.

Sammy, though, had used her monocular to spot him in the back of the lock.

Reggie was abruptly shocked awake from her vivid dream in Dan's apartment. She threw off the blanket, shouting out gibberish. The dream vanished, as if someone had shaken her head like an *Etch-a-Sketch*, and her sharp movements woke Dan.

Dan said, "Reggie, your phone is ringing." He shook her until she focused on him.

She picked up the phone and it was Mandy calling, so she answered, "What is it? What's happened?"

Reggie was sitting with the sheet around her and listening to Mandy report on a call Ray had just made to Steve requesting assistance. It looked like Frank Wagner was following him on the river. Mandy had hung up with Steve and immediately called Reggie.

Reggie said, "This is serious. Frank will kill him and Sammy as soon as he can. What are we going to do?"

They were soon back on the line with Steve, who was in the midst of getting his team in motion.

Reggie said, "There's a dock at the site where we found the skeleton, remember? The sheriff told us it was for bringing in equipment and loading excavated stone."

Steve said, "I remember it. I'll have him stop there, then get on land and run. I'll have a group get down there ASAP."

Mandy said, "What about us? Ray is our guy, and we need to help."

Steve said, "Get over to Pioneer Court in ten minutes." He dropped off the call.

Ray was at the junction of the Chicago River main stem with the north and south branches called Wolf Point, to the south of the Doucette sisters' apartment and in front of Northwest Engineering's building. Seeing a radar blip following him, he decided to test if Sammy had been right and they were being followed. Instead of going down the South Branch at the junction, he steered up the North Branch and kept the same speed. The blip followed. As he approached Goose Island, which stood in the middle of the North Branch of the river and had channels on both sides, he veered right and went up the east channel around the island. When he got to the northern tip of the island he took a hard left and proceeded south on the west channel. The blip followed the same course. Ray was now sure, and scared. He asked Sammy to take the wheel while he deployed a drone.

After getting the drone launched and flying it to the opposite side of Goose Island, he brought it up to the pursuing boat from behind. Ray pulled the drone to a close distance. He photographed the boat name and number, then he saw a figure in the boat. He immediately scanned the data into his shipboard computer and ran an identity check and came back with a name he didn't recognize. From the drone camera Ray saw that Frank Wagner was clearly the pilot. He must have adopted a disguise for his boat to avoid detection at the lock.

He asked Sammy to pull out two pistols, Kevlar vests and helmets from the locked cabinet below, then recalled and stowed the drone and took back the wheel. He was glad he'd used the trip across Lake Michigan to get Sammy familiar with the weapons. It turned out that she was a pretty good shot. He sped up and the blip followed suit. He called Steve to confirm that they were being followed by Frank. Steve told him the cavalry was on the way, and he should hurry to the dock near the McCook Reservoir, then get off the boat and run. The rain had started as drizzle while he was leaving Burnham Harbor, and now gained intensity.

––––––––––

Mandy and Reggie were waiting at Pioneer Court in front of LaSalle. They had persuaded Dan and Patrick to stay behind, promising they would not take any unnecessary risks. They had both argued about it but got nowhere. Within minutes, a black FBI helicopter swooped in from the river and landed, and the pilot gestured to them to get aboard.

Reggie pulled Mandy close and whispered, "Why do I have to do this? I hate helicopters. If this isn't absolutely necessary, I'm going to let Steve have it."

Mandy said, "It's like an airplane, which you do all the time. Do you have your St. Dymphna card?" Reggie pulled out her FBI badge wallet sleeve, which also carried her St. Dymphna card next to her Bureau ID. Mandy hooked her thumb at the FBI chopper and said, "Let's go."

They ran to the chopper and boarded. It took off in a hurry back down the river heading west.

––––––––––

Ray and Sammy had already reached the McCook Reservoir dock and tied up, as Steve had instructed them. Frank was some distance behind him and Sammy now, but within rifle range. He stopped and drifted while trying for a shot. He shouldered his rifle and found them in his scope scrambling out of the docked boat and up the embankment. He zoomed on the woman and said out loud, "You first, Hannah." He'd been fooled by her with that leak inspector ruse, but at least he'd had some fun that night. Little did he know that she'd provided a DNA sample the FBI wanted.

Scampering up the bank with helmets and vests were his two targets, and he aimed and shot them both, first Sammy and then Ray. They went down, falling over his horizon and no longer visible. He kept moving, docking behind Ray's boat and jumping off his boat with a Glock in his hand, running after them in driving rain. No trace of them could be seen over the lip of the embankment. It was a Sunday morning, and there was no activity. No guards were visible. They were probably at a site entrance to the north. He scanned the vast site and, without a glimpse of Ray and Sammy, guessed they'd headed down into a big tunnel shaft entrance ahead. They might be wounded or dead. Any other direction they'd have taken would have left them open to more rifle fire. Frank wasn't sure where it led, but he was going in. Rain was becoming heavy now.

He was making all this up on the go. No game plan of his had anticipated this. His only conceivable plan was to eliminate witnesses. He would handle Ray and Hannah and get back out and head down the canal before anyone understood what was happening. Frank was oblivious to the monitoring cameras playing out the chase. The guards were sharing the videos with the sheriff's office. But somebody still had to go in and get them.

Ray made another call to Steve Baker before he got too far down the shaft and lost cell coverage. He told Steve that he and Sammy had both been hit but their Kevlar vests had protected them, though they both hurt like hell. He might have a cracked or broken rib. Steve told him help was on the way and the Doucette sisters had insisted on coming.

Ray said, "Why did you let them come? How can they help?"

Steve said back to him, "Let them? They insisted on helping you. And who are you to talk? You brought Samantha down there, didn't you? We have to take him out of there and get the cuffs on him."

The farther they descended, the spottier the cell connection had gotten, so some words started getting dropped from whatever they were saying. What they'd heard was, "... a real menace ... we have to take him out ..." The rest was static.

He lost the connection but continued descending the shaft. Steve was racing to the site with sirens blaring and lights flashing.

Steve called Mandy's cell phone. "Mandy, where are you?"

"We landed and made it to the top of this big cavity with the scaffolding. I think they're all down there. Three deputy sheriffs met up with us, so we're good."

Steve said, "Try to distract Wagner by talking to him. Keep clear of the opening, though. My team and I are only ten minutes out."

Frank was making his way down the scaffolded stairs in the light from above, hearing steps and movement below him. Faintly he could hear the whirr of helicopter blades. Soon he heard voices too. He was staying put about midway down the shaft until it was clear what he was facing. The light was too faint to see below, and if he looked up, the daylight and heavy rain was too blinding for him to see clearly there, either. He made up his new plan on the fly. He would finish off Ray and Hannah, and then head out into the massive reservoir through the Deep Tunnel pipe exit. He'd have to figure out a way to kill the sisters later. There was no way he'd go back up into an unknown situation.

It was impossible with all the noise surrounding the sisters to hear down to the bottom of the excavation. Disregarding both Steve's and Ray's warnings, they started down the scaffolding stairs into the shaft. It was sheet metal, mesh steel stairs, and iron piping corkscrewing down to the bottom. Any one movement made sounds that were unmistakable and operated like a beacon.

Reggie hesitated, saying, "This doesn't seem too smart to me. What are we doing?"

Mandy said, "We're going to distract Frank to help Ray and Sammy until Steve gets here. We'll be alright. We're just following Steve's instructions. C'mon."

The hole was probably twenty feet in diameter, with scaffolding lining the sides so workers could toil away on the sidewalls and make their way up and down the hole. All along the way, equipment was staged, and supplies were stored for use as needed. The center inside the scaffolding was a clear open hole to the bottom, descending nearly three hundred feet below. A cage sat suspended from a cherry picker boom on the surface, no doubt for raising and lowering without the side scaffolding interfering. That wouldn't help now. It would be like sitting ducks for target shooting.

As Mandy started down the hole, Reggie said, "Steve told you not to go in, didn't he?"

"Come on. He wants us to distract Frank from going after Ray and Sammy. We can't do that from up here. He won't hear us with all this rain. Let's go." Without waiting for a response, she kept moving down the scaffolding stairs. Reggie reluctantly followed.

Suddenly Frank heard a woman's voice from above yelling, "Hey killer! Looks like you've come full circle with old Gus. This is where he buried Patrick Carney after killing him. Oh yeah, and you'll like this next part."

Frank was taking turns looking below for movement of his targets, Ray and Sammy, and then above for his sister pursuers.

Mandy started yelling again. "A video in Gretchen's condo caught you throwing her off the balcony. You even admitted out loud what you were doing, talking to a bludgeoned old, drugged woman before you tossed her. You also admitted killing Klaus. You're toast, Wagner."

Frank fired a volley of shots blindly up the shaft, and the sound reverberated in his ears. That was Mandy all right. He was blind with rage and had to get that bitch. All his troubles involved Gretchen, the Doucettes, and Ray. If he could eliminate them all, he might be able to squirm his way out of this and live in luxurious exile. He fired a couple rounds down the hole too, hoping to hit Ray or Hannah.

The sisters had made it down about fifty feet into the massive shaft. Reggie clung to the outer part of the scaffold next to the wall.

She was desperate, and whispered, "I can't go down any farther. You may have gotten me into a helicopter, but I can't go any deeper in some hole. Why did you pull me down here? Let's get out of here."

Mandy whispered back, "Stop babbling and keep your voice down. Here, take my St. Dymphna card. Now you've got double protection. Stay here, and I'll come back for you." She told Reggie what to yell at Frank once she'd started back down the scaffold, picked some items from the platform, and prepared to creep down the stairs again. She leaned over the rail and signed down to Sammy to fire up at Frank, hoping she would see the sign. Mandy and Reggie would draw him out over the hole and away from the scaffolding stairs. Hoping that Sammy had seen her and gotten the message, she then stuck an improvised target out into the shaft for Frank to go after.

Frank listened and tried to gauge the distance his pursuers were above him. The voices he heard dropped off, then he began to hear footsteps again on the scaffold steps. Then another voice yelled out, "Thanks for your DNA at lunch the other day, Frank. It nailed you, along with that hair we got from Hannah. Guess you won't be wanting a date with me after all, *Romeo*."

That was the other sister bitch taunting him. He chanced a look up over the edge of the scaffolding. He could see a silhouette leaning out over the opening, the light above providing a perfect target. He was determined to take the sisters along with Ray. With no family to live for, and his business empire bleeding out in front of him, what did he care what happened? He might as well go all out. He was already getting a vision of his father, Gus, Jr., berating him for his missteps, no matter what happened.

Ray and Sammy were on opposite sides of the tunnel bottom and were ready to crossfire up the hole. Sammy had been looking up the hole with her monocular and whispered across the shaft to Ray, "*Storm's a'brewin'*. The sisters signed they're going to flush him out into the open from the stairs so we can get a shot off at him."

"Why would he be so stupid to make himself a target for us?" he whispered back.

Sammy said, "He's in full predator mode right now and believes he's invincible."

After a set of taunts shouted by Mandy and Reggie, they heard Frank Wagner screaming at them and firing toward the surface. Frank leaned farther out over the scaffolding to get a better angle. He was also looking up into a massive thunderstorm burst coming down the hole. The storm that had followed them had finally reached the reservoir. Mandy had rigged a yellow construction raincoat onto a push broom she'd found. She texted Ray to fire at Frank as she drew him out into the tunnel shaft for a clear shot, but had no idea if Ray had cell coverage to see the text message. She was another fifty feet down the hole from Reggie. She'd thrust the raincoat-covered broom out over the edge of the scaffold and waggled it. To Frank's eyes from below it looked like a person. With the light and rain from above giving off a dreamlike appearance to the image above him, he couldn't quite place it. He hoisted himself out into the core of the shaft so he could get a clear shot up at the sisters. Then he started firing above him, and the raincoat jerked from the force of bullets hitting from below, with the gunshots reverberating in the tunnel.

Before the sound of Frank's shots could tail off, two deafening shots came from farther below and filled the shaft. Ray and Sammy used their laser-sited automatic pistols, and easily found Frank's back in the shaft above. Frank screamed with pain from two strikes to his back, twisting him around and pushing him out over the edge of the scaffold. The cold air on his face was the only thing he could feel as he lurched off the scaffolding and tumbled 150 feet to the bottom of the shaft. He never heard the screams of Reggie fill the tunnel after the gunshot sounds dissipated.

He was paralyzed. Bullets had severed his spinal cord near his shoulders and in his lower back, but he was still alive. Frank Wagner experienced his last few seconds of life with hatred raging through him. The image he was trapped with was the closed-circuit TV shot of Mandy Doucette dancing in the elevator, like the one he'd shot at above him in the shaft. The bottom of the drop was a bedrock floor of limestone, which would have emulsified him had he hit it. Instead, he was welcomed into a fast-moving underground river, moving laterally and pushing him into the McCook Reservoir.

More than three hundred feet above, Steve pulled into the McCook Reservoir construction site and made his way to the tunnel entrance. This was where he and Reggie had pulled Patrick Carney's bones out of the hole months ago. Three Cook County Deputy Sheriffs and a pilot were waiting in the rain at the entrance to the pumping station shaft, closely attending to two red-haired women.

Reggie was on the ground, with Mandy on her knees over her. Both had smiles on their faces and were laughing with relief.

Steve looked at them and wasn't sure who was who.

Reggie helped him by raising her hand and saying, "Reggie here."

Steve said back to them "Where's Wagner?"

Mandy and Reggie pointed to the shaft and gave thumbs down.

Steve said, "Damn you two. Where's Ray and Sammy?"

"Here," Ray said, as the two of them climbed out of the shaft, still wearing Kevlar vests and helmets. Both moved awkwardly, favoring the spots that had taken Frank's bullets.

To the deputies he said, "Why did you let them get near the opening?"

One deputy, acting insulted, said, "They pulled rank on us." Pointing to them vaguely, he said, "One of them flashed her FBI identification and said they were going down the hole."

Looking at the sisters, Steve said, "Reggie, aren't you strictly a surface person? And Mandy, I told you to stay away from the opening."

Mandy and Reggie shrugged their shoulders. Mandy said, "You told us to distract Wagner. We couldn't do that from up here, so we had to go into the tunnel. And we couldn't very well leave Ray and Sammy in danger. He'd already shot them and was following them down the shaft. We had to go in to distract him."

"Where's Wagner? Are you two alright?"

Ray said, "Thanks for asking. We're fine. Just some bruising. Wagner's probably dead, with some bullet holes in him. He's probably a bag of mush after that fall."

Steve said, "Bullet holes? From whose gun?"

"Mine," Ray and Sammy said in unison.

Steve asked, "Why did you shoot him?"

Ray said, "What are you talking about? You told us to take him out."

Steve shook his head, thinking back on his conversation, and muttering, "Huh? No, I didn't mean—are you serious? . . . oh, never mind," now remembering the gibberish at the end of that call.

Ray said, "He was shooting at us, and he'd already hit us once. It was self-defense, if you like that better."

Reggie had a big smile. "You think we could fit him into a barrel? I bet he's pretty pliable right about now."

Mandy said, "Pathologist humor?"

Ray hugged Mandy and Reggie and said, "Thank God for you two. Shooting up in that elevator shaft and seeing the figure you were holding above Frank, it made me think of one of the video clips I found at Northwest. It was of you in an elevator doing some crazy maniac dance. Your hair was wild and you were wearing big red dagger earrings. At least, I think it was you."

Mandy said, "What made you think of that?"

"Seeing that target you waggled at Frank in the tunnel."

Reggie said, "That creep filmed his elevator cabs?"

Steve said, "Oh yeah. I guess we'd better get the cherry picker operator over here. We need to get your next autopsy customer out of that hole before this next big storm hits."

Mandy said, "That should be one of my guys. I'd be happy to call out site superintendent to call the operator here, but I think it would be futile. With this storm they won't operate equipment anyway until the lightning is a minimum distance away. Will have to wait out the storm. Can you hear that roar? Isn't that the sound of the Deep Tunnel pipe pushing out water anyway?" A massive gushing noise was coming from the west.

Sammy said, "Yeah, we were just climbing up when it started to roar from below. Frank's in the reservoir by now. A cherry picker wouldn't help anyway."

Reggie pulled Mandy aside away from the group and said, "What were you doing in that elevator?"

With a shocked look on her face, she answered, "Nothing hinky! I was just testing the *tuned liquid damper.*"

"The what?"

Mandy said, "Never mind."

Reggie couldn't have been happier. It was even worth her underground terror, to get her hands on Frank. She'd have to wait for that pleasure, though. Six inches of rain had fallen on Chicago in a short time. The Deep Tunnel was pressed into service and water was pouring into the McCook Reservoir, taking Frank Wagner's corpse into the abyss, just like Sammy had warned. In another two days, the pump at McCook Reservoir slowly emptied the reservoir water. It would eventually be piped over and cleaned in the Stickney Water Treatment Plant, after foreign objects were first filtered out by the grille system. One of the objects found in the grille was the bullet-ridden, pulverized body of Frank Wagner.

Reggie and Dan performed an autopsy of the body and determined that 70 percent of his bones were shattered in the fall. Frank Wagner would now live in infamy at the Metropolitan Water Reclamation District of Greater Chicago for being first corpse ever collected in the grille at the pump site. Drowning was listed as the official cause of death. She also found the bullet-scarred vertebrae from the shots and concluded he'd have been instantly paralyzed.

Frank's corpse had been found at LaSalle's construction site, and over a hundred forty years before, Northwest's construction site in the same spot had held Patrick Carney's corpse. It was an irony that would later become a favorite part of Beth Carney's journalism series.

In the careful evidence search of Frank Wagner's boat, the FBI techs found fragments of broken glass on the fly deck recently covered with potassium cyanide residue, and much older traces of potassium cyanide in the crevices of the lower deck. Recalling that it was the boat he'd inherited from his father, Gus, Jr., Steve Baker had a theory. Although the murderer had been careful to remove the cyanide container, there must have been some that fell to the floor and was absorbed into the wood, waiting patiently until some enterprising forensic investigator discovered it so many years later. On the boat they also found a roll of duct tape, and later matched it to the tape found on the outside of the *Bogie* and the tape used to bind Jack Greer. Everything was sent to Quantico for analysis and what came back surprised Steve. The glass fragments were coated with cyanide as well and were determined to be from a set of glasses on board that were recent vintage. In fact, they'd come from Crate and Barrel and were only one year old, according to the store's inventory records and its record of a transaction with Frank Wagner. A later search of the Northwest warehouse would reveal a hidden vault containing several full vials of potassium cyanide.

Steve huddled with Reggie and voiced his confusion. "The glass was relatively new. How could it have been involved in Klaus Wagner's death at least ten years before that?"

Reggie answered, "We don't have any other victims, do we? Is anybody missing and unaccounted for?"

Steve looked at her and raised his eyebrows. "David Wilson hasn't turned up."

C H A P T E R

32

Aftermath

ED ROSEN CALLED a special session of the Northwest Engineering board of directors to assess the company's troubles. He was unable to put a happy face on the situation.

"We have an overwhelming set of challenges in front of us. First, we have shareholder suits for securities fraud. Next, the Carney family and LaSalle Enterprises filed a joint suit claiming intentional theft of intellectual property. Then Amanda Doucette sent a whistleblower letter and filed a wrongful termination suit. Next, the families of those who perished in the Great Fire have filed a class action wrongful death suit. The City of Chicago wants to rescind tax breaks and is researching an arson claim. Finally, the Canadian and Panamanian governments have put the canal awards on hold while investigating bribery in the bid process. It's a real shit show."

Ed looked around the room. There was total silence and stunned faces.

"Remind me why I took this job?" he asked.

Charles Winters said, "You were bamboozled like we all were. How much in financial terms are all those claims worth?"

"It would be what they call an *'existential event'* I think. Probably approaching a billion."

"Well at least we don't have the feds on us."

Ed said, "Not yet. They're just letting the Canadians and Panamanians do the heavy lifting for them on corruption. And the SEC will be here soon on stock fraud."

———————

The crowd size at the gravesite in Graceland Cemetery funeral was impressive. Following a service at Holy Name Cathedral, a funeral procession led through Chicago's north side to the cemetery near Wrigley Field. It was the final resting place of many famous historical Chicago figures. Now it was the final resting place for Chicago's hero after spending a century-long limbo inside a bridge abutment. At the gates, a gaggle of onlookers awaited the entourage, and followed at a respectful distance to the gravesite. After a few words were said over the casket, Patrick Carney's bones were lowered into the grave amidst the other family members interred there. Ironically, Carl Wagner had Frank's remains cremated and kept in an urn, awaiting an appropriate final site. Some had suggested they be mixed into the cement for a bridge abutment. Regardless of where his ashes went, his family name would take its rightful place instead of Mrs. O'Leary in Chicago lore.

The Carney family, along with the Doucette sisters and Dan, approached the grave and threw roses on the casket after the priest spoke. No tears were shed, given the 140-year time gap. A reception followed at City Gallery in the historic Water Tower building, one of the few structures to survive the Great Chicago Fire. There, Beth expressed aloud the family's grief for all the poor souls who perished in the fire. She also had kind words for the late Klaus and Gretchen Wagner, victims of their own family. And Beth being Beth, she promoted her new multi-week serial in the *Chicago History Journal*—the entire story of the Wagner-Carney feud.

Mandy and Patrick took the first possible opportunity to escape the media spectacle and walked south on the Magnificent Mile toward the river. As they neared the Pioneer Court site of the helicopter pick-up, Patrick suggested they duck into the Chicago Tribune Tower Building and visit the sales office for the upcoming condo conversion the tower was undergoing. He asked for a salesperson who seemed to know him. They were shown to a four-bedroom model on an upper floor, where they wandered around and enjoyed the views overlooking the river, with the Loop skyline at eye level.

Patrick said, "What do you think?" The unit faced south and gave a 180-degree view from the lake to the west Loop.

"It's spectacular, but why are you looking at this? Is there a problem with your place?"

Patrick said, "No. I've admired this place ever since seeing it from the window of our dingy family office. I think a bigger space is needed."

"Why? You'd be lost in it, wouldn't you?"

He turned her toward him and dropped to one knee, taking her hand and saying, "Not if you married me."

With his other hand he produced a ring box, revealing a huge diamond engagement ring inside and said, "I love you very much. Will you marry me?"

Mandy teared up as they embraced.

When they finally separated, Mandy said, "I love you too, Patrick Carney. Of course I'll marry you." She kissed him and then looked at him as asked, "Did you ask my dad?"

"Would I let Dan Aleri one-up me?"

"Did you ask Reggie?"

Patrick tilted his head and said, "C'mon. There's got to be a limit to this twin thing, doesn't there?"

She kissed him and said, "Just this once."

"OK, I can handle that. I'll bet Dan didn't ask for your permission either." She gave him an ambiguous raised eyebrow in answer.

"I need to call Reggie."

C H A P T E R

33

Takeover

THE YEAR FOLLOWING the collapse of the Wagner criminal enterprise and Northwest Engineering as a public company was chaos. The wall in the apartment shared by Mandy and Reggie was rearranged to allow for the newest objects to command center attention. Entirely unrelated to races, but nonetheless one of the longest endurance events, there hung two companion framed proclamations by the Chicago City Council. They honored the sisters for resolving the longest-running Chicago mystery—the cause of the Great Chicago Fire of 1871.

The Northwest Engineering juggernaut eroded with each passing week, as the many problems dragged the ragged management team along. One after another, senior leaders left to try to rescue their careers. Ed Rosen soon was managing a skeleton crew kept in place only by the hope of cash awards. Stock-based awards were obviously worthless, given the diminishing share price. Ed's goal was to salvage Northwest as an operating company, rather than let it die and be picked apart by the vulture economy. One bright spot was its continuing expertise in large-scale capital projects and its retention of the pending contracts. Despite facing corruption charges, there was still a business.

David Wilson, Frank's intermediary with the Canadians and Panamanians, had vanished without a trace. Steve's agents studied the video records of the Chicago River lock traffic and discovered Frank's boat entering and returning from the lake prior to Frank's death. They were able to zoom in on the outbound passage and pick out both Frank and Wilson on the fly bridge, but Wilson was missing on the inbound passage. Eventually Steve's investigators were able to pull all of Wilson's materials stored in the cloud. One of those was a cell phone recording between Wagner and Wilson walking outside and away from prying ears. They were talking about securing the Panamanian project and Frank was giving instructions to Wilson. The message was to get the Panama Canal work using the same corruption approach he had already used on the St. Lawrence Seaway. That recording was solidly incriminating, and even if they couldn't prove bribery, the tape would ensure a bribery conspiracy charge.

Carl was in for some extended examination and scrutiny in the whole mess. Yet even if he'd been pushed out and assuming he never worked another day in his life, his financial wherewithal would be substantial. He could land on his feet.

LaSalle's trade secret lawsuit had overcome its weaknesses, and Sammy had dug up the accounting records to prove the value of the pirated trade secrets. Ironically, these records were kept in the same warehouse Frank stored his explosives.

In her lawsuits, Mandy overcame the half-hearted defense from Northwest about attorney-client privilege. That meant she received a bounty in the securities fraud and bribery cases. Eventually the charges resulted in a settlement of $500 million, and Mandy received the minimum 15-percent bounty. Even after netting the $75 million to account for federal income tax, Mandy was left with over $40 million.

Ed Rosen's task was not done with the resolution of all the claims and fines. His goal of keeping Northwest a going concern succumbed to one final maneuver. Mandy had initiated a strategy discussion at LaSalle and was given board approval to pursue her idea. Her years in the DOJ anti-corruption unit taught her lessons in corporate reengineering. As companies reeled from self-inflicted injuries, there were consequences that were unthinkable before. She negotiated a tender offer of Northwest at a bargain basement price to LaSalle. A newly renamed LaSalle Northwest Corporation rose out of the Northwest Engineering ashes. It would consolidate the separate portions of the St. Lawrence Seaway and Panama Canal mega-projects, to be completed entirely under LaSalle's contract award. After collaborating with Mandy to make it happen, Ed Rosen was content to call it a day and retire again, to enjoy the fruits of his year of painful toil.

Not to be outdone as a celebrant, besides welcoming a daughter-in-law into the Carney clan, Beth Carney was also able to glow after her *Chicago History Journal* series on the Wagner-Carney feud raked in a Pulitzer Prize for journalism.

———

In the spring of the next year, Reggie and Dan exchanged wedding vows at St. Joseph's Catholic Church in Wilmette, the Doucette family parish. They were side-by-side with Mandy and Patrick. The double wedding was the high point of the year in the Chicago wedding season, with each of the brides serving as the other's maid of honor, and the same for best man role with the grooms. The brides were in matching dresses, of course. It couldn't be done any other way. Mandy's and Reggie's sisters served as the joint bridesmaids, along with Samantha Wong, and the joint groomsmen were Steve Baker, Rick Crawford and Ray Hanson, plus the sisters' brothers. Ray and Sammy had just returned from wintering in the Key West station of the Great Loop on the *Bogie*. A 400-person reception was held on the lake shore at the Michigan Shores Club in Wilmette. The event attracted significant media attention. Bob Doucette was in his glory, getting to give his identical twin daughters away at the altar with one bride on each arm, followed that night by a memorable father of the brides speech for his twins.

The two couples left the next morning for their honeymoons. Mandy and Patrick to Hawaii and Reggie and Dan to Tahiti. After a week they met back up together in Tokyo, where the sisters ran the Tokyo Marathon. While waiting for the start early on race day, and standing amid a huge gaggle of runners, Reggie said, "I guess I had you all wrong. I shouldn't have questioned you after all."

Mandy said back to her, "What are you talking about?"

"Just look at what happened. Northwest brings you over from LaSalle, and in four months you put them through the wringer. You expose and then kill their CEO, bring down a hailstorm of lawsuits on them, sting them for a huge settlement fine and whistleblower bounty, and then snap up their company at a bargain. You even get your old job back at LaSalle and get them a huge infringement payment. That was quite a trap you led them into. You were just being the provocateur, as usual. Right?"

Mandy shrugged her shoulders and said, "I am my father's daughter."

The End

APPENDIX

Timeline of Historical Events

1803:	Louisiana Purchase
1817–1825:	Erie Canal
1818:	Illinois Statehood
1825–1828:	Delaware & Hudson Canal
1825–1832:	Ohio & Erie Canal
1828–1830:	Chesapeake & Ohio Canal
1830–1835:	Baltimore & Ohio Railroad
1832–1853:	Wabash & Erie Canal
1835–1848:	Illinois & Michigan Canal
1837:	Chicago Incorporation
1840–1860:	First Generation of Chicago River Bridges
1848–1853:	Galena & Chicago Union Railroad
1851:	Chicago City Hydraulic Co.
1848–1853:	Cholera Outbreaks
1855–1870:	Raising of Chicago Buildings/Sewer Installation

1859–1869: Suez Canal

1863–1869: 1st Transcontinental Railroad Line

1864–1867: 1st Lake Michigan Tunnel

1865: Union Stockyards

1871: Great Chicago Fire

1872–1882: Gotthard Pass Tunnel

1871–1874: Rebuilding of Chicago

1873–1881: 2nd Transcontinental Railroad Line

1874: 2nd Lake Michigan Tunnel

1885–1900: Chicago Sanitation & Ship Canal

1890–1900: Chicago River Reversal

1891–1893: Monadnock Building

1903–1914: Panama Canal

1900–1904: New York City Subway System

1910–1914: Houston Shipping Canal

1911–1922: Calumet-Saganashkee Channel

1938–1943: Chicago Subway System

1946: LaSalle Enterprises Public Offering

1954–1959: St. Lawrence Seaway

1975–2029: Chicago Deep Tunnel System

2007–2016: Panama Canal System Expansion

2010–2013: St. Lawrence Seaway Improvements

AUTHOR'S NOTE

THIS IS A WORK OF FICTION. That said, the author attempted to give as accurate as possible a history of the water system in Chicago, the Great Fire of 1871, and the difficult period for Mary Todd Lincoln and Robert Todd Lincoln. He relied on the excellent works by the following authors: Benjamin Sells, *The Tunnel Under the Lake*; David M. Solzman, *The Chicago River*; Carl Smith, *Chicago's Great Fire*; Libby Hill, *The Chicago River: A Natural and Unnatural History*; Dan Egan, *The Death and Life of the Great Lakes;* William Maples, *Dead Men Do Tell Tales*; and Dr. Douglas Ubelaker, *Bones: A Forensic Detective's Casebook.* Any deviations in the history were either intentional to fit the story or accidental on the part of the author. Also, federal law does reward whistleblowers with bounty awards of 15-30 percent of amounts violators are fined for certain crimes, including corruption and securities fraud. Such fines have occasionally amounted to amounts of $1 billion or more. As to lip-reading in major league baseball, while it is tempting to believe that it takes place and was a fun idea to include in Samantha Wong's character, especially since the covering of mouths by players and coaches begs such an idea, but the author does not believe it really takes place.

The author also wishes to express his gratitude to his beta readers for their loving critique and insights: Elizabeth Roehlk, John Thompson, John King, Jim Evansizer, Bonnie Anderson, and Dr. Sarah Linden. I especially appreciated the insights of my technical experts: John Doninger on intellectual property law, and Dr. Orlando Gonzalez on pathology matters. Special thanks go out to the Metropolitan Water Reclamation District of Greater Chicago for its waterway diagram and for its permission to include it in this work. Finally, I am thankful for the great work done by my editors for this book: Leslie Wells and Debra Englander.